Tri Quarterly 105

Spring/Summer 1999

Editor
Susan Firestone Hahn

Associate Editor
Ian Morris

T0164124

Production Manager
Bruce Frausto

D...
Gini Kondziolka

...Editor
Josh Hooten

TriQuarterly Fellow
Brian Artese

Assistant Editor
Francine Arenson

Editorial Assistants
Gina Carafa, Russell Geary, Cristina Henriquez

Contributing Editors
John Barth, Rita Dove, Stuart Dybek, Richard Ford, Sandra M. Gilbert, Robert Hass, Edward Hirsch, Li-Young Lee, Lorrie Moore, Alicia Ostriker, Carl Phillips, Robert Pinsky, Susan Stewart, Mark Strand, Alan Williamson

TRIQUARTERLY IS AN INTERNATIONAL JOURNAL OF WRITING, ART AND CULTURAL INQUIRY PUBLISHED AT **NORTHWESTERN UNIVERSITY.**

Subscription rates (three issues a year) — Individuals: one year $24; two years $44; life $600. Institutions: one year $36; two years $68. Foreign subscriptions $5 per year additional. Price of back issues varies. Sample copies $5. Correspondence and subscriptions should be addressed to *TriQuarterly*, **Northwestern University**, 2020 Ridge Avenue, Evanston, IL 60208-4302. Phone: (847) 491-7614.

The editors invite submissions of fiction, poetry and literary essays, which must be postmarked between October 1 and March 31; manuscripts postmarked between April 1 and September 30 will not be read. No manuscripts will be returned unless accompanied by a stamped, self-addressed envelope. All manuscripts accepted for publication become the property of *TriQuarterly*, unless otherwise indicated.

National distributors to retail trade: Ingram Periodicals (La Vergne, TN); B. DeBoer (Nutley, NJ); Ubiquity (Brooklyn, NY); Armadillo (Los Angeles, CA).

Reprints of issues #1–15 of *TriQuarterly* are available in full format from Kraus Reprint Company, Route 100, Millwood, NY 10546, and all issues in microfilm from University Microfilms International, 300 North Zeeb Road, Ann Arbor, MI 48106. *TriQuarterly* is indexed in the *Humanities Index* (H.W. Wilson Co.), the *American Humanities Index* (Whitson Publishing Co.), Historical Abstracts, MLA, EBSCO Publishing (Peabody, MA) and Information Access Co. (Foster City, CA).

TriQuarterly is pleased to announce that Stuart Dybek is now a Contributing Editor to the magazine. We welcome him and thank him for his past invaluable contributions to our pages.

Contents

Cover photograph by Doug Macomber
Cover design by Gini Kondziolka

Two Poems

Laurence Goldstein

Through a Glass Darkly

> I predict that the world as we know it will cease to exist on August 18, 1999.
>
> —*Criswell Predicts* (1968)

Criswell, you were my favorite TV personality, fifteen minutes of high voltage prophecy daily on Los Angeles Channel 13.

"Pomp and Circumstance" announced your shadowed presence at a table, visibly straining at the last bars to start your rapid-fire reportage.

And then the spotlight, the camera dollying forward to catch the fervor of your mad eyes and throbbing baritone:

"I predict . . . that the strongest earthquake in the history of the U.S. will virtually wipe out the city of San Francisco on April 7, 1975 . . . I predict the destruction of Denver by some strange and terrible pressure from outer space . . . I predict the assassination of Fidel Castro by a woman on August 9, 1970 . . . I predict the renaming of every male child in the Soviet Union to Joseph in honor of the late Premier . . ."

You were the authentic voice of paranoid America, rattling off details of the apocalypse like the ticker on Walter Winchell's desk.

(That desperate old relic unmasked by television as everyone's lunatic uncle, telegraphing anti-Communist scoops to all the ships at sea.)

And then you would ask us, if we saw you on the street, to shake hands, embrace, "for that is the only way we can conquer our loneliness."

I knew your voice from Sunday School Bible readings at the reform synagogue. Yes, I could imagine Jeremiah on television, shaking a shepherd's staff and threatening no rain till Hollywood stopped making movies like *The Seven Year Itch*.

And then he too would show up at the Iowa picnic along with Vampira to plug his new half-hour format and remind the nomads of Bellflower and Tarzana that 87% of his predictions came true.

(The number is not implausible; even if you claimed constantly, as you did, that the U.S. would soon introduce contraceptives into the water supply to achieve less than zero population growth, you could cover yourself by intoning, after the show, "The sun will come up in the east. And set in the west. And then come up in the east . . .")

Criswell, I confess that you scared me with your sibylline prevision of the warlord you named "The Prince of Darkness" rising from the Asian steppes in 1976 to overwhelm the world—you hinted that he might land his hordes on Sunset Beach and herd my family into slave-labor camps.

The hydrogen bomb and your program made a perfect fit—one signified that the end of days might be next week, and the other was a covert message of hope:

The world would endure a few more decades, at least, until the runaway planet you called Bullarion annihilated great cities and caused every volcano to "wreak fiery havoc" for many years.

(There was a bonus: Atlantis would finally pop to the surface, as Edgar Cayce too had foretold.)

How eerie it was to walk in the doomed terrain of Culver City after your dinnertime broadcast,

Down the reeking mudflats of La Ballona Creek, past the Toddle House where realtors arranging the sell-off of Baldwin Hills could seal their deals and ogle some ladies of the night.

Hardly Babylon, I said to myself, spying some tired hooker and her john trudge two doors down Washington Boulevard to a cut-rate motel.

What did it matter which sins were performed or repressed? Enough to breathe in the pre-smog Pacific breezes, tinged with oleander and eucalyptus,

Enough to dance on the eve of destruction to rock 'n' roll denounced by city fathers as the devil's music channeled through the throats of Little Richard, Eddie Cochran, and the Ronettes.

Criswell, I miss your ravings about UFOs and truth serums and anti-gravity devices. Now it takes twenty stations to purvey the nonsense you distilled into a quarter hour.

Your brevity left me plenty of leisure to sit down with Poe and Lovecraft, and later with Yeats and Blake, and find their Orphic prognostications not so different from your own.

So—thank you for inoculating me as a youth fated to live through the last decade of the second millennium after the amazing birth prophesied by Daniel and Isaiah.

The sun came up today in the East, just like you would have predicted, and when I think of August 18, 1999, I don't panic;

Thirteen percent of the time you were wrong, including the day of your own death, scarcely noted even on Channel 13. And what about the fateful night of March 10, 1990,

When, according to you, citizens of Mars, Venus, Neptune, and the Moon would meet in Las Vegas to chart the future of the cosmos, and try their luck at the slots?

I'm placing *my* bet that on August 19, 1999, a few relieved stargazers like myself will lift a tall glass to you, Criswell, dreaming boy with no proper name on the banks of the Wabash, oracle of the infant electronic hearth, Nostradamus wannabe who made us war babies gasp in wonder and watch the headlines ever more keenly.

Perhaps you're walking the cloudy boulevards right now, with total prescience about the uncalendared eternity to come;

It's not heaven exactly, more like the microwave ether of a billion billion transmitted signals, a place of no unmediated word or person, Videoland;

Airtime erased in living rooms is perpetually present in this dreamspace, including you, Criswell, in your Liberace suit of purest white silk,

And who would have predicted how many fans are flocking to you on their angel wings, and dancing around your beaming spirit like happy geese in a halo of light?

Untimeliness

after Arthur Miller

They sauntered at shoreline where the breakers fell,
pensive husband and glamorous wife.
Today, Sartre had it right: hell
was other people who preyed on their life.

Distant objects relieved the eye:
four fishing boats by the peach-
colored horizon, gulls in the sky
and, suddenly, trucks on the beach.

A turning winch raised a net
bulging with fish, the sea's produce,
and dumped for transport the ill-fated
thrashing creatures, a silvery sluice

of never-ending energy, flowing west
into the insatiable guts of mankind.
"They know they're caught," she gasped, in her best
movie voice, and he, resigned,

steered her from what was more heartless,
the workers heaving aside inedible
sea robins, their corpses-to-be an artless
mosaic on the strand: waste as incredible

to tender souls as extinction of species
or triage in the traffic and brute neglect
of displaced persons, gypsies, refugees—
fish out of water fishermen reject.

"Why don't you put them back?" she said.
"Would they live again if they had water?"
Bending her beautiful body, she laid
fingertips on the day's slaughter—

too slippery! He intervened, a hero
flipping junk-fish to the waves,
one by one, back to a perfect zero.
He emptied all their sandy graves.

"They'll live as long as they can," she laughed.
"That's right, they'll live to a ripe old age
and grow prosperous," he chaffed
her as they strutted merrily offstage,

he blessing her, hope in his eyes.
"Oh, how I love you," she said.
Thinking, *for the moment nothing dies,*
nothing on this shoal of time is dead.

Five Poems

Yusef Komunyakaa

The 17-Year Locust

There in its tiny tomb of D
NA, held in the mute loam
It is made of, earthbound
& antediluvian, each nymph

Busies itself sucking sap
From a tree root. True
As twelve solid-gold watches,
When the time comes, the locust

Tunnels open a chimney
Of light—a mere eyehole
Of dust & sap that hardens
Into mortar. On the brink

It waits for green to draw out
God's praise & lamentation.
As if a new bead for a rattle,
It clings to bark & eats itself empty.

The God of Variables Laments

The other day I was dining out
With You Know Who, saying,
Don't worry if they call you PC
Lady, because they only want you

To question your heart till nothing
But a pinch of rock salt. The Master
Of Weights & Balances strolled over
To our table, favoring his right foot,

& stood glowering at us. I still
See his hate letters to Hank Aaron.
Finally, I said, Hi, Frank.
He said, Don't care what you say,

Property values are up. Manifest
Destiny is our liturgy. The god-
Forsaken moon is ours too, & you
Can't teach wood not to worship fire.

Neither/Nor

Gods, with your great golden
Shields & winged feet, you
Granted me a perfect wish,
& then threw in a second one

As bonus. I didn't know
One was a blessing, the other
A curse. You know I don't care
About gold, the bright burdens

It buys. I have seen a world
Of chains & ankle bracelets,
But I never could stomach pure
Unadulterated illusion or endless

Situation comedy. Lord, magicians
Sure can conjure an open-mouthed
Crowd. One wish grew worthless
After driving the other from my door.

Yesteryear

The sheriff slides a black knob
Of polished oak from its blue-
Velvet box, smooth
As a bull's horn.

His wife of twenty-two years
Sighs, gazing out at a jaundiced
Moon. He says, "Yeah, I truncated
The bastard's balls with my billyclub."

As if weighing good & bad, he holds
A breast in each hand. "The big one,
The tough sonvabitch, we took him
For a long ride in the graveyard."

His right hand slides down
To her wet sadness. Somewhere
A hoot owl calls. Somewhere
A moan opens a mouth, the eyes of many gods.

The Goddess of Quotas Laments

George Wallace is dead.
Few recant as he did, dropping
Skeins & masks, but I still see
The army of dragon's teeth

He planted like Cadmus of Tyre.
Fists of oaks clutch barbed wire.
How many replicas of him relume,
Wheedling east & west, here

To Kingdom Come, in vernal
Valleys & on igneous hillocks
That overlook god knows where?
I wish I knew why hatemongers

Drift to the most gorgeous
Spots on earth. I have watched
Choke vines & sunlight in cahoots,
Edging toward a cornered begonia.

Paragraphs from a Day-Book

Marilyn Hacker

for Hayden Carruth

Filthiest of cold mornings, with the crumbs
of my breakfast *tartine* and the dregs of tea,
to clear away. On the market street the bums,
long-term jobless, stateless, *sans-abri*—
meaning, those without shelter—
crouch on cardboard, wrapped in frayed woolens, filter
out the wind as best they can, discreetly beg:
a plastic bowl beside rag-swaddled legs.
They all are white, and half of them are women.
I talk with one: tall, stained teeth, arched nose and cheekbones
like Norman gentry. She's soft-spoken
as a fifth-grade teacher, who'd have shown
me fluvial maps, and pointed out the human
scale of geography. She huddles down
on the florist's doorstep in the rue Saint-Antoine.

Her friend camps daily on the *métro* stairs,
a tiny skinny woman with blue eyes.
I gave her my old gloves and a blue mohair

scarf when it was five below. Despite her size
and lack of an ounce of fatty insulation,
she vaunts her indomitable constitution
to layered housewives who pass the time of day
with laden caddies, homebound before noon.
In summer, they more or less live on the Quai
Saint-Bernard. The little one strips for the sun
to shorts and a tank-top, turning crinkled coffee-brown
around her aster eyes, and looks even thinner,
while her friend tucks a print skirt over her knees and relaxes.
Close to midnight, I sometimes see them sharing dinner
on a plastic plate, on the steps of the Bureau of Taxes.

But it's January now, it isn't summer
and even dog-walkers stay off the quais,
while I remain a late-comer
whose own taxes bloat strategies
of empire that bring sitcoms, sneakers, "fast food"
and strident tourists to the neighborhood.
Tired of their solipsistic booming voices,
I walk in parks they don't know. Under bare elms
and maples, Chinese schoolgirls draft their own
fables—homework, after La Fontaine:
a pigeon tells a mallard the advantages
he's gained from learning other languages.
They don't simper when they're joined by boys—is
subservience now merely one of their cultural choices?
"Our" foreign policy chair's Jesse Helms . . .

In winter, the produce on the stalls
is rufous roots, dark leaves, luminous tubers,
as if earth voided jewels from its bowels
for my neighbors'
Sunday stew-pots. Concurrent raucous calls
and odors waft among the vegetables:
merguez sizzles in a skillet, fowl
turn on a row of spits. Damp dogs prowl
between wool-stockinged calves and corduroys
Tissue-wrapped clementines
from Morocco (gold from old colonies)

salt fish from Portugal and Spain's
olives and oil; cauliflower from Brittany,
also the channel-crossing mist of rain
down from the northwest coast since yesterday

I almost gushed to my friend about a movie
I'd just seen: the son of a concentration-
camp survivor's homage. Mother tells son
the volumes she remembers. Now she's seventy-
something, tangoes in high-heeled elegance
over the abyss of memory.
But we were balancing fine points of translation
with forkfuls of ratatouille in a café
the freezing afternoon of New Year's Eve,
and both of us had other things to say.
Our plates were cleared. With habitual diffidence,
she handed a new manuscript to me
and took (to the Ladies') momentary leave.
I turned a page and read the dedication
to her father, who died at Bergen-Belsen.

A *Résistant* father died in a concentration
camp. A fifty-year-old father was a prisoner
of war from '39 till the Liberation.
The Germans shot another father
and his mother during the Occupation:
the Breton *maquis* betrayed by infiltration—
collaborators were everywhere.
A grandfather, eighty-four,
a grandmother, eighty-two, pacifists,
were gunned down by the *Milice*. They
left a note pinned to the old man's chest:
Le juif paye toujours. The Jew always pays.
Their son had shot himself at the end
of the *"drôle de guerre"* in 1940.
These are the absent fathers of my friends.

*

Wednesday night at the Comédie Française:
a hundred (white and slender) well-behaved

adolescents, from one of the good *lycées,*
file into balcony rows saved
for them to see Genet's
"Les Bonnes."
                    We're older than the actresses,
one of whose roles I took on
in San Francisco, our "salon
production"— two men and one woman,
in black shirts and tight
black jeans. I was "Madame"
for my friends' lyric vengeance five Friday nights.
Gerry, our "Solange," delivered her
last monologue, hands crossed, bald under the rigged spotlight,
like a condemned man awaiting the executioner.

James' gentle philologic daftness led
him to invent a language and its people,
both called "Prashad"
cognate with Slavic "Truth," simple and supple
enough for gnomic folk-tales. He had
written their history, which filled four hundred
typed pages, and three short plays
which we three, fresh from Genet's
ceremonies, undertook to memorize
and then, to perform.
I was a fag-hag in my early twenties;
shared with my friends their thrift-shop retro charm
and the facility of a linguist
for recitations in dramatic form
in a language that didn't quite exist.

But James died youngish, twenty years ago
and Bill, our "Claire," my friend then, doesn't speak
or write to me (still from San Francisco)
because I wrote a book
he didn't like. We shared a vast bay-windowed
flat with Paul (Chip, sometimes). Bill lives, now,
alone in a room at the "Y"
from which he goes to work every day
and returns, a wall away from homelessness.
In our rundown wooden

Victorian south of Market, east of Van Ness,
a trestle table in the kitchen
seated ten for feasts provisioned at
a cut-rate market called "The Dented Can."
No—it was Bill and I who named it that.

And Bill and I imagined lives in France
where he had sojourned as an army brat
while I had merely a Romance
Language degree. Often, we sat
among Paul's convalescent kitchen plants
gossiping avidly, with flawed accents,
over coffee-mugs and *pan
dulce* from the Mexican
grocery next door.
                                    Tunisian
Jews have a new snack-bar downstairs
featuring bagels and American
soft-drinks, favored, it appears,
by Sunday shoppers in the neighborhood
where I've lived these past twelve years,
decades eclipsed, accent somewhat improved.

                        *

Cherry-ripe: dark sweet *burlats*, scarlet *reverchons*
firm-fleshed and tart in the mouth
bigarreaux, peach-and-white *napoléons*
as the harvest moves north
from Provence to the banks of the Yonne
(they grow *napoléons* in Washington
State now). Before that, *garriguettes*,
from Perigord, in wooden punnets
afterwards, peaches: yellow-fleshed, white,
moss-skinned ruby *pêches de vigne*.
The vendors cry out "Taste," my appetite
does, too. Birdsong, from an unseen
source on this street-island, too close for the trees:
it' s a young woman with a tin basin
of plastic whistles moulded like canaries.

—which children warbled on in Claremont Park
one spring day in my third year. Gísela
my father's mother, took
me there. I spent the days with her
now that my mother had gone back to work.
In a brocade satchel, crochet-work, a picture-book
for me. But overnight the yellow bird
whistles had appeared
and I wanted one passionately.
Watching big girls play hopscotch at curb's edge
or telling stories to V.J.
under the shiny leaves of privet hedge
were pale pastimes compared to my desire
Did I hector one of the privileged
warblers to tell us where they were acquired?

—the candy store on Tremont Avenue.
Of course I don't call her *Gísela*.
I call her *Grandma*. "Grandma will buy it for you,"
—does she add *"mammele"*
not letting her annoyance filter through
as an old-world friend moves into view?
The toddler and the stout
grey-haired woman walk out
of the small park toward the shopping streets
into a present tense
where what's ineffaceable repeats
itself. Accidents.
I dash ahead, new whistle in my hand
She runs behind. The car. The almost-silent
thud. Gísela, prone, also silent, on the ground.

Death is the scandal that was always hidden.
I never saw my grandmother again
Who took me home? Somebody did. In
the next few days (because that afternoon
and night are blank) I don't think I cried, I didn't
know what to ask (I wasn't three), and then I did, and
"She's gone to live in Florida" they said
and I knew she was dead.

A black woman, to whom I wasn't nice,
was hired to look after me.
Her name was Josephine—and that made twice
I'd heard that name: my grandmother's park crony
was Josephine. Where was Grandma; where was Gísela,
she called me to her bench to ask one day.
I said, "She's gone to live in Florida."

Second Retreat: Knife-Sharpening at Vajrapani

Peter Dale Scott

Day One

The jay with his chatter
like the trees

with their gesticulations
cannot communicate

except by becoming silent
the times he comes up close

hoping to share breakfast

Day One: Stone

to clean this stone
drop it in a pot

of boiling water
over the next hour

the grease and dirt
will slowly breathe out

into the water
leaving underneath

a photographic image
of its identifying

pocks and scratches
on the metal

Day Two

Stillness eludes me
the dark leaves

of the tall bay tree
reflected in my mug

rippling
each time the yogi

at the other end of the table
stirs his tea

Day Three

Light between the shoulders
of those sitting in front

remains on my retina
a blue goblet

which when focused upon
becomes a lake

with rushes round it
the ripples enlarging

till the far shore disappears
and you can see within

which is to say
darkness

My first meditation
was when my father

taught me to walk
Indian-style

one foot in front of the other
out to the granite point

to look for a moose
making no noise

Day Three: Steel

The gap between knife and steel
should be small

if you hone in
at too wide an angle

the blade will be sharp at first
then quickly dull

Day Four

Beneath the eyes
of the White Tara and Green Tara

Shakyamuni and Medicine Buddha
black angry Mahakol

on this cushion
I am three-and-a-half feet high

and when a grown-up
steps on my foot

the powerlessness I feel from age
from having so little in my will

to leave to my children
so little done those absent years

so little to show
(this going inside

the pain of self-revelation
will it leave me impotent?)

is suddenly overwhelmed
by the hot tearful

powerlessness of childhood
Am I sixty-seven or four?

I am suddenly angry
at this teacher who cannot ease

the confusion of injustice in the world

Day Five

I walk on the gravel road
taking baby Indian steps

I am twenty miles high
and risk toppling over

I am walking on the moon
my head so far from earth

it might roll off course
and not come back

Day Five: Cleaver

This heaviest cleaver
my steel cannot sharpen

could it be meant to stay blunt?
Consider: how much pain

in a family
where there is love

Day Six

I say to my teacher
Is it common for you to hear this?

my retreat has been so profound
I have come wonderfully into touch

with how completely rotten
I feel about my life?

And he answers
Things are as they are

but you can feel regret
and I feel regret

become compassion

Day Six: Chef's Knives

The chef's knives in this drawer
this gompa near Boulder Creek   meditation hall

where we are given the freedom
to be silent

none of this would be here
if not for the persecution in Tibet

the anonymous benefactors
who brought the lamas here

and now the logging
blue ominous crosses

on the redwoods around us

Day Seven

The room so desperately hot
you can hear the sweat

roll down your sides
even the teacher is losing it

his head almost hitting the floor
from lack of oxygen

and when trucks finally arrive
to empty the Portapotties

scent wafts over us
I find myself saying

I am being mindful
of the noise and smell

of human feces
being sucked up through a tube

and a breakthrough
from laughter

the human condition
stercus mundi   the shit of everyday life

suddenly so comic
it is an escape

Day Seven: Orange

Perspiring beneath
the Tibetan prayer flags

and bunches of home-grown herbs
I remember my sons Mika and John

singing to me
(where is that tape

I promised to listen to again?)
as I slice an orange

the blade falls cleanly through

Day Eight

As the end comes into sight
each breath becomes more precious

each footstep I take
moves me closer

at any minute
I might sob disappointed

that we will soon have
to talk again

or else with joy
admiring the courage

it took my young wife Ronna
to marry an older man

Day Eight: Techniques

Here I am still sharpening
as my father did

at the head of the Christmas table
back and forth

flashing blade and steel
outwards towards the guests

even after Shanti
the cook has showed me

her trick of sliding
the edge quietly

inwards
towards the navel

Day Nine

On this last morning
as one or two car

engines start up
beyond my tinnitis

just continue
to breathe in and out

with the same concentration
walk this strict

tight-rope
between light and darkness

death and life

Interior: The Kill

Carl Phillips

The last time I gave my body up,

to you, I was minded
briefly what it is made of,
what yours is, that

I'd forgotten, the flesh
which always
I hold in plenty no

little sorrow for because—oh, do
but think on its predicament,
and weep.

We cleave most entirely
to what most we fear
losing. We fear loss

because we understand
the fact of it, its largeness, its
utter indifference to whether

we do, or don't,
ignore it. By then, you
were upon me, and then

in me, soon the tokens
I almost never can let go of, I'd
again begin to, and would not

miss them: the swan
unfolding
upward less on trust than

because, simply, that's
what it does; and the leaves,
leaving; a single arrow held

back in the merciless
patience which, in taking
aim, is everything; and last,

as from a grove in
flame toward any air
more clear, the stag, but

this time its bent
head a chandelier, rushing
for me, like some

undisavowable
distraction. I looked back,
and instead of you, saw

the soul-at-labor-to-break-its-bonds
that you'd become. I tensed
my bow:

one animal at attack,
the other—the other one
suffering, and love would

out all suffering—

Dogs

Marcus Cafagña

Tonight in Michigan
  dogs are barking, whining
    and barking through walls,

keeping the woman
  next door awake; two albino
    German Shepherds in cages

without food or water.
  Dogs that send the woman
    in 2-B back under the fingers

of electrodes and restraint,
  white shoes nipping her heels
    as she moaned and fought

for balance. If she could
  just focus on something else.
    The chipped walls, the buckled sill.

Impossible to do
  more than swirl paint
    around the can, with these dogs

barking, whining, yipping, crying.
  The smell heaving against her
    senses until she squeezes

the lid back, stands all her weight
        so the rim snaps shut, then returns it
                to the closet. Every surface clean,

magazines stacked, hands
        turning clockwise. A good year
                to be alive, a good place to rest,

but not with this colitis,
        these dogs howling pain
                in her bowels, the bowl

white as their flanks,
        their soft thin ears.
                Nothing to worry about,

this blood keeping her
        up late, these ulcers
                inside hammering their fists,

the walls bleeding,
        the door whining back
                on its hinges, crying against dogs.

    after Michael Van Walleghan

Shibusa

Mary Yukari Waters

"You have a sensibility for elegant manners," my tea ceremony teacher once told me, "the way a musician has an ear for pitch." Even before I could read, mothers were pointing out my floor bows as examples to their daughters: spine straight, its line barely breaking even when my head approached the floor; rear end clamped to heels the entire time with tensed quadriceps. As a teenager I performed the "admiration of vessel" step at tea ceremonies with an artistry beyond my years. I held out the ceramic bowl before me with arms neither straight nor bent, but rounded in a pleasing curve. Tilting my head just so, rotating the bowl in my hands the requisite three times, I lost myself in the countless subtle ways glaze changes color when shot through with sunlight. Such rituals of etiquette lifted me to an aesthetic plane, where often I had the sense—though I could not have articulated it then—of life being a dance, to be performed with stately grace.

But my bearing lacked that ultimate essence of refinement, described by elders as *shibusa*. It had to do with something more than mere maturity and was hard to define. The Buddha's smile of sorrowful sentience had this quality. A maple leaf in autumn, slowly twisting during its long fall to earth, evoked *shibusa*; that same leaf in midsummer, growing healthy and green from its branch, did not.

"Aaa, it will come—" I remember my teacher saying with a sigh.

*

As a young bride, I was besotted with my husband Shoji. He was square of face, with a firm, straight line of a mouth and hair slicked back from his brow with immaculate comb lines. More than once, others commented on his likeness to those fine three-quarter profiles of samurai painted on New Year's kites. Like a samurai, Shoji was well versed in martial arts—fifteen years of kendo training—and displayed, unconsciously, those fluid transitions of movement so prized in Noh theatre. He was successful in business as well: a fast-rising executive at Kokusai Kogyo, an import-export conglomerate. Years later this company would be disbanded in the aftermath of our military defeat, but at the time it had the clout and prestige of today's Mitsubishi.

Early in our marriage Shoji was transferred overseas, to the Chinese province of Pei-L'an. It was 1937, seven months after the province had fallen to Japanese rule.

"Don't forget to write!" my girlfriends clamored; then, in hushed tones, "And give us details! Those women's bound feet . . ."

One would think that sailing away to China would have exposed me to the cruelties of life. Today there is fervent talk on the radio of our soldiers' atrocities there: villages burned, women raped, soldiers butchered in prison camps. But all I knew of Pei-L'an Province was our executives' housing compound: nineteen eaves sweeping up, pagoda-style, their ceramic roof shingles glazed a deep Prussian blue. The high wall enclosing our compound was white stucco, and the large main gate (through which we women passed only when escorted by our husbands) was topped with a miniature stylized roof in matching blue tile. I had little curiosity about how the region beyond had been defeated, and it would have been ungallant, ill-bred even, for Shoji to disclose the morbid details of war to a young bride. I wonder now how much he, as a mere civilian, knew of all this at the time. At any rate, I was more interested in immediate events, like the ripening of persimmons in autumn. That fine play of color—bright orange globes against the dark blue—gave me stabs of delight; it added an exotic touch to this new foreign experience.

The company had hired nineteen housemaids from the local village—one for each house. They arrived each day at dawn and were let in by the compound guards. Sometimes Shoji and I, drowsing in our futon, heard their faint voices coming up the main path, the harsh grating of consonants making the women sound as if they were perpetually quarreling.

Xi-Dou, the maid assigned to our home, was about my age. I sneaked curious looks at her while she worked; back home, domestic servants were rare. Her feet, far from being bound, were even bigger than mine. But despite her calloused hands and faded mandarin tunic she had a pleasing face, with full lips and wide-set eyes. She never laughed and only rarely smiled—wistfully, with a slight pucker of brows. Those smiles caused me intense guilt over my own newlywed bliss, which seemed shallow and coarse in contrast. "Shoji," I said one night when we were lying in bed gazing up at the shadowed beams of the ceiling, "I wish Xi-Dou could join us for dinner."

I heard the slow crunch of his bean-stuffed pillow as he turned his head in my direction. "Xi-Dou? The maid?"

"I saw the poor thing crouching on a stool in the kitchen," I said, "eating our leftovers. It ruins the harmony of this home for me, seeing something like that."

"*Maa*, such a gentle heart you have . . ." Shoji murmured, his forefinger along my cheek as slow and deft as the rest of his movements, "and a face to match . . . but," his finger trailed away, "that's the procedure with servants. I assure you she doesn't take it personally. The food here is a lot better than what she's getting at home."

"It seems impolite, when she's already right here in the house," I said.

Shoji propped himself up on his elbow, looking down at me with his handsome samurai face. "Darling?" he said; in the moonlight his brows lifted in amusement like dark wings. "We just defeated these people in a *war*."

I did not reply.

"I'm not suggesting," Shoji said finally, "that etiquette—or consideration, whatever—shouldn't exist in wartime. Far from it. People need it to cope with life. But your nebulous gesture isn't practical. *Ne?* It would give her false hopes, make her life look bleaker in contrast."

"Wouldn't it give her—dignity? Or—" my voice trailed off in embarrassment. He was right, I saw that now; what would Xi-Dou want with the company of Japanese strangers?

"True kindness, in my opinion," said Shoji, "is good pay." He kissed my forehead once, twice, then fell back on his pillow with a scrunch. "Give her occasional tips, how about that? It'll do you both good." Momentarily I heard his soft snore.

I was not fully satisfied by Shoji's solution. On one hand it pleased my sense of order: for each situation, there should be a proper and logical course of action. Yet some additional dimension was missing, though I could not have defined it.

His comment interested me: *people need it to cope with life.* That had not been my own experience. I had never used etiquette to "cope." But I understood how its ethereal quality, like temple incense, might lift one out from the realm of daily cares.

I continued gazing up at the ceiling. These Chinese roofs were lower than I was used to; I sensed the weight of the beams pressing down upon me in the darkness. *Maa*—I thought—whether in kendo or in matters of judgment, Shoji always hits the heart of a matter with one sure blow.

*

Shoji soon became friends with another executive in our compound, Mr. Nishitani. They were the only two men in management who were still in their thirties. Both were tall and striking, with that genial assurance which comes from a lifetime of excellent schooling and privileged treatment. Nishitani-san, a bachelor, began dining frequently at our house.

In certain ways Nishitani-san was the opposite of my husband. With Shoji one got the impression that behind each word or motion was a hidden reserve of strength, of discipline. It was evident in the way he told jokes at company parties: so deadpan that when he delivered his punch line it took a moment for his audience to react. Only after they burst into laughter, roaring and shrieking, did Shoji give in to laughter himself, his rich baritone notes pealing forth from well-conditioned lungs.

Nishitani-san, on the other hand, carried all his energy on the surface. His smiles were dazzling, sudden and unexpected like flashes of sunlight on water; the older wives whispered among themselves that those smiles took your breath away, quite! Somebody once said that even the air around Nishitani-san seemed to shimmer. In excitement his voice rose and his cowlick shot up like a tuft of grass; in a burst of good humor he was not above breaking into some Kabuki chant—right in public—or improvising a silly jig. "Won't you ever learn to behave?" I chided him with motherly resignation, though I was five years younger than he. Compared to Shoji, Nishitani-san was just a bit boyish for my taste. But that quality would later endear him to my little girl Hiroko, with whom I had recently learned I was pregnant.

Xi-Dou, our maid, fancied Nishitani-san. On the evenings he came over she plaited her hair loosely, draping it over one shoulder in a long gleaming braid instead of pinning it up into a bun. On a few occasions I could have sworn her lips were faintly stained with lipstick. One of mine? I wondered. I never mentioned this to Shoji, but it did occur to me, once or twice, that "coping with life" was not such a clear-cut business as he had implied. Certain needs, however impractical, will transcend all others. From the corner of my eye, I watched Xi-Dou as she backed away from our table, clutching the empty serving tray to her chest, then turned to the door with one last look over her shoulder at Nishitani-san. As far as I could tell, he was oblivious to her presence.

Nishitani-san brought out a side of Shoji that I did not often see. When it was just the two of us, my husband was reverently tender or else serious and philosophical. But when Nishitani-san came to dinner he became witty, full of one amusing anecdote after another. Nishitani-san, who flushed easily when drinking sake, responded in kind, determined not to be outdone. I would laugh and laugh, gasping for breath, forgetting even to cover my mouth with my hand, till the muscles in my cheeks ached.

Those were such happy times, right before the Second World War.

Sometimes I left them—either to give Xi-Dou instructions or else to use the bathroom, something I did frequently now that I was expecting. I was not yet far enough along to feel the baby inside me, but surely it was soaking up all this laughter, growing stronger and finer as a result. In the privacy of the hallway I often stopped to tuck in wisps of hair which, on such evenings, invariably came loose from my chignon. Before me was a small window with a view of the Xiang-Ho mountains. Beyond the pagoda-style roofs I could make out their blue outline in the gathering dusk, high and jagged in the distance. And I, heartbeat still high from the hilarity of the evening, would stand in the hallway and gaze out for a while before going on my way. I thought of Shoji's deep laughter, of his large hands; of this coming child and of business continuing to boom—and I forced myself to be calm, to concentrate on those somber mountains darkening and fading beyond the compound walls that enclosed us.

From the next room I could hear the men's deep voices, laughing.

*

I have learned since that no experience lives on in memory. Not in the true sense. Its essence becomes altered, necessarily, by subsequent events. My memory of China is steeped in a sense of encroaching doom that was surely not present then, like a scene flooded with the last rays of sunset.

War was declared in 1941, when Hiroko was three years old. Kokusai Kogyo pulled up its Pei-L'an branch, and we employees sailed home in shifts to our various homes in Japan. Our family came back to Kyoto; Nishitani-san sailed home to some town near Nagasaki. Three years later, Shoji was killed in action on Iwo-Jima. Bombs dropped on our city; there were fires. Little Hiroko, weak from malnutrition, caught pneumonia two months after her sixth birthday. She died eleven days later.

Over the decades, this period has faded in my memory. Only occasionally now will its essence seep out into my body, staining my saliva with a faint coppery taste which makes me think that somewhere, within the tissues and nerves of my body, I am bleeding.

*

One morning a year after the surrender—Hiroko would have turned eight by now —an odd thing happened.

I was crouched beside the kitchen door out in the alley, watering my potted chrysanthemums. In one hand I held the watering can; with the other, I was twisting off a browned leaf here and there. Hearing the slow *k'sha k'sha* of gravel, I twisted around to see a seafood peddler pass me in the alley, bowed under the yoke of his pannier. His blue jacket looked unfamiliar; he was not from our neighborhood.

This was not unusual; residents of other areas often used our alley as a short-cut to Kamogawa Bridge on their way downtown.

As the man bowed slightly, in gratitude and apology for using this short-cut, our eyes met briefly. Then he stopped, a startled look on his face. He lowered his baskets, brimming with shijimi shells and tangles of pickled seaweed, onto the gravel before me. Something about him looked familiar—perhaps the shape of his lips, curled up slightly at the ends as if to get a jump start on a smile. But I could not place him.

The peddler stepped toward me, then bowed deeply. It was a well-trained bow, slow and straight-backed, unsettling in a man of his station. I hurriedly rose, still holding my watering can. "Goto-san, do you remember me?" he said. "I'm Nishitani. I once had the pleasure of your friendship, and your husband's, back in Pei-L'an."

Again our eyes met, and I glanced away. The shame in his look made my heart contract with pain. Even for such times, this was extreme misfortune. I fancied I could feel his loss of face pulsing out toward me, like heat waves.

We exchanged pleasantries. Nishitani-san had lines on either side of his mouth, like parentheses. Had they been there before? Something seemed different about his features—he had lost that shimmer, I think now, which had once played upon them.

"Nishitani-san, do you have a moment to sit down?" I sank down onto the kitchen step. "Here with me?" My voice came from far away. Even the weather had a surreal quality to it, I remember. It was overcast. The sky was not grey but whitish, like thick membrane, and light glowed behind it with a brightness almost brutal.

"*Saa*, that would be fine," he said. A faint version of his old smile brought back China to me, like a whiff of old scent. "Just for a few minutes."

Nishitani-san offered no explanation of his situation, nor did he mention what he was doing in this part of the country. I avoided looking in the direction of his baskets, for I wanted to spare him as much discomfort as possible; I kept my gaze trained on his face and never once glanced down at the hip-length vendor jacket he wore, cobalt blue with the store owner's name written in white brush strokes down the length of its collar. Nishitani-san smelled so strongly of fish blood, sitting beside me, that my temples were tightening into a headache. And he had once used such lovely cologne, from Paris.

He asked after Shoji and Hiroko, and I told him, in the briefest terms. "Aaa, here too . . ." he murmured. I remembered then that he had lived near Nagasaki. "How you must have suffered," he said after a silence, gazing at my face. I knew he was registering the premature streaks of white in my hair, the sun damage on my once flawless complexion.

"Do you remember," Nishitani-san said abruptly, and he began to reminisce about the delicious roast duck at our dinners, Shoji's old jokes, the comical quirks of our compound neighbors. I heard in his voice a new gravity, a new tenderness, that seemed to lift up each memory—like some precious jewel—and hold it up in wonderment to the light.

"You know," I said, "Hiroko missed you for almost a month after we sailed home. 'Uncle *Nee*-tani,' she kept saying with that lisp of hers, and she looked so worried with her little forehead all wrinkled up that everybody just had to *laugh!*—"

"A whole month, really?" Nishitani-san said. His lips curved up into his old dazzling smile. "That was unusually long for a three-year-old!"

"You see, *hora*, you're the type," I said with my old playful air, "who makes a huge impression on everyone he meets!" I froze then at my choice of words, for it skirted a little too close to the impression he would be leaving me with today. But Nishitani-san seemed not to mind, for he tipped back his head and laughed.

I pictured him back in China, on a sunny Sunday afternoon a few months before war was declared. He had been striding away after luncheon at our home, a tall, confident man; the force of his gait made the back of his white shirt, always immaculately starched, balloon out above his belt like a full sail. "Uncle *Nee*-tani! Uncle *Nee*-tani!" Hiroko had shrieked, running after him through the dappled light beneath the persimmon trees, losing her red sandal in the dirt, fumbling to put it back on then losing it again after a few steps.

Nishitani-san had glanced back. "Escape, Nishitani-san, escape!" I called out to him, laughing and shooing him away with both hands. He had flashed me a big white smile and, with a boyish laugh, trotted away in mock haste, leaving Hiroko bawling in the middle of the path.

Remembering all this, I felt the prickle of approaching tears and lowered my eyes to hide them. Nishitani-san was still laughing; it surprised me that his hands, red and raw like a laborer's, were trembling on his knees.

*

"The aristocrats of the ancient court," I say, "were devout Buddhists." It is decades later, and I am lecturing to my older tea ceremony students on the origins of etiquette.

"Buddha taught that life is filled with pain," I tell them. And suddenly an image of Nishitani-san's hands comes to mind, as they looked one day in the year 1946. There were dark scabs on his knuckles, hard as horn and soon to become callouses; on the rest of his hands were thin red scratches. I remembered my first glimpse of his baskets, full to the brim despite the lateness of the morning hour.

Clearly he was new to this, and struggling; he had not yet perfected that peculiar air vendors have, the bland unthinking cheerfulness which attracts customers.

"Filled with pain," I say to my students, "and sorrow."

"*Hai*, Teacher," the girls murmur in their high-pitched voices.

On that long-ago morning I pulled out my coin purse from my apron pocket—my hands, too, were trembling now—but before I could speak, Nishitani-san shook his head no. It was quick, a mere jerk—the imperceptible warning one gives in the presence of a third party. I slipped the purse back in my pocket.

"Those aristocrats, influenced by Buddha's teachings," I tell my students, "felt that nobility of spirit was the grace—or ability—to move through this world voluntarily, as a game or dance. And they passed down their ideal through the rituals of etiquette, *ne*? Polite speech, for example. Even today we refer to an honorable person not as having been killed, but as having condescended to play at dying."

The girls nod politely, blankly.

Today, what strikes me most about that morning—for memory will always shift focus—is our wordless farewell as Nishitani-san and I bowed to each other. It would be many years before I linked the essence of our bow with that of Kenryu's famous poem about a rice plant: *weighed down / with grain / making graceful bows / in the wind*. How lovely our bows must have seemed to a casual onlooker: stately, seasoned, like movements in a sacred dance.

Tusk

A. A. Srinivasan

Hindi, Tamil, Bengali, Gujarati, Malayalam, Marathi, Punjabi. I brought all of them to the cyberworld of local advertising and graphics. Of course, without the help of scholars who felt themselves quite intimate with each of the languages, I could not have accomplished this task. I have earned my fortune in the world of technology, and I assure the squeamish entrepreneur there remain princely amounts of money to be made in the realm of electronic reality, after my own small contribution.

I began my career in a more mundane field, developing electronic mail transferring programs. My software development served as a better way to send memorandums, documents, haiku and love letters through fiber optic lines quick, bang. Within the next two years, my program would have become obsolete due to my lack of enthusiasm for the business, but for a stroke of genius; I sold the project to Permasoftware for a hefty sum. At thirty-two I am more than ready to retire, emotionally as well as financially. I will work again one day. When? I don't know.

To say I do not work is not entirely true. Some might term me a type of physician of the future; for many people, I am more important than their own GPs. I carry a pager, and when a new computer enters the home, I feel a gentle vibration on my hip. An anxious voice on the line pleads for my help.

Nitin Aggarwal was my first house call after I sold my company. "Vinay," he boomed, "we've bought a new computer. Bigger than my own son! But, you know, this thing, I can't get the damned monitor to show a bloody . . . uh, you know . . . this thing. When are you available? Are you going to Ganapati Chathurthi on Sunday? We are. Priya wants the priest to bless the computer, but there is no way in hell I am going to drag it all the way down there. Almost three-thousand dollars we spent on this thing. I bought a lot of software stuffs to go with it. You will have to come over and teach me how to use it."

This same man never did have This Thing blessed by a priest, but three years later, it seems to work fine. He gave it to his son (who is now bigger than the CPU) and bought himself another component which refuses to fit under his desk. Now he possesses the perfect excuse to purchase new office furniture.

I make regular house calls to Nitin. Today he expounds on the same subject I hear about every time I pay a visit. "You know, Vinay, you are like family to me, like my own son. Why is there a giraffe walking across my screen? Damn thing. Parag must have loaded one of those . . . screen-savers on there. Wait until my clients catch a glimpse of this. Don't you want to have children, Vinay? Don't you miss having a home cooked meal?"

He doesn't realize I am served a home cooked meal every time I make a house call to set up, repair, or remove a computer from a residence. "Vinay," they say, "you must be hungry. My husband can wait to set up his computer. Come, sit down. Have some dosai. Have some puris. Have some naan. Have some rice, yogurts, alu, dal, bharta, raita, sambar, bhindi, vada, papadums picklejalebisgulabjamuns."

I smile at my old friend sitting across from me, who tinkers with his computer, running the giraffes, monkeys, and toucans off the screen with the click of a key. I rub the heftiness around my middle and laugh to myself. As far as meals are concerned, I am well taken care of.

My mother also tries to please and appease everyone with food. It is her way of getting my father to shut up for a few minutes. And my mother *does* spend most of her time attempting to pacify my father, just as I had tried years ago. My parents are champions of domestic strife, and when they are not engaged in verbal combat, they immerse themselves in silence. No one knows why my father is so angry. He never discusses anything with us. My mother always says: "He's a businessman, Vinay. Rich people didn't get rich by being nice."

As a child, it was imperative for me to gauge my father's moods before I said anything and especially before I made a request. The first time I asked him for a computer, he nearly knocked my head off, for he had lost big time in the stock market that day. I learned to decipher the Dow Jones at an early age. I spent most of my days watching television while my parents were at work, until they did finally buy a computer for me. Television became only a memory. My father bought me a new computer every two years, a bribe, I think, a way of preventing me from pestering him. I loved my first computer the same way a child loves a pet, a sibling, a parent, even. My mother would come in with my dinner in hand, and she would play with the keyboard and the mouse while I ate.

This was her way of getting me away from my personal terminal for a few minutes; she knew I would always move for her.

Nitin's wife reminds me of my mother. She is one of the best cooks around, and after eating one of her meals, I feel as if the whole universe (or perhaps just a decent-sized computer) will fit into my stomach. For his wife, I developed a Hindi script on the computer, enabling her to write a well-designed cookbook for the Venkateswar Temple fund-raiser. All the women ooh-aahed at her designs and typesetting skills, then immediately placed an order for her cookbook, as well as for a copy of the homemade program, which created the visual feast. The husbands phoned me, one by one, shouting, "Vinay, you're a bloody genius! Why didn't you think of this sooner? Why didn't *I* think of it sooner? Do you want to work for my company? We're thinking of getting into import/ export, you know? I have a friend who wants to publish a SoCal Gujarat newsletter *in* Gujarati, but I said, 'No way, *bhai*, no way. You'll have to pub-lish it in English, or nothing.' But, when Seema showed me that cookbook of yours, I rang him *immeedjiatly* and shared the news, my genius friend." When I reminded him the font was in Hindi, not Gujarati, he replied, "Yes, but you know Gujarati, no?" No. I don't even know Hindi. A con-sultant and friend wrote out the alphabet for me since English is my one and only language, I'm afraid.

I hired a Gujarati doctor to write the alphabet to aid me and delivered the program to Mr. Shah the following month. Before I finished with the Gujarati text, Sri Subramanian phoned, asking for the development of a Tamil alphabet and a collection of clip art depicting Rama, Sita, Arjuna, Krishna, Ganesha. I hesitated for a moment, wondering how long it would take me to develop a South Indian language. Too long, I thought, and too many headaches. Already, I dreamt of demonic dancing alpha-bets all night, but Subramanian begged, "*Enna?* What's wrong? South Indian languages are beneath you?" I replied, "Not beneath me, perhaps beyond me." He chuckled and phoned me three more times before I agreed.

For him, I developed all of the items he requested: an unrefined ver-sion of the Tamilian alphabet as well as a screen-saver of Krishna and Arjuna rolling across the battleground with Hanuman dancing around behind them, setting the field alight with his tail. I seemed to have got-ten a bit carried away and muddled my myths, but Subramanian cared lit-tle and overlooked any flaws. We both viewed it as an experiment any-way, a highly successful one.

A designer helped me develop a Ganesha screen-saver as a gift for my mother. The elephant-headed god rides along on his mouse and falls off of his vehicle, His stomach bursting open from the collision with the ground. The animation is fantastic, as balls of rice pudding and other sweets come tumbling out of Him, brightly-colored desserts fly across the screen. He scoops up his food and places it all back inside of Him as the Moon watches and laughs. Ha ha ha! The Moon rotates round and round, gleefully, while the mouse scampers back and forth! An indignant frown settles across the face of the god. He breaks off one of His tusks and hurls it at the laughing lunatic, but the Moon catches the sacred ivory in his mouth and refuses to return it. Then, the scene begins again, with a jolly Ganapati strolling across the monitor on his mouse-steed. The program has become very popular with children.

In came orders of all sorts, forcing me to produce more and more alphabets. A poet friend insisted I develop his native language on the computer, for his earnest labors were presently dedicated to a collection of Bengali haiku. Also, a married Punjabi woman was having an affair with another Punjabi, but her husband, a man originating from the state of Karnataka, could not read the love letters they sent back and forth via the electronic mail's attached documents.

And every time I delivered a new alphabet to a family, they sat me down at the dinner table, asking if I wanted any pakoras, bhajees, bharta, khatrika, rasgollah, basmati pillau, thair sadham, dum-alu . . . food flying at me from all directions.

Nitin now reminds me of my age and of the enormous house I bought last year, all empty and sad. "It is *sooo* sad and lonely, I can't even bear to visit you there. Why do you own such a big place, *bhai?* A palace isn't a palace without a woman and couple-of-three kiddies running round." I shake my head and smile, thinking it might not be such a bad idea if I begin a family, have someone to help me spend my money, but still, I don't know if it's wise to take advice from an accountant who believes couple-of-three is a legitimate numerical description. I tell Nitin how to turn off his Jungle Life screen-saver and head home.

I share my house with a boarder named Subash, who, when he is not at work, sits in front of the television waiting for the next cricket match. "Vinay, you are my godsend," he told me when he moved in. "In New York, I had to ride down to Greves Cinema in the middle of the night and catch the matches there, but that satellite dish you've got makes for the happiest home in the whole world." I am unsure of my reasons for buying the dish in the first place. I hate watching television, and I usually pick up *India West* if I want to know cricket scores, but Subash's passion for the sport refuses to be appeased by a few lines in a weekly dis-patch. He threatens to kill himself if India fails to win the World's Cup this year. "Its been too long, Vinay, too long for us."

When I arrive home, Subash sits at the dining table grinning like a jolly Buddha. "Good chances! We're in the running. Australia and Sri Lanka are the big opponents this year. West Indies, not so good. South Africa, Pakistan, no way." He rocks back and forth, rubbing his palms together like an anxious fan waiting for the bowler to let go of the ball. "You are good luck. Did you know that? Ever since I met you, good things have been happening. There is some fish curry in the fridge. Have some. Have all you like. You need to eat. You'll bring me good luck, won't you?" He smiles at me, enjoying his own little joke.

I envy Subash sometimes. The look in his eyes during a cricket match, the tightened fist on his lap, the roaring of his voice, make the house come alive, as if there are a hundred people pumped up, living under one roof, this roof.

His passions extend beyond cricket. Subash threatened to kill himself once before, said he intended to jump off my balcony (which probably would *not* have killed him) if he missed the chance to put his hands on the brand new Microsoft Windows software the very day of its release. At 2:00 A.M., he danced in the street, waving his box back and forth in the air after standing in line at the computer store for two hours. I should have been embarrassed to be with him.

"We're having a cricket party on Tuesday, and you're coming. You need to bring the dessert."

"I can't come."

"Why not?"

I can't think of any reason.

"Of course, you're coming. You never go anywhere. You sit in front of your computer all day, researching God-knows-what, and you need to start getting out more, dating, doing something. I'm not going to be here forever, satellite dish or not. I have plans for my future: parties to attend, food to eat, countries to visit, weight to gain, women to charm. You are wasting your life making house calls and sitting in front of a computer. I can barely remember what your voice sounds like. Say something."

I laugh.

"Say something."

"Hello. My name is Vinay."

"Something interesting."

"I don't care much for cricket."

"Say something that isn't blasphemous."

My stomach growls, and I wander to the refrigerator for some fish curry.

"Ganesha has a fat stomach and big ears. That's why my mother named me Vinay."

Subash laughs, staring down at his stomach. "Then, most of us should be named after dearest Ganapati."

I once dated a girl who said, "Vinay, you don't talk much and this bothers me. It makes one think you might, perhaps, be a murdering psychopath. A silent man is a bad sign, means he might combust at any given moment. Please say something. Don't just nod like that. You look like an imbecile. Do you sing? You aren't an imbecile, but you need to speak up. Speak up, speak up. I need to know what you're thinking, and for gods' sake, don't whistle. That is another sure sign of a lunatic." I loved her, although I never discovered where she derived her knowledge of psychopaths. She married her singing teacher, and the two later opened a sari shop. Her name was Leela. The store has been named after her.

She asked me to set up a computer inventory system for *Leela's Palace* before they opened to the public, and I agreed. While I unhappily loaded the software onto their computer register, Leela took a rest from decorating the mannequins in the front window. "You are the only one I trust to do this, to not rip us off," she said, sipping on a Coke. She held the can out to me and I ignored the gesture. "Some might say I've taken advantage of you because I knew you couldn't say 'no.' In fact, you can't say a damn thing. How did a man without a tongue become so successful? I always thought you would amount to something if you could just burst out of that feeble life you lead." I said nothing. The computer system was ready for operation. Leela picked up a bag of samosas sitting next to her chair and dropped them in front of me, then turned on her heel and resumed her dance with the half-naked mannequin.

Subash points a finger at me. "You haven't dated anyone since Leela. What you saw in her, I don't know. There is a woman I want you to meet at this party, so you must come."

I put up a struggle but not a terribly convincing one. Something in my voice or the way I concentrate a little too hard on reheating the fish displays a glimmer of excitement. When Leela left me, she asked, "So, what will you do now?" I shrugged, replying, "Work. I have a lot of work to do, projects. I'll have more time for them now." She laughed, no, she guffawed at my response. It took me two years to understand the meaning behind that roar of laughter.

"Does she like computers?" I ask casually, poking at the fish in the microwave.

Subash bangs his palm flat on the table and laughs the way Leela laughed when she left. "My god, you must be kidding, chap! You think I would set you up with someone who liked computers? No way! Vimmi hates most things with a plug attachment. For a while we all thought she was the Unabomber. She said she'll be carried into the information age weeping."

I laugh, agreeing with him that an egghead in my life might not be the best woman suited for me.

"Although," Subash says, scratching his chin, "If you're curious, you can find a picture of her on the Web. Her brother created his own page."

"What is her brother's name? Maybe I know him," I say.

"Vimal Narayan."

Bingo. The only clue I need. "Never heard of him." I sit down at the table, next to Subash, with my dinner in hand.

"Will Vimal be at the party, too?" I ask, still attempting an air of nonchalance.

"I think he'll be in Detroit until next week, but *you* must be there! She knows all about you now. I told her she needs to save you from your sorry life, my friend. And I am doing this for my own selfish reasons, too. The happier you are, my dear Ganapati, the more luck you will bring to me! Pakistan, get ready to give up your title!"

"We haven't even met each other yet," I say. "I wouldn't place any bets on account of me. What if she hates me, makes my life miserable? What if I hate her in return? What if we never even speak to each other?"

"Look, Vimmi is a hundred times nicer than Leela, and she doesn't have a mouth like a turbine. She's a little shy sometimes, but not *too* shy, always smiling. She's a painter."

"Really?" I ask, too quickly. "Have you seen any of her paintings?"

"No," he says, picking out the onions from the fish curry, one by one, and dropping them into his mouth. "She's a big cricket fan, so she's all right with me."

"Then why don't you ask her out, yourself? All this makes me very suspicious."

"She isn't Bengali, and that *is* a must. She has got to speak my language, chap."

"The only language *you* know, *chap*, is cricket. Your vocabulary is limited to batsman, bowler, wicket, Azharuddin, and Tendulkar."

He laughs. "True, very true, but Mums wouldn't like her very much then, would she?"

After polishing off all the onions, not bothering to leave me any, Subash washes his hands and heads out the door to collect betting money from his friends for the Cup finals. An hour later, he arrives home with two fistfuls of cash accompanied by a check or two. He drops everything on the table, in front of me, covering the newspaper I read half-heartedly. I want to wait until Subash has gone to sleep before looking up the picture of the woman who doesn't possess a mouth like a turbine.

"Okay, Vinayaka, here it is. All on Mother Bharat. Six-hundred whopper-oonies." He snaps a hundred-dollar bill in front of my face. "Tomorrow it all begins. Do your thing."

"Stop it," I say laughing, pushing the money out of view. "You're incorrigible."

"Alas, chap, only one of my many virtues."

"Then I don't think I want to know what your other virtues are."

"Oh, but dedication is my finest one!" He leans over the table and scoops up all the money to his chest. "Who else would sacrifice a week's vacation to monitor their team's performance?"

"I can only think of nine-hundred-million other people." He waves my comment away with one free hand.

True. Subash did in fact use up his vacation time, a whole week, to watch the last of the Wills Cup matches. Beyond the subcontinent, a person such as this might prove difficult to find.

He yawns and says, "I'm going to bed. Get plenty of sleep tomorrow. The match is live, live! 1:30 A.M." He fondles the green lump of bills close to him as if it were his teddy-bear.

I wait for the light to turn off in his bedroom before I head upstairs to my office. Subash has a tendency to barge in, late at night, yelling, "God help me, Vinay, I'm going to smash that thing to smithereens if you can't fix my damn computer. Everything lost! Who asked Microsoft to make my life easier anyway?" After I would fix the problem, he would simply slap his hands together in an overly dramatic *namasté* and sigh, "I worship you, *bhai*, I really do."

I sit down at my desk and log in. My sister often laughs at me, at the fact I have a password to get into my personal computer at home. "Who the hell will break into your files here, brother dearest?" She's right. I disable the program, allowing me to enter my files without logging on the next time I use it. I have been using my computer less and less and will eventually forget my complex password anyway.

I enter the realm of the World Wide Web and perform a search for Vimal Narayan. After arriving at the correct address, the colorful page explains that the creator is an attorney, originally from Kentucky. His favorite sports are badminton, squash, and tennis, none of which I am remotely good at. In college, he was the head of a speech and debate team, which I now interpret as a euphemism for an argumentative and confrontational person. (Dearest Leela was also the head of her speech and debate team.) Vimal is handsome, with his evenly proportioned features and muscular physique. The photo shows him holding both a tennis racket and a gavel. His ambition is to serve on the United States Supreme Court. Click HERE, it says, to meet my MOTHER, FATHER, SISTER, SAINT BERNARD. I click where it says, SISTER. The image loads while my fingers drum against the mouse.

A photo of a woman comes up, crisp, clear. She casually holds a sculpture under her arm of a rat or hamster with wings. Her hair falls to her shoulders, one side tucked behind her ear. Her round eyes question why a camera sits in her face, a face which resembles a cherub in its perfect circularity. Her incisors nervously gnaw on the edge of her bottom lip. She wears an AUDUBON shirt which shows a hedgehog or beaver sitting under the logo. The screen reads: My sister Vimala is an artist/sculptor. She lives in Los Angeles with a dog, a parrot, a mouse, and a ferret. She has just finished a Ph.D. in bio-chemical engineering at the University of Illinois, and plans to do absolutely nothing with it! But I love her anyway. Her favorite sports are diving for clams and bungee jumping, and she loves to cook and paint. She doesn't have an e-mail address. Click here to meet my MOTHER, FATHER, SAINT BERNARD, ME. I click on all of them, one at a time, to see if there are any more pictures of Vimmi. There are none.

I turn off the computer, bored with everything else it has to offer. Attempting to sleep tonight seems futile now. Too bad India isn't playing a match today. Then I would have a reason for pacing the hallways during all hours of the night, although I really could care less about the outcome. Subash would know something else haunts me; he is spastic but far from stupid or unobservant. Perhaps I should wake him, ask him what he has told her about me. Does she *really* want to meet me? No, it will excite him too much. Then I'll feel foolish and embarrassed when I meet her. What am I saying? I can't date a woman whose favorite sport is bungee jumping. I'm terrified of heights. Clam diving? What is that? It doesn't sound like much of a sport to me. And what does one do after picking up the clams? She can't possibly eat them. Can she? How disgusting. All right, I *have* tried squid. I can live with clams—I suppose. And why a ferret? Where can I get one? What is it? Are they rodents? Marsupials? Felines? I'm allergic to cats. Will I also suffer an allergic reaction to ferrets? Women always choose animals over me, complete beasts. How do the mouse and the ferret interact? What about the parrot? I've met one before, and it never shut its yap, sort of like Subash, but I like *him*. Perhaps Vimmi's parrot doesn't speak, or enunciate properly. Do all of these various creatures get along? It is obvious that she's already too complicated for me. There is no way I can go through with this, no way. Subash will call me a coward, no doubt. I've done this to him several times before, but then, he didn't understand I was afraid of another Leela, and I was afraid of *not* having another Leela. Perhaps I should rid myself of my computer, throw it to the dogs . . . and the mice and the ferrets and the parrots and throw myself at Vimmi. God, why didn't I take speech and debate? I think I'm hungry again.

*

In the early morning hours, I dress and hurry to my office in the same way Subash has been running around for a month like a mouse in a plastic ball. I print out the photo of Vimmi and hide it in my shirt pocket after folding it neatly into a square. A few pens prevent the photo from falling out. I remove it two or three times when time passes too slowly, then fold it up straight-away every time the house creaks. I train my mind to erase any thoughts of computers. Should I ask her about her animals? How would I know of her interests? I can't betray myself, divulge my late night research. Subash flies through the door just as I tuck the paper to my chest.

"Hey chap!" I feel a heavy slap on my back. "What are you doing? You *really* need to get out more. I am going to throw that computer out the window if you don't stop sitting in front of it all day, all night, all day. You make me want to scream. How can you fiddle with things like that when, in only seventeen hours, the match of the century will begin?" Subash waves an arm in the air as if he is rounding up cattle, then scampers out of my office. I hear him shouting, "Ganapati, ho!" as he runs down the hall, toward the kitchen. The countdown has begun.

*

The shouting, booing, hissing, cheering begins at 1:30 A.M. Five cricket fanatics, a sleeping wife, and me, sitting around a fifty-two-inch television watching the first semifinals televised from Calcutta's Eden Gardens. Not a word was mentioned about Vimmi. I sit at the table in back of the sofa, where I pick at the gulab jamun I bought from the Indian grocery shop. The five men help themselves at different intervals to the snacks, the dinner, and the dessert. One of the men has lost his voice from his inability to contain his emotions over the last month; however, he does manage to croak, "Hi, Vinay." Subash stands up and stretches after shouting, "Dammit! Let's beat those Ravanas!" During a lull in the match, he says, "I forgot about dessert. Hand me some of those, my 'Good Luck Ganapati.'" (This is how he has introduced me to his friends.) He holds out a plate to me, and I ration out three fried dough balls. He rolls his eyes to the heavens and yells, "Brilliant!" After finishing the second gulab jamun, he turns to his mates and says, "Hey, where is Vimmi?" The men ignore him. One man shrugs. "I don't think she lives too far away," Subash mumbles, his eyes now glued back on the television screen. "Maybe she only wants to catch the end of the match." He wanders back to the sofa.

The Bengalis are now rioting. (In Calcutta, not the living room.)

I've eaten half of the gulab jamuns. I should save some in case Vimmi comes.

Shouldn't she have arrived by now? Perhaps I'll meet her another time. We always tend to run into one another, we Indians, somehow, somewhere, sometime, in Los Angeles. I know what she looks like. I wonder if she would be impressed by my artistic creations, my alphabets. Maybe I could bring her slowly into my own world, show her a few things on the computer. I feel one side of my chest. Yes, the printout is still there. Would Vimmi and I cook together? Would she create a cookbook of her own? She would probably hand write the damn thing herself. Or maybe I could entice her into using the computer. Would she eventually develop a fondness for it, the way I once developed an insatiable appetite for gulab jamun? Would I, one day, find love letters from her to someone I didn't know, written in a language foreign to me?

I see Subash eyeing the last gulab jamun, but I snatch it up first, placing the sweet ball near me.

I wander out onto the back porch and seat myself near the pool. What if Vimmi and I hit it off like long lost friends? I wonder if she wants to have children. Wouldn't this surprise my dear friend Nitin? Would I entertain him in my home and compare my couple-of-three kiddies to the size of computers? Probably not in Vimmi's presence. Or would she and I have pets only?

Subash beckons me inside before I can make myself comfortable. "They've lost! We've lost. Forfeited. Damn riots started again!" He turns away, his despair expressed by silence. The guests leave one by one. Subash manages to open his mouth to say something, though he looks like someone dying of malnutrition. "Hey, Vinay." He called me Vinay, not Vinayaka, Ganapati, Ganesha. I would even settle for chap. "Vimmi phoned while you were outside. She said she didn't set her alarm correctly. She sounded half asleep."

"Who?" I ask. "Oh, yes. Vimmi." I shrug and laugh. "Well, she didn't miss much then, did she?"

He nods weakly, turning his eyes toward the blank face of the television.

I drive home, carrying the last gulab jamun in a plastic baggie. Subash stays at Shankar's house for the night, the best thing for him right now. He needs the company of someone with whom he can share his grief.

The night is clear and cool. I look at the moon, its half-smile. Sometimes I wait for something to happen when I stare at it for too long, wait for it to give something back to me, and at other times I think it is simply laughing.

Events Leading to the Conception of Solomon, the Wise Child

Dannie Abse

And David comforted Bathsheba his wife, and went into her, and lay with her; and she bore a son, and he called his name Solomon: and the Lord loved him.

I

Are the omina favorable?
Scribes know the King's spittle,
even the most honored
like Seraiah the Canaanite,
and there are those, addicted,
who inhale
          the smoke of burning papyrus.

So is the date-wine sour, the lemon sweet?
Who can hear the sun's furnace?

The shadow of some great bird
          drifts indolently
across the ochres and umbers
of the afternoon hills
          that surround Jerusalem.
Their rising contours, their heat-refracting
          undulations.

The lizard is on the ledges,
the snake is in the crevices.

It is where Time lives.

Below, within the thermals of the Royal
        City,
past the cursing camel driver,
past the sweating woman carrying water
        in a goatskin,
past the leper peeping through
        the lateral slats
of his fly-mongering latrine
to the walls of the Palace itself,
the chanting King is at prayer.

        Aha, aha,
attend to my cry, O Lord
who makest beauty
to be consumed away like a moth;
purge me with hyssop and I
        shall be clean.
Wash me and I shall be
        whiter than the blossom.
Blot out my iniquities.

Not yet this prayer, not yet
        that psalm.
It is where a story begins.
Even the Bedouin beside their black tents
have heard the desert wind's rumor.
They ask:
        Can papyrus grow
where there is no marsh?
They cry:
        Sopher yodea
to the Scribe with two tongues,
urge him to tend his kingdom
        of impertinence.

II

When the naked lady stooped to bathe
  in the gushings of a spring,
the voyeur on the tower roof
  just happened to be the King.

She was summoned to the Palace
  where the King displayed his charms;
he stroked the harp's glissandos,
  sang her a couple of psalms.

Majestic sweet-talk in the Palace
  —he name-dropped Goliath and Saul—
till only one candle-flame flickered
  and two shadows moved close on the wall.

Of course she hankered for the Palace.
  Royal charisma switched her on.
Her husband snored at the Eastern Front,
  so first a kiss, then scruples gone.

Some say, "Sweet victim in the Palace,"
  some say, "Poor lady in his bed."
But Bathsheba's teeth like milk were white,
  and her mouth like wine was red.

David, at breakfast, bit an apple.
  She, playful, giggling, seized his crown,
then the apple-flesh as usual
  after the bite turned brown.

III

In the kitchen, the gregarious, hovering flies
where the servants breakfast.
A peacock struts
                in its irradiance,
and is ignored.

On the stone floor and on the shelves
the lovely shapes of utensils,
great clay pots, many jugs of wine
                many horns of oil,
the food-vessels and the feast-boards.

On the long table, butter of kine, thin loaves,
bowls of olives and griddle-cakes,
wattled baskets of summer fruit,
flasks of asses' milk and jars of honey.

What a tumult of tongues,
                the maids and the men,
the hewers of wood,
the drawers of water,
                the narrow-skulled
                and the wide-faced.
What a momentary freedom prospers,
                a detour from routine,
a substitute for mild insurrection.

They ask:
      In his arras-hung chamber
      did the King smell of the sheepcote?
      On the ivory bench, did he seat her
            on cushions?
Did she lie on the braided crimson couch,
beneath her head pillows of goat hair?

Who saw him undo her raiments?
Who overheard Uriah's wife,
Bathsheba of the small voice,
           cry out?
Was it a woman made love to
or the nocturnal moan
           of the turtle dove?

Will the priest, Nathan, awaken
who, even in his sleep, mutters
           Abomination?

Now she who is beautiful to look upon
leaves furtively by a back door.
She will become a public secret.
She wears fresh garments of blue and purple,
the topaz of Ethiopia beneath her apparel.
But a wind gossips in the palm trees,
the anaphora of the wind
              in the fir-trees of Senir,
              in the cedars of Lebanon,
              in the oaks of Bashan.
It flaps the tents where Uriah, the Hittite,
is encamped with Joab's army
on the Eastern open fields.

Does purity of lust last one night only?
In the breakfasting kitchen, the peacock screams.

IV

The wind blows and the page turns over.
  Soon the King was reading a note.
Oh such excruciating Hebrew:
  "I've one in the bin," she wrote.

Since scandal's bad for royal business
  the King must not father the child;
so he called Uriah from the front,
  shook his hand like a voter. Smiled.

Uriah had scorned the wind's whisper,
  raised his eyebrows in disbelief.
Still, here was the King praising his valor,
  here was the King granting him leave.

In uniform rough as a cat's tongue
  the soldier artlessly said,
"Hard are the stones on the Eastern Front,
  but, Sire, harder at home is my bed."

Though flagons and goat-meat were offered
  the Hittite refused to go home.
He lingered outside the Palace gates,
  big eyes as dark as the tomb.

Silk merchants came and departed,
  they turned from Uriah appalled—
for the soldier sobbed in the stony heat,
  ignored his wife when she called;

sat down with his sacks, sat in the sun,
  sat under stars and would not quit,
scowled at the King accusingly
  till the King got fed up with it.

"Stubborn Uriah, what do you want?
  Land? Gold? Speak and I'll comply."
Then two vultures creaked overhead
  to brighten the Hittite's eye.

"Death." That's what he sought in the desert
  near some nameless stony track.
And there two vultures ate the soldier
  with a dagger in his back.

The widow was brought to the Palace,
  a Queen for the King-size bed,
and oh their teeth like milk were white,
  and their mouths like wine were red.

V

Should there be merriment at a funeral?
Stones of Jerusalem, where is your lament?
Should her face not have been leper-ashen?
Should she not have torn at her apparel,
               bayed at the moon?

Is first young love
                always a malady?

When Uriah roared with the Captains of Joab,
                the swearing garrisons,
the dust leaping behind the chariots,
                the wagons, the wheels;
when his sword was unsheathed
amidst the uplifted trumpets
and the cacophony of donkeys;
when he was fierce as a close-up,
                huge with shield and helmet;
when his face was smeared with vermilion,
did she think of him less
                than a scarecrow in a field?

When she was more girl than woman
who built for her
                a house of four pillars?
When his foot was sore
                did she not dip it in oil?
When his fever seemed perilous
                did she not boil the figs?

When the morning stars sang together,
face to face, they sang together.
At night when she shyly stooped
                did he not boldly soar?

When, at midnight, the owl screeched
                who comforted her?
When the unclothed satyr danced
                in moonlight
who raised a handkerchief to her wide eyes?

When the archers practiced
                in the green pastures
whose steady arm curled about her waist?

True love is not briefly displayed
like the noon glory of the fig marigold.

Return oh return
pigeons of memory to your homing land.

But the scent was only a guest
                    in the orange tree.
The colors faded
                    from the ardent flowers
not wishing to outstay their visit.

VI

The wind blows and the page turns over.
  To Bathsheba a babe was born.
Alas, the child would not feed by day,
  by night coughed like a thunderstorm.

"Let there be justice after sunset,"
  cried Nathan, the raging priest.
Once again he cursed the ailing child
  and the women's sobs increased.

So the skeletal baby sickened
  while the King by the cot-side prayed
and the insomniac mother stared
  at a crack in the wall afraid.

Nobody played the psaltery,
  nobody dared the gameboard.
The red heifer and doves were slaughtered.
  A bored soldier cleaned his stained sword.

Courtiers huddled in the courtyard,
  rampant their whisperings of malice.
The concubines strutted their blacks.
  The spider was in the Palace.

Soon a battery of doors in the Palace,
  soon a weird shout, "The child is dead."
Then Bathsheba's teeth like milk were white,
  and her eyes like wine were red.

Outside the theater of the shrine
  David's penitent spirit soared
beyond the trapped stars. He wept. He danced
  the dance of death before the Lord.

That night the King climbed to her bedroom.
  Gently he coaxed the bereaved
and in their shared and naked suffering
  the wise child, love, was conceived.

CODA

Over the rocky dorsals of the hills
the pilgrim buses of April arrive,
one by one, into Jerusalem.

There was a jackal on the site
                of the Temple
before the Temple was built.

And stones. The stones only.

Are the omina favorable?
Will there be blood on the thorn bush?
Does smoke rising from the rubbish dump
                veer to the West or to the East?
So much daylight! So much dust!
This scribe is
                and is not
the Scribe who knew the King's spittle.

After the soldier alighted,
a black-bearded, invalid-faced man,
stern as Nathan, head covered,
followed by a fat woman, a tourist
wearing the same Phoenician purple
                as once Bathsheba did,
her jeweled wrist, for one moment,
a drizzle of electric.

But no bizarre crowned phantom
will sign the Register
                    at the King David Hotel.

Like the lethargic darkness
of 3000 years ago,
once captive, cornered
within the narrow-windowed
                    Temple of Solomon,
everything has vanished into the light.

Except the stones. The stones only.

There is a bazaar-loud haggling
                    in the chiaroscuro
                    of the alleyways,
tongue-gossip in the gravel walks,
even in the oven of the Squares;
a discontinuous, secret weeping
of a husband or wife, belittled and betrayed
behind the shut door of an unrecorded house.

There is a kissing of the stones,
a kneeling on the stones,
                    psalmody and hymnody,
winged prayers swarming in the domed hives
of mosques, synagogues, churches,
ebullitions of harsh religion.

"For thou art my lamp, O Lord . . ."
"In the name of God, Lord of the Worlds . . ."
"Hear the voice of my supplications . . ."
"And forgive us our trespasses . . ."
"The Lord is my shepherd I shall not want . . ."
"My fortress, my high tower, my deliverer . . ."
"The Lord is my shepherd I shall not . . .
                    . . . my buckler, my hiding place . . ."
"I am poured out like water . . ."
"The Lord is my shepherd . . ."

" . . . and my bones are vexed . . ."
"The Lord is . . ."
"Allah Akbar!"
"Sovereign of the Universe!"
"Our Father in Heaven!"
"Father of Mercies!"
"Shema Yisroael!"

There is a tremendous hush in the hills
above the hills
where the lizard is on the ledges,
where the snake is in the crevices,
after the shadow of an aeroplane
has hurtled and leapt
below the hills and on to the hills
that surround Jerusalem.

Married Love

Mark Rudman

Every time Levin walked into the bathroom area when Kitty was quietly
submerged in the tub or standing under the shower
and he could see her body behind the curtain's scrim,
he was startled that he still stared
as if he'd never seen her naked before
and shocked that his desire was as keen
after these years of domestic life as when
he first found the nerve to speak to her
that evening at the skating rink
while every other young unmarried man
was at that instant skating in her direction.

Levin was never sure of anything in this life
except the fact of his unworthiness,
and his gratitude for the miracle that such a serene
and perfect creature as Kitty—
who was above everything earthly
and whose smile opened
the doorway to the enchanted
world of his early childhood—
knew no bound. He didn't believe

that a woman as sought after as
the eighteen year old Kitty
would have bothered to see that his scowling
eyebrows disguised the kindness in his eyes
so that in time she consented to marry

this low, earthly, and chaotic man,
who changed his mind like weather
and was neither dashing nor handsome.

He was roused from reverie by the vague
feeling she didn't want him there so he'd usually
back out of the bathroom
yet before going downstairs find some excuse
to return when she was about
halfway through drying off with a towel
and he could see her body all the more clearly.

More clearly than during lovemaking
late at night in the demanded upon dark
when he didn't see what he was
touching or entering in any detail,
and lingered, and though acutely self-conscious
of his own tactlessness he wasn't embarrassed.
She was his wife.
No one could say he was a voyeur.

How long had he known her?
Three weeks, three years, three months, ten, sixteen years,
he couldn't remember;
all that he knew was each time he came upon her in this way
he was still awed, and fascinated,
as he was the first time.

It was always the first time.

Countless encounters blurred; merged:
he heard the sounds that drove him on;
and saw her raise one leg, close
both of them while they lay moderately still;
then open.

This was the image he often held while
he wielded his scythe, yet never became
dangerously distracted.

"What is it?
Maybe it isn't good.
Maybe it bothers her.
Maybe I should apologize.
Maybe I should confess.
I'll talk to Stefan—he lives in the city.
He'll know the right thing to do.

No, if it bothered her she would tell me.

You'd think that after all this time—
and we do have three children—
she would have said:
it's not as if we don't know each other.

Could she be shy about her body
after so many births?
I, I . . ., I don't know."

Stammering: a sign to change the subject.
Losing himself in work he loved was his one chance
to slow his wheelspinning mind,
going round round and round,
like prisoners in a yard.

The thought of going nowhere made him wretch.
But it was September. Carts, oats, harvest.
Now Levin could lose himself in labor.
Plunge his pitchfork into the hay.
And as the sweat soaked through his clothes
and he looked up at the peasants working all around him
he felt some reprieve from the torture of this self-questioning
which otherwise would never leave him alone.

"Everything . . ." he muttered to himself,
"why do I have to question everything.
Why do I have to care, especially if it doesn't bother her."

At dusk, Levin returns in a transported state,

goes running through the rooms to share
his ecstasy with Kitty.

Before she registers the radiance on his face
and he gives her his long-anticipated hug, she says:

"You know Nikolai, it really bothers me
that you always find your way into the shower
when I'm in the bathroom or taking a shower.
We have several bathrooms.
Why can't you use another one."

"Yes darling you're right and I apologize I'm sorry.
Not sorry, mortified!
I DON'T KNOW WHAT IT IS
PLEASE forgive—something
comes over me—but I don't know what."

 "You don't want me to put a lock on the door."

"But we have never held anything back from each other.
I'm more exposed in my diaries than you are in the shower."

"You're so honest—but also use your bluntness to get your way
and I won't let you. You'll take apart any reason I give.

I want to be able to bathe alone without being interrupted.
I want a lock I can lock from the inside."

 "Oh no you can't do that because what if
one of the children has to see you immediately."

"They can knock. And I didn't say the door
would always be locked."

Stalky the Clown

Ira Sadoff

Mrs. Dandridge was dying. Mr. Severinson was dying. The cranky Mrs. Zwick was dying. Little Tammy Wynette Rawlings was dying. According to the different clocks of their diseases, but surely all of Quin's patients were dying. After nearly ten years on the oncology ward, though she still loved her work, Quin was wearing down. She was helping Anna Zwick down the hall for a CAT scan, walking so slowly that Anna asked her, "Are we moving?" but then she added, "What's that coming toward us?"

"That's my ex-husband," Quin replied.

Randy waved with both hands, and seeing Quin he did a somersault and pulled a balloon shaped like a giraffe out of his coat. "He's funny," Anna said.

"He starts out funny," Quin said.

"Like life," Anna said.

"He's a clown," Quin said. "Professionally, I mean."

He crossed his hands behind his back and circled them as they pro-ceeded down the hall. "You haven't answered my last letter about Leo's golf lessons. He's going to fall behind his classmates. Life's shorter than you think."

"Not short enough for some," she said. "You know I can't afford anoth-er forty dollars a week. We've had the golf discussion."

"Well, we're having it again."

Randy told Quin again it was important for his five-year-old to learn how to play golf. When the boy grew up he'd need to make contacts, and the golf course was a great place for doing business. In the interim they could play at Randy's mother's club, where they can drive around in cus-tomized fiberglass golf carts made to resemble their real cars. In his moth-er's case, a Lexus. Leo loves it. Randy gets to drive and spend real time with Leo: they can learn the game together. Randy had already written to Quin that he saw through her "too much money" ploy. "You're really afraid Leo will enjoy his father's company; you can't think of anything better to do with Leo than bake. Baking's not a job for a boy with a half-time father," Randy wrote. It's important, as Arnold has told him, that parents keep open lines of communications, that they maintain consistent standards.

"Randy, you confuse consistent standards with *your* standards. Now please go. I'm working."

Randy closed his eyes and grabbed his stomach. "You gotta get me some kind of antacid. I think I'm getting an ulcer."

"I wish I had an ulcer," Anna said, then turned to Quin. "You were right. He did start out funny."

Quin had decided on being a nurse when her father came down with lung cancer: she'd been encouraged by two elderly nurses who took care of her father as if he had been their only son. Taking care of people was what Quin did well, what she'd always done well. It was what hooked her on Randy (he really did need her) and was tied up loosely with her father's death. That she stroked her father's face a few moments before he died, telling him, "I'm here, Dad," and that he turned his face away, muttering, "for what good it does," made it necessary for her to prove to herself she was a generous and responsible person, and assured her of long-term penance with her Randy.

She and Randy had married only months before the initial diagnosis, and though Randy agreed to come to the funeral, he'd sneered during the service because it was religious. "A better place, my ass," he muttered. Then he loosened his tie and fiddled with the colored handkerchiefs he kept up his sleeve. Two days later, on their kitchen floor, he told her he was having a seizure.

"You just ate pizza," Quin said.

"I know what I ate," he said. "Call 911."

She laughed. But she called 911. And rode in the back of the ambulance with him. And when he broke out in hives, she rubbed hydrocortisone cream on his back.

"I'm going to be scarred for life," he said.

She once thought Randy was funny. Remarks like that were funny. He couldn't possibly mean them. He said them with his clown face on. He giggled afterwards. He brought her paper flowers to cheer her up. Even his neurotic routines had an air of comedy to them. He always said he was "working on things." He did his job, going to therapy weeks and then months on end. He pursued what he thought of as a passion. She'd been charmed by his boyishness, soothed by how much he needed her. Unlike her father, Randy would never leave. During one of their long talks about ending their relationship he'd said, "I think we have a good relationship. You like to give, I like to receive."

And it was most often worth giving, because after he received, conflict abated, a brief calm ensued: he might even be contrite or at least let her be.

> *Dear Quin,*
>
> *Hygiene is important. Leo comes home from school filthy from lunchtime baseball. I've supplied his knapsack with a change of clothes and I require Leo to take a bath every night before he goes to bed, or he loses TV for the next day. Please adhere to this regime: cleanliness is good for his self-esteem.*
>
> *Love,*
> *Randy*

Now he was coming in the windows, coming in the doors. The front door, the back door, the garage door. He followed Quin to work at the hospital, he followed her to the market, he followed her home. He scribbled letters and shoved them in her mailbox, sometimes twice a day. One night she'd fallen asleep, and when she opened her eyes in the dark there was the specter of him, standing over her in his clown suit, dropping tears on her face. No, it was not a dream, it was Randy, a fifty-year-old clown who did not understand the meaning of the word separation.

Randy had not always been a clown. While his father was alive he'd worked as one of his staff attorneys at the Vanderhollen Zipper Company. When his father died suddenly and his company was bought out by International Garments, their corporate legal staff rendered Randy's job unnecessary. The buyout, accompanied by a sizable inheritance, did free Randy up to live out his childhood dream: he became a partner in the Ring-a-ling Happy Time Circus, a seasonal outfit that made weekend stays at malls, flea markets and the parking lots of Wal-Marts all over the northeast. During the winter, Randy worked for Jolly Wally's outfit: a group of clowns who entertained at birthday parties for children who studied at prep schools like the Musée Lycée. Virtually Randy's only happy memory of his father had been their yearly visits to the circus. Randy would sit on his father's lap while Trevor explained how every magic trick worked. Didn't that take the fun out of it? Quin once asked. Of course, Randy said, that was the point. With the birth of his son, of course, Randy had even more reason to want to be a clown: what kid didn't love a clown?

"I'm devoting the next seven years to our child," Randy said, talking to her through the shower curtain.

"Poor Leo," Quin muttered. "Would you hand me a towel, please?"

"If you weren't so sex starved," Randy said, "*you'd* have time to pay him some attention."

She snapped a towel off the rack. "I'm not sex-starved now. I was sex-starved while we were married."

"I did everything I could to make you happy."

"Oh please. Damn it, what are you doing in my bathroom? How did you get in here?"

"What if there were a fire and my son were trapped? I'd have a right."

"You don't have a right to walk in on me in the shower."

"I've seen you naked before."

"That was my mistake."

Randy sat on the edge of the tub, put his head in his hands, and quietly began to sob. "I've come to ask you to delay the divorce. Experts have told me Leo needs time. It's traumatic." When Quin said nothing, he added, "Then there's the matter of his golf lessons."

"Let's talk about it in the morning."

"You're so stubborn. Come in for one session with my shrink to discuss it."

"Oh Randy," she said, but she could hear her voice softening. The trembling, the pain in his voice, traveled through her like an injection.

"And if Arnold thinks now's the time and you're sure you've given it enough thought, I promise."

"Arnold? The bearded lady's husband?"

"He's fully credentialed. He studied with someone who studied with Anna Freud."

"I'll think about it," she said. "Now please. I'm not getting out until you leave the house."

"What kind of shampoo are you using? Your hair looks like a robin's nest."

"Since when does Bozo give cosmetic advice?"

"I thought Leo would like to see me in my working outfit."

"Is there no place safe from you?"

"You think your son is *safe* while you're showering with the door closed? What if he chokes? Safe? Who was it who broke into my house and stole . . . well, you know what you stole."

Randy had once called the police and asked them to search Quin's house for a missing cutlery set. The cutlery set Quin's mother had given as a wedding gift. Except for an end table and a few chairs, it was all she had taken out of their house. The next day, though, when the police refused to enter what they called a legal matter, Randy replaced the set with an exact replica and mailed her the bill.

After she put on her robe, she watched him thumb through her mail, searching under the couch for who knows what until he told her.

"Why don't you admit you're seeing someone? You've been seeing somebody for the last two years."

"Who? Who?" She shook her head.

"I trusted you. Why else would you leave?"

"Isn't it self-evident? How many times have I told you?"

"Tell me again: I forget." When she didn't answer him, he added, "Is it O.K. if I just sleep on the couch?"

"Get out," she said. But he was already sitting on her couch, taking off his enormous clown shoes.

Tonight *she* felt she had no choice but to call the police. When two burly twenty-year-olds arrived, though, Randy was throwing Leo up in the air and making hysterical noises. Never mind that it was eleven o'clock at night. One of the cops asked, "Is he bothering you, ma'am?" What could she say about a five-foot-three balding clown with a bubble nose, with a slumped over frame like an arthritic grandmother's, a voice that still cracked like an adolescent's, a man who broke out in hives when he started to worry? How could she say he bothered her? What bothered her is that she'd married him.

"Could you just ask him to leave?" she muttered.

"Everybody loves a clown, Miss," one of them said.

"Officer," Randy said, "talk some sense into this woman. She's hysterical."

"We don't get involved in domestic disputes of that nature," one of the kid cops laughed. "That's a job for a true professional."

"Never mind," she said, closing the door of her bedroom and placing a chair under the knob, shouting, "You'd better be gone by the time I wake up," and he was. And with him the original set of knives.

Dear Quin,
    I saw you driving through downtown Danbury with Leo in the car going

*at least 40 miles an hour. It makes me wonder: how can I trust you to
drive our son to school? Slow down. Please.*
Love, Randy

> *P.S. I didn't see Leo buckled in. We should double check, given the cir-
> cumstances, don't you think?*
> *Yours truly,*

Randy

Some days—when her shift allowed it—she got home from the hospital before three, so when the school bus dropped Leo off in her driveway
she spent time reading to him and he to her—Leo liked books about animals and adventure stories where children get to fly or sail away to distant countries—and he was getting good at not only sounding words out
but understanding the flow of entire sentences. He asked good questions,
Quin thought. He was trying to figure out the bounds of fiction and nonfiction, what's real when an animal is hurt or a child is in danger. "I like
fiction better," he said, and Quin agreed. Sometimes Leo would even
occupy himself for a short time with his Geo-Safari game and Quin could
read on her own, a luxury not available to her during her marriage.

Leo was shy but sometimes brought home friends. They played soccer
and basketball and Legos, all in sight of her kitchen window. What she
noticed was that he shared his toys, he was gentle with his friends, he
liked to be goofy and imitate sounds from audio tapes she's bought for
him. She looked at her son, his blonde hair darkening, his face blooming
into her lips and mouth, his father's eyes, her sloppiness, his love of
repeated ritual (he'd seen *Fly Away Home* fourteen times), her this, his
that, and somewhere in there qualities which resemble neither of them
but were becoming discretely his (a love of science: she's proud he can
change a light bulb), and she was happy for him, worried about him. She
couldn't define the happiness she wanted for him, she was just beginning
to figure that out for herself.

Leo came into the room carrying a stack of books. "Mommy, will you
read to me?"

"Sure Sweetie. In a second."

"What time do we eat? Can we have macaroni and cheese? Brandon
says macaroni and cheese is his favorite."

"I'll look to see if we have any left in our stash." She got up from the
dining room table, opened the cabinets and sighed. "I have to go shopping."

"Daddy says," Leo adds, "we might all go to Disney World and see the real dinosaurs. Grandma's treat."

"We'll see, Darlin'. We'll see."

"Daddy says you won't let me play golf. Is that true, Mommy?"

"Daddy and I are working things out, Leo. You don't have to worry about it."

"And Daddy said it was wrong of you to take his property without asking."

"Sweetie, this is a grown-up problem. And we grown-ups," she said, lying to her son for the first time in his short life, "can take care of it."

Dear Quin,

Perhaps you're not aware that condoms do not offer reliable protection from AIDS. I enclose an article that proves condoms are only 75% effective against the virus. As Leo's mother, do you want to take that kind of chance? Who knows, after you've been with complete strangers for a couple of months, whether or not it would be a health risk to take you back. You might enjoy a fling or two, but reality will set in. What happens to Mr. Right when the magic rubs off?

Concerned,

Randy

Arnold's office was in the guest bedroom of his and Marla's apartment, so clients walked through the foyer, passing through the living room to sit on a wooden bench, looking into Arnold and Marla's open bedroom. Arnold had called Quin, confidentially he said, to warn her he was worried not only about Leo but also Randy's stability. Randy and Quin sat on opposite ends of a wooden bench waiting for Arnold to finish with a circus client whose fear of heights had been intensifying. Quin had to go straight to work after the session so she was wearing her nurse's uniform. Randy wore a cobalt-blue golf blazer and yellow slacks. For a white noise machine, Arnold piped in late John Coltrane, which sounded like a nervous breakdown in progress. "You've seen him here, often?" Quin asked, squinting as she looked into the bedroom.

"Usually in more informal settings."

"I don't know why I let Arnold talk me into this," Quin said.

"Because Leo's welfare's at stake," Randy said. "We have to put ourselves aside."

"That's a novel idea, Randy."

"Since when did you become so cynical?"

"You think I like it?" Quin said. "It's my only defense."

"Against what?"

The door opened and a tearful acrobat, Antonia, in sequined pink leotards and ballet slippers stepped out, slowly putting one foot directly in front of the other, extending her hands to the side, teetering, almost losing her balance.

"It must be an exercise," Randy said. "He's brilliant, you'll see. He studied with somebody who studied with the son of the son of Freud."

"Sounds like a monster movie," Quin said. "Didn't you say last week it was Anna Freud?"

Arnold waved them into his office. He moved from behind his big desk to the middle of three folding chairs, and sat, legs spread wide, between Randy and Quin. "Nice to see the two of you," he said, extending a hand to each and squeezing hard. "Together."

When Quin cringed, he held her hand tighter. "I know what pain you must be in. It was good of you to come, Quin. To think of Leo's needs before your own. Randy, I know you'll do the same." Randy nodded enthusiastically, then without missing a beat listed several reasons why golf was important.

Arnold ritually bobbed his head up and down. "You see Quin, given the tension between you two, and given the looming possibility of a separation agreement and other legal struggles, I'm sure it wouldn't be in Leo's interest for you two to fight over something as silly as golf. Conflict's damaging to children. Randy, in his sadness over the loss of the marriage, has attached tremendous symbolic importance to these lessons. If he's willing to put up half of the expense for lessons, could you put up the rest? After all, what do lawyers charge an hour these days? Randy's convinced that Leo's really excited about playing golf . . ."

"Why shouldn't he be? Two days ago Leo came home from school and said, 'Daddy says you won't let me play golf.'"

"Well," Arnold said, rubbing his chin as if he had a goatee, "is that true?"

"Ask Randy." Arnold leaned closer to her, as if to ask the question again. "Whatever Randy wants to do on his time with Leo's acceptable to me," Quin said.

"But if he had a golf lesson on a weekend he was with you," Arnold says, "he'd miss it, wouldn't he?"

"If I couldn't take him. My hours are very irregular. You know there's a big discrepancy between Randy's income and mine."

"You could have had everything," Randy's voice broke. "I offered you a round-trip vacation to Paris. All expenses paid."

"Please . . ." Quin begged.

"You know," Arnold said, "A team sport would be a good thing. To be a part of something when the rest of the boy's life is so unsteady."

Arnold stood up and moved behind Randy, rubbing his shoulders as if he were a boxer between rounds. "You see, Quin, this whole transition's been so difficult. With the death of Randy's father every separation's exaggerated, like an earthquake aftershock: he somatizes, he gets paranoid." Randy smiled. "It's going to take a while for him to adjust . . . assuming you maintain your choice."

"You can assume it."

"So there: you see how wounding it might be."

They both looked at Randy: his hands covering his face. He began to emit slow moans, moans that reminded Quin, not happily, of their sex life. "I think I have to go," she says.

"Think it over, Quin. If you give him time he'll come around. But if you don't, you can see he can't help himself: if he can't have you in his life, he feels strongly enough about the subject so he's willing to litigate. In his state he has only two choices: to internalize or to make your life difficult. He's not used to losing something, I mean someone he cares for. It's not in his experience: I don't know if he's capable of it. Whether we approve or disapprove, it really doesn't matter. So it's in everyone's interest to show a little extra compassion. This golf thing, it's not that important . . ."

"Precisely," she said. A half-hour later, as she finally stood up to leave Arnold's office, she said aloud, "How does he do it? How does he get everyone to cater to him?"

"You don't remember," Randy said. "I'm charming."

When two days later she was served papers from Kidman, Argyle and Shaw for a court hearing on golf, she took stock of the stacked-up letters on her desk, the state of her checkbook and Leo's sleeping peacefully in the bedroom. She could fight Randy, she was strong enough now, but it was Leo who'd pay the price. She left a message for her lawyer. "All right, I give. Golf it'll be."

Dear Quin,

Leo's next lesson, chip shots, is Tuesday at four. He needs new shoes and if I were you I'd schedule a haircut. Marla and Arnold thoughtfully wanted to know if you wanted to attend their Lila's birthday party with Leo. If so, please try to think of an imaginative costume. I've got mine. Guess.

Love,
Randy

After staying up with Anna Zwick all night, injecting morphine, discussing with the children and grandchildren whether or not they ought to take extraordinary means to keep her alive (the children agreed, but one grandson, young and self-absorbed, could not be persuaded), after watching Anna's shaking become so severe that the end of the IV needle kept slipping out of her emaciated arm, after all that and more Quin couldn't remember, at four in the morning Quin finally came home. In the days before, half-awake, half-mumbling, almost talking in her sleep, Anna told her how she didn't want her husband with her when she died (although he had died five years before); she didn't want that son-of-a-bitch to have the satisfaction of seeing her in pain again, the pleasure he got seeing her washing a kitchen floor, locking her in the bedroom when she talked back to him. She'd been looking at her friends to see if they had it any better—and to her way of thinking they hadn't—so tonight she screamed, the only time, with all the pain the cancer elicited from her—and her last words were, "Rot in hell, you bastard," with a scream so shrill and high-pitched that Quin heard a ringing in her ear for the next hour and a half. Then Anna Zwick closed her eyes, and with a spitting noise, a clack-clack coming from her chapped, feverish lips, died. Oh, Quin thought, drained, depleted, raw, as she put her keys in the door, if only she had heard Anna's screams years ago, when she was with Randy, if only she could have, but just for one moment, put herself in Anna's place, it would have been impossible to stay in that house, with that family, with that man. But of course, Quin thought, putting her coat in the closet, mechanically removing her uniform, stripping down to her slip, it wasn't as if she didn't know she'd regret giving her life up to someone else, it was just that the knowledge was useless. Like a recipe when you only had half the ingredients.

Two weeks on the night shift had set her clock all wrong, she was having difficulty sleeping, so she sat in the kitchen, put some chamomile tea in a cup of water and waited for the microwave tray to run its circles beneath it. Her head was spinning, crowded with Anna Zwick and a half dozen other women in the ward who weren't going to make it. And behind the shadow of those women, her own father, her own father who hadn't heeded a single warning about stopping smoking. She'd brought him Nic-o-ban, she flushed his cigarettes down the toilet, she paid for him to go to hypnosis, and he never went. There was something about him that wanted to die. But no, though she was the nurse, there was something about him she could not save. She had the information he needed, even if he wouldn't follow her advice, even if he'd ask what he called a "real doctor" to check up on her; nothing seemed to give him more pleasure than to bring back a doctor's disagreements, as if to say, you don't know any more than I do.

With that voice in her head, she heard, from what she thought was Leo's bedroom, a cough. But she was sure Leo was with Randy, though for a moment she panicked and wondered if, in her distraction and busyness, she could have gone to work and left Leo in his room. That's all that had to happen. If Randy found out he'd have Leo taken from her in a minute. But then she heard the cough again, and because perhaps she had some experience with coughs, she recognized the first as a real cough, but the second as the cough of an adult. It was a throat-clearing cough, not a cough from deep in the lungs.

She picked up her car keys off the kitchen table, tiptoed back to the front closet, put on a winter coat, and was about to open her front door when from the corner of her eye she caught a ghostly image walking out of Leo's room: it was Randy: his eyes were red and teary, and he held a Kleenex in his hand.

She screamed, and though it might have come out as a gagged mutter, to her mind it had the force of the scream of Anna Zwick.

"We have to talk," he said.

"What the hell are you doing here?"

He dropped to his knees. "Please, Quin, I beg of you."

"How did you get in here? Where's Leo?"

"I brought him with me."

"You what?"

"You should see him sleeping. He had a terrible night: he was asking for you in his sleep, asking where were you: I didn't know what to tell him. Look in his room: isn't he the most adorable thing alive?"

She walked back into the kitchen, and dropped her body down of the chair. "I'm too tired for this, Randy. Go home."

"I'm not a dog, you know. I'm your husband."

"You're not my husband. Not any longer."

"That's what I want to talk to you about. I can change. I've already changed. I made a list," he took a folded piece of paper out of his pocket, "of all the things I do differently now. Here, just look at it." She shook her head. She couldn't call the police again. She did not want to say, as she'd said so many times when they still lived under the same roof, "it's over." Instead, though she had words in mind, nothing came out of her mouth.

"You know how I used to tell you how selfish you were . . . well, I'm turning the guest room into a study for you, a place where you can be by yourself. I wouldn't bother you. I wouldn't knock. I'd even take care of Leo. No complaints. Darling," he said, getting on his knees. "I'm devastated. This is all I can think of to get you back. I need you so much. Otherwise—I have to tell you the truth—there's nothing for me."

She closed her eyes. It was worse when he told the truth. "I'm sorry, I can't even tell you how sorry I am. But Randy, please, you have to stop."

"No strings attached. You won't hear a word out of me. No siree, I'll . . ." he put his thumb and forefinger to his mouth and moved them across his lips, "I'll zip my lips and throw away the key."

"Jesus Christ, Randy, you're in your pajamas."

"I've been here since two."

"I don't want to be heartless, really I don't, but I don't want to see you in your pajamas. Really I don't." Even though she tried to hold back, she started to cry. "I just want to go to bed."

He moved toward her. "Well come on then, get some sleep. And when you're rested we'll have a talk." The tears came from way back: she couldn't stop crying. "I know," he said, and reached for her hand. "You know, Quin, remember when I used to say, 'I'm feeling Randy,' and I made you laugh. Remember? And then I put my red nose on and rubbed it against your nose, like Eskimoses . . ."

"Please stop," she said, over and over again, in lower and lower tones, as if she were descending an elevator; when he placed his hands on her shoulders they weighed a hundred pounds: it was as if they were still in their old bedroom of the old house.

"Even if you don't feel *that* way about me, you must be . . . you must need it the way I do," he said. "I know you do."

"Get your hands off me," she said. "Or I'll call the police."

"Go ahead," he said, gritting his teeth as if suddenly there was another Randy, full of fury, inside him. "We're both in our pajamas. You saw what happened last time."

She stood up, and looking at the spittle gathered at the edges of his lips, for the first time since she met him she stopped seeing him as a person with qualities; he was feral and insatiable, undeniably the man *she'd* once said yes to. "I'm getting out of here," she said. "If you don't get out of here now, I will."

"Where will you go? All our friends were *our* friends. I had to tell them what you did."

"This is a bad movie," she said. "Get out, you bastard, or I'll kill you."

"That's what I've been waiting for," he said. His body stiffened, he strode mechanically from her toward Leo's room. "They'll want to hear that in court," he pointed at her. "You're an unfit mother, Quin. Your son's lying in that bedroom there, scared to death, and all you can think about is yourself. Poor you. Well you don't know poor, believe me." Then he disappeared and came back with Leo draped in a blanket, half-asleep, muttering something she couldn't understand.

"I'm taking my son home," he said.

She waited till nine to call her lawyer, then drove to the police station to file a restraining order.

Her hearing was almost as brief as her sexual encounters with Randy. Randy's mother sat primly by his side. She took out her checkbook and wrote out checks while the judge asked Randy, "Was this the marital residence?" "Was there violence involved?" "Was there a history of violence?" The judge listened while Quin told him about Randy's breaking into her house. Randy explained that the boy had been screaming at home uncontrollably, and since Quin was so good with him, he brought the boy over. She'd never required permission before. After all, he'd been given a key, which he showed to the judge. Quin glared at him: he smiled in her direction. The judge did not bother to take the matter into his chambers: restraining order denied. In the future, he requested of Randy that he call in advance of his arrival and not enter Quin's house unless there was clear mutual agreement.

"You'll be served with papers," Randy's mother told Quin as they walked out of the courthouse. "Shame on you."

She watched them leave in his mother's Lexus while she watched from the courthouse door. There were golf clubs in the back seat. There would be more letters, more arguments about Randy's lists of activities for Leo, more visits to court: they'd pick and pick at her, until there was nothing left. Unless she went back to her place right now and started to pack. And took out a map of some state where Randy couldn't find her. Some small town without a circus. Without a golf course. Without her son.

Sweet

Edward Falco

On the way to work I meditated on the sunrise, which I watch every morning through my bedroom window, and then when I got to work, the barn doors weren't completely closed, which meant someone had arrived at the stables before me, which was unusual, so I was quiet as I approached the gap between the sliding doors and then I stepped back out of sight when I saw Sweet. She was in her stall, eating out of her colt's feed bucket with a white plastic spoon. The galvanized steel bucket looked huge next to her small body, looked as though she might as well swim in it as eat out of it. She had on work boots and faded jeans and a yellow halter top that caught slices of morning sunlight shooting through the bars of her stall's high window. Behind her, His Majesty watched as she leaned over his mix of oats and molasses. His head was lowered, as if he were thinking of using it as a battering ram, but he appeared more confused than angry at the sight of his groom eating his mash. I waited a minute and then made a big production out of opening the barn doors, and when I walked onto the floor of the stable, His Majesty was at his feed and Sweet had her tack box open and a curry comb in her hand.

"Sweet!" I said, pretending to be startled. "What are you doing here so early?"

She answered, without looking up from her tack box, "Do I need your fucking permission asshole? I'm here early. What do you care?" She went back into her stall and began brushing out the tangles in His Majesty's tail.

I ambled over to my stall and looked in on Miss Payday. She was lying peacefully in a bed of straw, head up and alert. When she saw me, she whinnied. "And good morning to you too, Sister Payday," I said, loudly. I settled myself down on my tack box, using it as a bench, and slowly went about unwrapping a pair of chocolate croissants that I bought at the

French bakery by my apartment. I like to eat my breakfast at the stables and say hello to the other grooms as they stumble in to work. Most grooms, they're a sorry lot: drunks, gamblers, illiterates, fools. Mostly drunks and gamblers. Myself, I guess I fit into the fool category because I've always liked grooming horses, ever since I started doing it as a kid, more than thirty years ago, and I've never tried to make anything better of myself, though I know I could.

When I finished unwrapping the croissants, I arranged them attractively on a pewter plate from out of my tack box, and I poured myself a steaming cup of coffee from my thermos. Across the stable floor, Sweet was getting His Majesty ready to jog. Sweet was such a tiny, frail girl, probably no taller than five-three, five-four at the most, maybe a hundred pounds. When she first showed up at the stables—during the season, about two years ago, at the Meadowlands in New Jersey—everyone knew she was a runaway. She couldn't have been older than fourteen. She had short blond hair and bright dark eyes and a fresh-scrubbed look, and she was wearing good clothes, khaki shorts and a nicely-fitted blouse and high-quality sandals, like a child of some upscale, uptown couple. When she told Victor she was seventeen, he laughed, but he hired her anyway, which no one could figure out because she didn't know shit about horses. He arranged for her to work on his farm in Orlando for the rest of the meet, and then when we all came back to Florida for the winter, she was already here, at the stables, grooming. Some of us were thinking he had helped her out, that he might have had a spark of decency he had been keeping hidden—but then it turned out he was screwing her. We shouldn't have been surprised. We all know Victor. But she was so tiny then, it didn't hardly seem possible.

"Sweet," I called across the stable. "I've got some coffee and an extra croissant, if you're interested." She didn't answer, but I could see she had heard me. She was brushing His Majesty's mane.

I liked watching Sweet as she worked. I had lately discovered in myself a spiritual bent. A while back, I found a book by Kahil Gibran in a New Age bookstore in town. I was attracted to the store by crystals hanging in the window. Several large crystals were positioned to catch the late evening light and break it into rainbows. I wandered around through the store, enjoying the thick scent of incense, checking out the books, and fingering small vials of brightly colored aroma therapies. I found the Gibran book next to a genuine crystal ball that cost several hundred dollars, and I bought the book after reading only a handful of pages and being impressed.

Though I never actually read the whole book cover to cover, Gibran's words affected a deep change in me. His observations awakened a place within me that had long been sleeping. Suddenly I began seeing all the ordinary things of the world in a new light. The sunrise is a good example: what used to be just part of every morning—watching the sunrise from my bed, through my bedroom window—became something spiritual, as if the light were like God's love, His love washing over the world. But also other simple, everyday things, like the way light reflected off stalks of straw in Miss Payday's stall, turning the straw gold and casting a golden tone throughout the stables; and the horses, the beauty of working muscles under sleek hides glistening with sweat; and Sweet, too, her beauty. Sometimes I used to just quit what was I doing and lean against the bars of my stall to watch Sweet as she put down a bed of straw or bathed her colt. I liked especially the lean muscles of her legs as she stood on her toes and stretched for something; and the way her breasts moved and shifted as she worked. Watching Sweet used to be about the favorite part of my day until Paul, who was going out with Sweet at the time, told me he'd put my fat ass in the hospital if he caught me staring at her again. And I knew he would. He told me that Sweet had asked him to tell me, but Sweet never said anything to me herself about it, and I'm sure she would have, if I were really bothering her—which I'd never want to do.

Paul was the real beginning of Sweet's problems. She took up with him after Victor dumped her. Paul was the stable manager and second trainer, and it was him that got Sweet into crank. Now she was living with Robbie, another groom, and she made the stuff herself, getting the ingredients she needed, somehow, from Wal-Mart of all places.

I finished my first croissant, and had my hand on the second one. "Sweet," I called again. "Last chance. This extra delicious French chocolate croissant is tempting me sorely."

Sweet stopped working on her colt and turned around to give me a look.

"You'd be doing me a favor," I said, and I patted my gut, which extended way out over my belt and sort of rested on my thighs. I've always had a problem with weight.

"You bet your fat ass, I'd be doing you a favor," she said. "You have a cup for me?"

"Hell, yes!" I shouted. "For you, Sweet, I'd run out and scramble up some eggs, just say the word!" I folded my hands over my belly and laughed.

Sweet mumbled, "Oh, for Christ's sake," and tossed her curry comb down into the dirt outside her stall.

I pulled a cup out of my tack box, and had her coffee and croissant waiting for her by the time she crossed the stable.

"Jesus," she said, holding the steaming cup of coffee to her face, "this smells fucking great."

"Should!" I said, my voice that high-pitched, fat man's whine that I hated and tried hard—with no success—to suppress. "It's only Colombian Supreme," I said. "Fresh ground last night, ten bucks a pound over at Starbucks!"

Sweet sipped the coffee and nodded appreciatively. "It's good," she said. "What kind of coffee maker you got?"

"Brüne," I said. "What's Robbie got, Mr. Coffee?"

Sweet snorted, making a kind of half-amused, half-disgusted sound that came from way down deep in her chest. "The cocksucker," she said. "The asshole . . ."

I smiled but looked away, out through the stable doors to the training track, where a couple of grooms already had their horses out jogging. I didn't like to hear Sweet curse. She didn't used to curse at all. In fact, when she first started, she didn't used to say hardly anything at all. She was a sweet thing. That's what we started calling her, Sweet Thing—and then it just worked its way down to Sweet.

"What's the matter, Fats?" Sweet sat down next to me on the tack box. "My language offend you?" She held the croissant to her nose, inhaling its chocolate fragrance, and then took a small bite which she chewed with her eyes closed.

I said, friendly as could be, "Please don't call me Fats. I've asked everyone here not to call me that."

"I don't even know what your real name is." She looked me in the eyes, curious, as if I were about to reveal something of interest to her.

"It's Winston," I said. "I prefer to be called Win."

"Son of a bitch," she said. "I never heard anybody call you anything but Fats."

"That's because they're no-class fools around here. You know I tell the truth!"

"Got that right," Sweet said, looking back toward her stall and His Majesty, who was looking back at her.

"You mad at Robbie?" I asked. "I thought he was your old man?"

"Was," Sweet said, with her mouth full. "The prick threw me out last night. I had to sleep in the goddamn stall."

"Threw you out?" I said, my voice doing its high-pitched squeal again. "Just threw you out on the street? Just left you with no place to spend the night?"

"That's what I said," Sweet answered. She covered her face with her hands and rested her elbows on her knees and massaged her temples with her fingertips. "Jesus Christ," she whispered, almost as if she were talking to herself. Then she sounded angry. "I'm strung out on speed, I've got no place to stay, I don't have a fucking cent to my name . . . I'm such a fucking mess."

I surprised myself and put my arm around her shoulder and then kind of moved back a little when I realized what I'd done, expecting her to haul off and punch me. She didn't though. She just kind of stiffened a bit and swallowed hard.

"Sweet," I said, "You're welcome to stay at my place till you get yourself straightened out."

"I can't stay at your place," she said, dismissing the idea as if it were totally absurd.

"Why not? I got an extra room with a fold-out bed. It's not like I'd expect anything from you. There's no strings attached or anything. Nothing at all."

"Right," Sweet said. She pulled away from me, out from under my arm, and went back to her stall without saying another word.

"Just remember," I called after her. "No strings!"

Back in her stall, His Majesty nipped Sweet's shoulder, and she slapped him hard on the muzzle and cursed him out a blue streak, and then went about putting him in harness. I watched her awhile, until I heard another groom's car pull up to the stable, and then I got to work on Miss Payday. Rest of the day, I kept thinking back to when I put my arm around Sweet, a natural thing, wanting to console her, and how she didn't resist me at all, and I knew there was bound to be something between us. I felt it in my heart, and I thought she felt it too, and then that night when she showed up at my apartment lugging two big cardboard boxes full of her things, I felt my feelings were being confirmed.

"Sweet!" I said. "I'm overjoyed!" And I was. Honestly. It was a little after ten at night, and I had been thinking about her constantly since that morning.

"I'm sure you are," Sweet said. She crossed her arms under her breasts and gave me a hard look. She seemed tired, and she was bedraggled, as if she hadn't showered or cleaned up or slept well in a long time. Her eyes were red and puffy, from crying it was obvious. "Look," she said. "Before I come in, let's get it straight. You said no strings, right?"

"Of course," I said, my voice shooting up high. "Sweet," I said, sincerely, "you don't know me at all if you think I'm wanting anything other than to help you out when you need it."

"Right," Sweet said, and she shook her head and whispered "motherfucker." She picked up her boxes and toted them into the apartment.

I closed and latched the door behind her, and when I turned around I saw her standing in the center of my living room, checking the place out. She had a ferocious look about her, like a cat ready to tear something up, and I had to remind myself what a kid she was, still only sixteen at the oldest, and that underneath that mean-looking exterior there was a scared girl who needed someone to help her get straightened out. "Put 'em down, put 'em down," I said. She was clutching her boxes, holding them to her chest, her arms wrapped around them. I pointed to the floor next to the Lazy Boy recliner that was against the wall.

Sweet wouldn't let loose the boxes. "Where's the extra room?" she said. "Where's the extra room you said you had?"

I folded my hands over my belly and leaned back against the door. "You're standing in it," I said. I opened my arms. "This is it."

Sweet looked around the room: at the Lazy Boy and the 19-inch TV positioned on a stand a dozen feet in front of it; and at the table and two chairs by the room's only window. "Fats," she said. "This is your living room."

"You can have it," I said. "You can move right in here long as you need—"

"Fats—"

"Win. Please."

"Win. You said you had an extra room."

"Well, this is an extra room!" I said, my voice soaring.

"The living room isn't an extra room, Fats! It's the fucking living room!"

"Well, this is the room I meant, Sweet. My bedroom's over there." I pointed to the red bead curtain that separated my bedroom from the living room.

"Son-of-a-bitch . . ." She dropped the boxes. "And you said you had a fold-out bed." She looked around. "All I see is a table and a recliner."

"That Lazy Boy's better n' a bed! That's where I sleep most nights!"

Sweet covered her face with her hands. She rubbed her temples. After several long moments, she took her hands away from her face and looked at me. "I'm supposed to sleep in the recliner and make myself at home in your living room?"

"Sweet," I said. I was quiet awhile. I gave her a paternal, loving look, trying to communicate to her that I cared and was concerned and was just trying to do a good deed, to help her out.

She sighed. "Fats," she said. "Win . . . Win, do you have a shower?" She ran her fingers through her hair and rubbed at a spot on the back of her neck, looking away from me. "I need a damn shower," she said.

"I smell like a fucking horse." Her voice trailed off, getting softer, almost inaudible. "I haven't had a fucking shower in days. . . ."

"Do I have a shower?" I yelled. I laughed loudly. "Of course I have a shower!" I opened the door to the bathroom and flipped on the light. "Tell you what," I said. "You take a shower and I'll whip us up a late-night breakfast: eggs, bacon, toast, and juice. The works. What do think?"

She nodded and gave me the slightest smile, and I could see that her eyes were watery. She picked up her boxes and carried them into the bathroom, and after she closed the door, I heard her slide the lock closed and then it was quiet. I listened awhile, just looking at the door, and I couldn't help imagining her getting undressed, taking off her clothes only an arm's length away from me.

"Win!" Sweet's voice boomed from behind the door. "Are you just standing out there or what? I haven't heard you move."

I tiptoed quickly to the kitchen and then called back: "What was that, Sweet? I had my head in the refrigerator."

She didn't answer. A moment later I heard the shower going, and I started cooking up the bacon. By the time she turned off the water and pulled back the shower curtain, I had set two places at the table and dropped three slices of bacon apiece on each plate. Next to each plate was a glass of orange juice, and in the center of the table a stack of toast rose up off a white, ceramic lazy Susan that pictured a standard-bred race horse trotting across a finish line. When everything was ready but the eggs, which I planned on cooking up once Sweet was at the table, I hurried to my bedroom and brought out my leather-bound blank book, which I had been writing the best of my sayings down in for the past year. I put it on the far end of the table, away from the plates, hoping it would look like I just happened to lay it there.

Sweet came out of the bathroom wearing light-weight, silk-like pajamas that hung loosely from her body, but clung to all the right places. I almost fainted.

"Win," she said, "Do you have a robe?" She gestured to her pajamas, showing she was aware of how sexy they were. "These are the only P.J.s I've got," she said, "and I don't want to sleep in my clothes again."

I shook my head.

"Great," she said. She looked at me a moment, and then added, "Well at least you could quit fucking staring at me, all right?"

"Oh," I said, startled. "I didn't realize. I'm sorry." I looked away from her, toward the kitchen, and then I remembered what I was doing. "I'll whip up the eggs!" I yelled. "You sit down, Sweet! Make yourself comfortable!"

In the kitchen, I cracked two eggs into a bowl and dropped a fat slice of butter in my biggest cast-iron frying pan. "Scrambled okay?"

"Scrambled's fine," Sweet answered, softly, as if distracted.

When I glanced back at her and saw that she had my book opened and was reading in it, my heart did one of its flutter things that scares me sometimes.

"Did you write this stuff?" Sweet said.

"What stuff?" I said. I didn't turn around.

"This stuff," Sweet said. *"The heart is like a broken furnace. The heat of its love is squandered."*

"Oh, that," I said. I carried the frying pan to the table and portioned out the scrambled eggs. "That's just my notebook where I write down my thoughts."

Sweet put the book down alongside her and dove into the eggs and toast. "Jesus," she said. "I'm starving. This is the first thing I've eaten today since that croissant."

"That's terrible, Sweet," I said. I brought the frying pan back into the kitchen and by the time I sat down to my eggs, Sweet had finished.

She propped her head up on her hands and smiled at me, and I think that may have been the very first time she ever gave me a genuine smile. The food obviously had a good effect on her mood. "What's it mean," she said. *"The heart is like a broken furnace? . . . "*

"Well," I said. "That's hard to explain, Sweet. You have to think about it."

She nodded and made a cute face, as if she found me entertaining, and then she opened up the book again. "How about this one," she said. *"The life of a wounded soul is a Ferris wheel that spins wildly out of control.* What's that mean?"

"Well," I said. "There again, you know. Same thing. Got to think about it."

"Got to think about it," she echoed. Her appearance seemed to shift as she watched me, as if she might be seeing me differently, as if it might be occurring to her that I was a deeper person than I might look to be. She folded her hands in front of her on the table. She said, "Are you sure *you* know what you mean?"

"Well," I said, "Sweet. It's not that simple." I clasped my hands over my stomach and leaned toward her slightly. "Sometime you have to let your thoughts lead you into deeper waters, if you know what I mean. You have to be willing to ponder things. A deep thought's always going to be a little mysterious, at least at first."

"Oh," she said. She nodded, her eyes fixed on me. "You mean, something like this: 'The stupidity of the good is unfathomably wise.'"

"What?"

"'The stupidity of the good is unfathomably wise.' Friedrich Nietzsche."

"Who?"

"Nietzsche. German philosopher."

When I didn't say anything more, Sweet offered me another smile. "My father read me Nietzsche at night. He was obsessed with Nietzsche. He'd read to me from Nietzsche's books, and he'd give me sayings to memorize, like that stupidity one. This is from the time I was five or six. My mother thought he was reading me Winnie the Pooh." She laughed.

I couldn't figure out anything to say. Sweet fiddled with her plate and looked a little antsy. I repeated the name, "Nietzsche," and the sound of it felt strange. "Do you remember any other sayings?"

"Lots," she said. "You don't want to hear."

"I do," I said. "I've been reading Kahil Gibran myself lately."

"Never heard of him," Sweet said.

"He's a philosopher too," I said. "Eastern."

Sweet looked away, out my window, which overlooked a junk-strewn alley. "'Woman was God's second blunder.' That's one that stuck in mind."

"Nietzsche said that?"

"So sayeth my father."

"Lord," I said. "What kind of thing is that to say to a little girl? What was His first blunder?"

Sweet shrugged. "How about this: 'Morality is the herd-instinct in the individual.'"

"What?"

"Enough," Sweet said. She twisted around in her chair to look at the recliner, and then looked back at me. "Fats," she said. "Let's work this out." She crossed her arms in front of her on the table, very businesslike. "I'm desperate for money and a place to stay, but I'm not going to fuck you, so you can just forget that."

"Sweet!" I said. I grasped the table with both hands. "I can't believe that you'd—"

"Oh, cut the shit, Fats. You've been jerking off over me for two years. Tell me it's not true."

I could feel my face turn bright red. "It's— It's not—"

"Oh, please . . ." She stared at me a moment, and then sighed dramatically. "Listen," she said. "How about this? I'll share your bed with you at night and walk around naked and stuff, and we can even cuddle some. You can even touch if you want," she said. "I don't mind being touched. But that's it," she said. "No penetration, no bodily fluids. Period. Nothing except nakedness and light touch." She smiled and winked at me. "It'll be fun," she said.

"Sweet," I said. I was shocked. I tried to make my face express my sadness and disbelief. "If you think for a moment that I was offering you a place to stay because—"

"Right," Sweet said.

"I was trying to—"

"Do a good deed," she said. "Right."

"Honestly, Sweet. I swear."

"I believe you," she said. "I know." She rubbed her temples, and then sat back in her chair with her eyes closed as if she were doing a meditation exercise meant to calm her. When she finally opened her eyes and spoke, her tone was friendlier, less businesslike. "Win," she said. "I'd appreciate it if you'd let me share your bed with you tonight, because I'd really rather sleep in a bed than a recliner."

"Well," I said. "I mean . . . it's a big bed. If you really want to . . ."

"I do. I'd appreciate it." She propped her head up on her hand, cutely, and smiled. "And, listen, I know this is a big thing to ask, but if you could let me have some money, just, like, a hundred bucks maybe, to hold me over, I'd be in your debt. Can you do that?"

"You mean," I said. "Like a loan?" When she didn't answer, I said, "Well, sure, Sweet. For you, I'd do that."

"Thanks," she said. "And if you could take me shopping tomorrow, after work, I'd appreciate that too."

"That wouldn't be Wal-Mart where you want to go shopping, would it Sweet?"

"Yes. Wal-Mart," she said.

"I don't know about that, Sweet."

When I said that, her face hardened and she swiveled around in her seat, turning to look at the recliner.

"But," I said. "Okay. If you really feel you need to."

"I do," she said. "I need you to help me out there, Win."

I nodded. "Okay, then," I said. "I will. I'll help you out."

"Good." She slid her chair back and patted me on the knee. "Why don't we get to bed then, all right?"

"Okay," I said. I gestured toward the dishes. "I'll clean this up and you go ahead."

She winked at me and then got up and went to the bathroom, and when she closed the door behind her, I noted that she didn't bother to pull the latch. I cleared the table and scraped the dishes and when I turned on the water to wash the plates, I heard Sweet leave the bathroom and get into bed, and then this wonderful, intense moment happened. I had my hands under the running water, which was warm and soothing, and I was running a sponge over the surface of the plate, and I realized—it just sort of hit me—that Sweet was actually getting into my bed. Sweet. She was getting into my bed. We were going to sleep together, me and Sweet, and when that dawned on me, I was just, suddenly, like, miraculously happy. It was a transporting feeling. It was like God was placing this gift in my hands, putting Sweet into my care—delicate, beautiful Sweet. In my bed. I almost couldn't believe it. I almost thought it was all going to turn out to be a dream.

I finished up the dishes, and turned off the lights, and when I got into bed, it wasn't a dream. Sweet was there, her back turned toward me, the covers pulled up to her neck, her head snuggled into the pillows. I pulled back the covers to get into bed and saw that she was naked, and my heart fluttered so wildly I was frightened for a second that I was going to die right there, before I ever had a chance to get into bed with her. I had to just stand there a long moment, holding up the covers, waiting for my heart to quit jumping, and it occurred to me then that she might already be asleep, since she didn't turn around to see what I was doing.

When I finally got into bed, I was careful not to touch her, I don't know why, but after awhile I regretted it, because I was just dying to put my hands on her body, just to feel her skin. Then I did something that I had no idea I was going to do. I turned on my side and put my arm around her, touching her forearm first, letting the palm of my hand follow the length of her arm, and I touched her breasts and whispered my great secret to her, something I hadn't told a soul: that I had never been with a woman in my whole life. Not one. Not one single time, and I could feel the heavy tears splashing down onto my chest as I told her. She reached back to pat my thigh. "It's okay," she said. "But that's enough touching for now, all right? Let's go to sleep." She took my hand gently by the wrist and pulled it away from her. "Okay," I said, and I settled onto my back with my arms crossed over my chest. I was breathing hard, kind of choked up. It took awhile for me to get calm again, and then I wasn't at all sleepy. After I lay there for several minutes, I realized that the blinds were pulled closed, and we wouldn't be able to see the sunrise in the morning. I got out of bed and went to the window to open the blinds.

Sweet said, "What are you doing, Fats?" Before I had a chance to explain, she added, "You are going to be a gentleman, aren't you Fats, and not tell anyone about this arrangement?"

"What arrangement?"

"My sharing your bed. Others don't have to know about that. You can just tell them you're doing me a favor, giving me a place to stay."

"Well, that's the truth," I said. "That is what I'm doing."

"Okay," Sweet said. "Good then." She was quiet a moment, and I thought she was going to say something else, but she just said, "Good night."

"Good night," I answered, and I got back into bed. For a long time I lay there quietly, listening to Sweet breathe, and thinking about what I might be able to do to help her. I'd buy her stuff for her tomorrow, because I didn't think I could stop her. But maybe over time I could help, maybe even get her into some kind of program. I lay there thinking about that for a long time before my thoughts shifted to the morning, and I fell asleep imagining the sight of the two of us in bed, imagining what we'd look like with morning sunlight coming through the window, with God's light washing over both of us, golden and brilliant and clear, the way His light is, always.

Speed Bump

Stephen Dixon

This woman says "You know, I didn't want to spring this on you, or not at this time. But as long as we're speaking of accidents, even if this isn't the kind we mean, you almost ran me over today." He says "What? What? Say that again. I almost ran you over today?" "I'd say an hour ago, minus a few minutes." She looks at her watch. "No, exactly an hour ago, to the minute. Isn't that amazing? And that I bumped in to you so soon after it. Because I looked at my watch then, I don't know why—maybe . . . well, anyway—and recorded the time in my head, one-oh-two. I was sitting by the Carver entrance, waiting for my daughter to come out—" "What was she doing in school today?" "A group drama class she takes every Saturday for six weeks, not for credit, but given by Mr. Donalson, the theater teacher there. And it was warm inside—I don't think anyone bothered opening a window in the whole building, or maybe they're not allowed to on weekends, and the theater isn't air-conditioned—so I went outside. I was sitting under a shade tree on the curb near the entrance when you came tearing through the lot. Yours is a gray minivan, right?" "Yes, dark gray, it almost looks black." "Of course I didn't know it was you or your car when it was first coming towards me. And I suppose, to avoid the speed bump a few feet from where I was sitting, since your head would have gone through the car roof if you had rode over it at that speed, you suddenly swerved right, where the bump ends and it's only flat pavement, and I literally had to pull in my legs at the last moment or they would have been run over, at least the feet." "It's true. I was driving back from the mall at around that time and used the school parking lot as a cutoff— I mean a shortcut—to Kenilworth." "You were thinking, with that 'cut-off,' that you almost cut off my legs, am I right?" "I don't think so. Just that the words are very close—the two syllables and the 'cut'—but I don't remember seeing anyone sitting on the curb there. I don't even recall a car parked in the entire lot when I was cutting through it." "There were about five, all of them, including mine, parked head-in to the curb on the other side of the entrance from where I was sitting. Don't ask me why we all parked on that side, but we did. It could be that one followed the other and then when the fourth saw the three, he did also, and so on. I only remember those cars because I was sitting for a while with nothing to read or do and had lots of time to look around. I think that you were going so fast that that could have been why you didn't see the cars or me or anything but the speed bump you were so determined to avoid." "Well, I'm certainly sorry that the incident ever happened, and I apologize. I still find it hard to imagine how I got so near the curb you were sitting on—" "I was sitting on it, believe me, for a half an hour or more, right where I said." "I know; I'm not disputing that. Nor do I remember driving so fast, but if you say you saw it, then I guess I was, or close to that speed, and I'm really sorry about that too and for the scare or alarm or whatever it might have caused you." "It was pretty scary, but I'm over it," and she picks up her frozen coffee drink, sips it and looks at her daughter sitting with his daughter on the grass about thirty feet away.

He looks at his wife across the small table they're all sitting at. She gives an expression that seems to say "It doesn't sound like something you'd do. Did it really happen?" He raises his shoulders and looks at his wife's friends whom they're also sitting with and they had arranged to meet on the patio of this coffee place. The woman he met when his daughter and he went inside to get everyone's drinks, saw his daughter's friend and her mother, whom he'd spoken to briefly a few times when they were both waiting to pick up their kids at school and things like that, and invited them to join them outside. "Sounds as if you went through something quite frightening," his wife's friend says to the woman when she turns back to their group. He thinks does she have to continue on it? Where's her brains? Can't she see how potentially embarrassing it is for me and that the conversation about it was over? "But as we were saying regarding our children's proneness to accidents, life for everyone—even kids in a crib—is filled with near collisions and lucky escapes and it's only the infrequent time when the accident actually takes place and you're affected physically by it." "But it's so odd how I still can hardly believe it happened," he says to the friend. "Again, I'm not saying it didn't, and I'm sincerely sorry and anguished and all that for my part in it, but how did I ever not see her?" "Beats me," the woman says. "I wasn't hiding. I was definitely there, seated, looking around, and I feel— though I don't want to build this to a point way out of proportion to what ultimately resulted, but as long as your friend here is referring to lucky escapes and such—damn lucky not to have lost a foot or leg, or worse, for that's how close the car got." "I'm really glad it turned out the way it did," he says, "meaning that nothing serious happened except for the scare, which was bad enough," and sips his hot coffee and looks at several people coming out of the coffee place and taking a table nearby and then at his daughter and her friend on the grass.

He works his face into what he thinks is a slight smile and freezes it, as if he's enjoying looking at the girls and content they're getting along so well, while inside he feels awful. Stomach's tense, neck's tight, sweat's on his forehead and running down his back, which if anyone notices, he can blame on the warm day and that he just happens to sweat more than most people. What he must seem like to the others now, though that's not important, so neither should be the sweating. Glad his daughter's over there and didn't hear what he'd done, though this woman's daughter might tell her, since her mother could have told her during the drive here. Well, all of that he can work out with his daughter and wife, even if he has to lie, and his wife can later explain to her friend that it wasn't as bad as this woman had made out. But to himself: What was on his mind when it took place? What the hell was he thinking of? he's really asking. How could he have been inattentive or oblivious or just plain out of it when he was heading for the speed bump and then after while he was cutting around it? And the parked cars. He honestly has no recollection of them either and he could have crashed into one of those, or did he quickly see them out of the corners of his eyes and instinctively, without consciously realizing it, which is what happens a lot when you drive, established where they were in relation to his car and gave himself plenty of room to get past them? But if it happened with the speed bump and the woman this time, it could happen again with something or someone else, and much worse. He could have killed her or run over her legs or feet, as she said. Right now she could be in a hospital with a leg or two amputated and he could be in a police station or a police car driving to one. He could be saying to the officers or himself, pulling at his hair while saying it, "I can't believe this has happened. It's horrible. I feel miserable and I'm stupid and reckless and I shouldn't be driving and I'll feel miserable about it for the rest of my life, what I did to that woman, so do what you want with me. I'm guilty and that's it and all I can say is I know what I did is wrong and I'm deeply sorry, as sorry as anyone can be about it, but that doesn't help anything, I know that." The woman's daughter would have found out soon enough in school and run out of her class maybe just around the time the emergency medical ambulance and police cars had shown up. That's what could have got her out of the school—got the whole class out. They heard the police and ambulance sirens, wanted to know what was happening outside. There might be a fire in the building, some of them could have thought, or the teacher did and because the school was officially closed for the day he thought the fire alarm system might be turned off, so he hustled his class outside. Or someone could have run into the theater and told them what had happened. "Wasn't it your mother who was so hot in here that she went outside to wait?" So the daughter could have run to the school entrance and seen her mother being wheeled in a gurney to the ambulance or being given emergency treatment on the ground. If one of the woman's legs had been torn off, the medical people would retrieve it. And while some of them would be trying to stanch the bleeding and giving the woman something to prevent her from going into shock, another would be packing the leg in ice or whatever they pack it in today. Because of the advances and successes of microsurgery and limb reattachments the last ten years or so—you read about it a lot in the newspaper—all these ambulances might now have special packing equipment or even a freezer for amputated body parts. The woman would be screaming if she hadn't been sedated yet or the sedation hadn't taken effect or she wasn't unconscious. The daughter would probably be screaming too. He would be standing somewhere near, giving his driver's license number and information like that to the police and saying the things he thinks he would: "I did it and I feel absolutely miserable about it and I have no defense or excuse for it: it was the worst thing I've ever done in my life." But, suppose—he's thinking, would he do this?—he realized at the time that he'd hit someone—didn't see who it was, so didn't know he'd possibly be identified by the person—and drove, if she wasn't caught underneath the car or in front of one of the wheels—away from the parking lot without stopping? She would have told the police, if she could, who had hit her. Told them at the accident scene. Perhaps just had enough strength to give his name, or his daughter's name, and her daughter could have filled in who he was. The police would be after him by now. They would have first gone to his home. His other daughter, who stayed behind to work on a school science project due Monday and knew where her parents and sister had gone, would have told them where he was. The police might even be here by now and would be questioning him about the accident and saying he'd been identified as the driver who hit the woman. How would they know it was him sitting here? His daughter could have told them what he was wearing and looked like—tan shorts, a dark T-shirt, almost bald, "exactly six feet," he always said he was, which wouldn't help them if he was seated—or they just asked all the male customers of a certain age till they found him or made an announcement inside the coffee place and then on the patio: Is there a Mr. So-and-So here? He would raise his hand, be questioned, say that he had driven past the school at the time they say the accident happened but he doesn't think he hit anyone—that is, if he did flee the parking lot. They'd ask to see his car. He forgot about that and he probably hadn't checked, after he got home, if there was any sign on it that he'd hit someone. They'd probably find blood, maybe hair and skin and a telltale dent on the part of the car they'd say she was most likely hit by and he'd be arrested for leaving the scene of an accident he was involved in and taken to the police station and booked. But if he did stop in the lot after the accident, stopped by choice, which he's almost sure he would—almost a hundred percent sure—the police would probably still bring him in but not arrest him in the lot. They'd politely ask him to accompany them in their car, he thinks, and if he said he didn't want to—though again, he's almost a hundred percent sure he'd go without a fuss—then they'd probably arrest him, maybe even put cuffs on him, and bring him in. And from then on he'd feel, though with a gradual reduction over the years but never where he'd completely get over it, if he had hurt the woman as seriously as he thought he could have, that his life would be ruined and he'd never be the same after the accident, or something like that, but perhaps not as extreme. What he's saying is that it'd affect him as deeply and disturbingly as anything wrong he's ever done and continue to affect him, though perhaps less so over the years, for the rest of his life. That too extreme or exaggerated too? No.

The three women have been talking for the last few minutes about fatigue and several ways to combat it: a certain Korean tea that the woman says gives her quick energy and some leg, arm and abdominal exercises the friend says she does to increase her physical strength. "Let's face it," his wife says. "The worst time in life to cut back on your activities is when you get to around our age, which is really the beginning of the great physical slowdown, when you find yourself suddenly getting pooped over the things you used to do effortlessly. So you have to fight it with all the things you've said. A good strong cup of strong cappuccino helps too."

He thinks Why was he in such a hurry when he drove through the school parking lot? Cutting through it made sense, since it was a short-cut, but he's saying why so fast? Because he'd gone—this is what led up

to it—to the mall to buy a pair of running shorts, it so happens—the elastic in the old pair had stretched so much that the pants were coming
down over his waist when he ran—and after he bought the shorts and a
pair of shoelaces for his running shoes and was having a cup of black coffee in the mall's food court, as a pick-me-up and just for a break from
things to sit and read, he realized he and his wife were to meet her friend
at this coffee place in ten minutes and that it would take him fifteen minutes to get home from the mall once he got in his car, another five minutes or so to get his wife and daughter in the car and it was about twenty minutes from home to the coffee place. As it was, when they got here
and started apologizing to her friend for being late, she said she only just
arrived a few minutes ago and was worried she'd be very late and had
thought of calling them but then thought they were already here or at
least on the way. The only thing he can say—he's saying, if there's anything to be learned or gained from all this—is that he won't drive as fast
when he takes that shortcut and from now on—though he'll see if he
sticks to this—to go no more than ten miles over the posted speed limit
on the road.

His wife's friend says his name and he says "Yes?" and looks up and she
says "So what do you think of what we were saying?" and he says "I'm
sorry, what?" and she says "I knew you weren't listening. Off in your own
thoughts, where you're probably better off, since we really weren't saying
much," and the woman says "Oh, I don't know. They weren't break-
throughs we made, but we were discussing something important." "Truth
is," he says, "I was still berating myself for my dumb speeding through that
school parking lot, which is maybe what you were discussing," and the
woman says "No, and I thought we were over that. I didn't originally
bring it up, you understand, to make you feel bad or guilty, although I
would caution against traveling through lots of any kind at that speed,
even if they appear empty. For your own safety, and of course others',
drive slower. But I mostly brought it up to show something about coinci-
dence. For here I was, minding my own business, the one person on a few
thousand square feet of asphalt, it seemed—only visible person. And
entertaining these nice thoughts about my family and the upcoming summer and also feeling good because it was so delightful out—soft breezes,
cool shade—when a car roars through and scares me out of my wits, and
wonder of wonders if it isn't, out of the million plus people in this city and
no doubt half of them drivers, someone I know whom I'm then having
coffee with an hour later." "I know. Amazing," he says, "amazing."

Later at home he thinks could she have been exaggerating? Not lying, just exaggerating. Some people do to make their stories better. He does-n't know her well—for instance, if she has a history of embellishing the truth, he'll say—but he's almost sure she was this time. Because he just doesn't remember speeding through the lot. Going about ten miles over what's probably a fifteen-miles-per-hour speed limit for a school zone, okay, but it was Saturday and he thought nobody was around. But why would he speed forty, fifty miles per hour, the way she described it? He means, he had a reason—to get home fast because he didn't want his wife angry at him for making her late and possibly even miss her appoint-ment—but he remembers, not distinctly, just vaguely remembers not going at the speed the woman said. He did turn to the right—not swerve—to avoid the speed bump. But the bump didn't come up at the last second where he had to make a sharp right to get around it; he had intended to avoid it. And because he knew the bump was there long before he reached it, he slowed down. He always slows down when he's about to make a turn. And she described it as if her legs or feet were a few inches from his car when he made that turn. But the speed bump ends some twenty feet from the curb so as to make room, he assumes, on regular school days for cars to park head-in. What he's saying is that there must have been plenty of room for him to drive around the bump with-out getting near her, if he was driving slowly or relatively slowly when he made that turn, since there was no reason for him to get so close to the curb if he could be ten to fifteen feet from it. Scaring her he probably did—this big car approaching the curb for a couple of seconds before making that left turn—but there couldn't have been a moment when she was in any real danger, even if he didn't see her. If she didn't say it was close just to make her story more exciting, then she did it, despite what she said at the coffee place, to make him feel bad, guilty, any of those things. So that's it: she was exaggerating. He'll never know exactly what happened or what their exact positions were in the lot in relation to each other, but he knows the incident wasn't the way she said. He feels better about it now, and he didn't just make up this solution to have himself feel that way. He gets out of his chair in the living room and goes to the kitchen to tell his wife what he thought.

Crawfordsville Confidential

G. E. Murray

1.

In the land of milk and cream delivered early
and daily, and always in glass bottles, we care
about good grooming and, of course, news
of slurs and curs . . . Can it really be that home

becomes a place to be stranded?
"I don't see a single storm cloud
anywhere in the sky, but I can sure smell rain,"
out on the edge of Crawfordsville, Indiana,
where the answers and questions become identical
as evil twins.

2.

Basketball ghosts bounce and sweat again
in that second-floor gym in the middle of July—
that never-to-be-forgotten home
of the first-ever Boys State Championship.
Rusty jump shots and long ago corner hooks
rim out in a stream of dusted sunlight.
"Just to play the game, don't you know,
you know, no matter how much the sacrifice . . ."
How searing afternoon's vagueness now,
dreamed in a daylong haze of headache pills
downed at the General Lew Wallace Motor Lodge:
how the pure arc of the ball rises

to echoes of split-jump cheers
in lubricated air, when phantom bodies
strive and leap and go prostrate
to that squeak of rubber on polished wood—
all in the name of shirts and skins.

3.

You can only wonder how Ezra Pound dissected his time here,
among tractors and proctors and temples of antebellum style,
as he cooed sweet Greek in the ear
of his secular madonna . . . Just now, two pigeons
greet first daylight on the Green of Wabash College.

Something to be said for being scandalized silly,
and in more than one language
when life becomes holier than the Crusades.
And what's more—didactic passions
eventually drive you insane, thinks young EP, so what?
Sew buttons, ha!

And make it new always . . . and always
leave the door cracked open, a light on,
and one foot on the floor.

4.

"The meatloaf here's not very good,"
warns waitress Lucy, a pretty girl
with a tooth missing. Indifferently,
day proceeds utterly.
Off Country Road X-10, out by Carcus Creek,
driving past Minnie Betts' florist shop
and what's left of the old city jail,
you figure each small detail adds
glory to any story.
                    "Relax," says Elton Bidwell,
the county's dead buzzard collector,

"I'll take care of us all
when we com' on home."

5.

The town goes dark in a killer storm.
Collective forgetting and forgiving
occurs. But safety comes in many forms.
In this vast black you get to thinking
about giddy joys and little sorrows,
the curse of full employment at minimum wage,
and those conspicuous professors—
their bowties and braces speaking to the ages
and marking moments of learned unworthiness.
Maybe, it's vacuum-packed fear
in a stage-managed town. Time to guess
what's behind each tiny crime and local leer,
at once rancorous and baffling. Strangers
need not apply. A few lights click on
at the Shortstop Grille. These cruel weathers
turn asphalt slick. The old intramurals begin again.

6.

Early Sunday morning and a drunken Elton Bidwell
is strung like a scarecrow on the front porch swing,
deposited by grand wizards from the Odd Fellows Lodge bar
late last night, a reminder to those devoted folks
heading up Church Street with song-books in hand,
that home sure proves just another place to be stranded.

Two Poems

Ann Townsend

A Door

In the clinic, the palsied boy thrashes
against his mother, who holds out the last

vestige of childhood, that he cannot see,
a rocking horse inside a clear bowl.

"Look," she pleads, while the therapist
persists at her lonely task, stretching

his arms past their limits, past their cramping
musculature, above his head. He's half-blind,

and his eyes explore the region of the ceiling
bright with pasted-on stars. His mother shakes

the toy to call him back, while those assembled
in the waiting room shudder through their pain

on plastic chairs, and the boy struggles
and shouts. All this takes place just beyond a door,

half-opened, that anyone may see, and know,
and bless themselves for their luck.

Geraniums

As if their rough fans had too much
of the light, the geraniums "fail to thrive,"

as one mother said of her frail baby,
reporting with some confusion the doctor's term.

What does it mean, she asked, and I had
no good answer but raised the infant

to be weighed and measured once again.
He hung between my hands like an empty

pocketbook, leathery, limp, his abdomen
paling where I held him. All summer,

despite our watering and tender care, the flowers
wilted. I watched the boy die, leaf by leaf.

I kept wishing I had something else
to turn to for the comparison.

Two Poems

Peter Cooley

Language of Departure

Late afternoon and the man finds himself,
his face in his hands at his desk,
nodding, about to drop off a few minutes.
He'd better wake up, shake himself with coffee.
It's past the middle of middle age:
soon he'll be asleep for the next millennia
and the gods may or may not wake him.
There are only a few decades left if he's lucky
to tell his wife, his children, all he feels
they've given him, and already he knows
his language of departure comes from that other country.
He must learn a new alphabet, open his mouth farther
to form vowels. Where he is going there are no words
except those given as they enter to the chosen.

Rochester

Reader, you will tell me as you lift your eyes
from my last line: why would I choose to be

this immortal one if I took on another body?
This sleepless, wounded, never-handsome rook

brooding at the novel's beginning and its end
before a fire, Jane Eyre at his side?

Reader, answer me: isn't it true
you have that attic, too, where we all hide

our madness whom we call some other
we married early, when passion would declare itself?

And now we must feed and clothe and visit it
and flee the monster guiltily, to be driven back

that she attack us and draw blood with open jaws.
I do not know the name, the date, the place

you slept with madness and I would not confess
the exact features of my own: all this is metaphor.

I will admit my wife has witnessed many nights
the demon when it walks out of my skull.

Then I shake from head to foot as she shakes
her nights, and she indulges me my faults

as I do her, as you yourself must. Reader, confess,
you have mansions you set on fire, too.

Three Poems

Paul Breslin

To a Friend Who Concedes Nothing

You arrive, yes, but you bring your distance.
Even at parties—those tributes to the surface
(still intact, with its houses,
through eons of rain and lightning)—your smile
looks hammered from something intractable,
long withheld from the sun. None of us
but descends in his time to the heart's forge
and bears some scar from its boiling metals.
But to *live* there, regarding the world
through cracks in its heavy door:
blinding sword-blades of light, cleaned
of the transient objects they once carved.
For us, this comfort: that the place
must be bearable a moment longer,
since you are bearing it, indifferent
whether the work of your anvil rust in darkness
or shine at a stranger's hearth.

Home

1.

It will take time, your postcard says, but you will get better.
You miss us; moreover the food where you are is terrible.
It is boring there, with nothing to do but read and wait.
For me and my sister, postcards, but sealed letters to mother
one of which, unsealed to me thirty years later, said:
The harm done me, and done by me, has gone too far.
We should kill the kids in their sleep to spare them suffering,
then kill ourselves and be done.

2.

Once, during your stay in the hospital, I sat in the sunroom,
until my attention wandered from the backyard's
red fence, single flourishing maple, garage, and swings,
to the curtain. The sun shone through the weave of bright orange,
yellow, and apple green, making each thread transparent.
I saw how the colors crossed and meandered
jaggedly sideways, then returned to their horizontal
or vertical course. I stared, it must have been several minutes, at where
one green and one orange thread met, twined, and parted.
I memorized the shape of that crossing, then tried
to take in a larger pattern, a whole square inch at once.
With a fierce concentration I envy now, I struggled
to hold it in memory, as if by pulling this small domain
into my consciousness, I could save my life. When I closed my eyes,
I could not recall it. The sun was falling behind
the house across the alley, and soon the curtain would be in shadow.
I pulled back my gaze to the scale of the room,
and saw how tiny the realm that defeated me was.

3.

We left on a sudden "vacation," and you came home to an empty house.
To my sister and me, who had not read your letter, this seemed
   unnaturally cruel.
We returned to find you waiting for us, alone.
It was overcast, late afternoon, but no lights were on.
When you raised your face from your hands I was frightened:

your hair was almost gone, and what remained
was the white of extreme old age. Your skin, always pale
and smooth, looked friable, like your father's.
Your eyes moved no more than a blind man's—
they took nothing in and gave nothing back.
Your shoulders pulled forward and in, so the body
I used to be proud to inherit, compact and powerful,
looked too compact, too dense, as if some enormous weight
had been pulled inside
and would never get out.

I had read about stars, how the sun would shine steadily
for millions of years and then swell to the size of Antares,
swallowing all of its planets closer than Jupiter,
and then collapse to a pale dwarf of itself,
pulling the matter around it down and in. Later,
they would discover black holes, that could bend light
from its path and never release it.

                    When you finally spoke
I could scarcely hear you, the voice was so listless
and indistinct, as if the words formed
in the back of your throat never touched tongue or lips.

The Lesson

Could he trust what she gave
in the openly sensual gaze

she poured on him as he poured
out his story? Not once did she glance

at her watch, or the sunlit window.
"You need an audience"

(which was one thing he needed),
"but that's all right. I like that."

She offered to rub his back. The tension
disappeared down his spine, then rose

where he dared not ask her to follow.
She was dating his roommate, for whom

he'd found her waiting, an open book
spread on her lap. But why

hadn't he called her after
the break-up the following weekend?

He lay awake most of the night deciding
she'd liked him too much, too quickly:

bad taste, bad judgment. Only one
who despised him as he despised himself

could teach him how to resemble
the confident ones she accepted

whose fathers, shouldering others aside,
got what they wanted; whose mothers

doted on them till they understood
that any girl would be mad to refuse them.

Two Poems

Charles Rafferty

Sculpture

She is making a sculpture of me
with cigar ash
instead of granite or bronze.

It has taken her weeks
to amass enough of it,
smoking the cigars herself

or visiting the bars
and barbershops—cradling
homeward in the heel

of her palm
the thumb-fat berries
of pure immolation.

The work is difficult.
She uses a needle
and her own saliva—

relying on gravity
and steadiness, the air vents
crammed with pillows

and sealed with cardboard
and tape. The sculpture
is a constant

crisis of impermanence,
for there is a wind
around her wrists

as she stitches at the ash—
turning my features
to flakes, then dust,

a finger-smear
across her chin
as she stops to take her tea.

When she is out
trying to locate more ash,
I sneak inside to see how I am

coming. I seem always
just below the surface—
as if my body were seen

through inches of ice
on a January pond,
a rising toward oxygen

that could take many months.
My entire semblance
could be crushed into her

pocket, the lovely one beside her hip.
Even her music,
turned on low,

could carry me floorward,
crumbling and soft
and still unformed.

Fire-Eater

She dated a fire-eater
for two months
one summer. He stunk

of kerosene and claimed
he couldn't taste her.
It was like dating

someone blind
in the mouth. She stopped
bathing. Her hair

became tangled.
She wore the same panties
day after day.

Her general sense
of grooming
degenerated

in the presence
of this man, the way
the girlfriend of a thief

might offer to drive
the getaway car
or one day hold the gun.

When asked by friends
why she went
with such a man,

she had no answer ready.
All she could think of
was the way he ate fire

late at night
in his circus trailer:
the blazing sword,

the illumined throat,
the blackness of the air
as he held her down.

Teatro Natura

Ricardo Pau-Llosa

A strip of islands cropped in seagrape,
grass and other natures, splits the clean
shaven beach like a compass needle.
On one side, the motels and condos,
and, after scaling a little bridge
over the tourist desert's Giverny,
another spasm of sand
and then, as always, the sea.

We walk upon a hardness that skirts
these guarding designations
where bug and bird gather
to their sullen pretense
of an open world,
all roost and pollen,
sleep and nest. And we stop,
lined by the fall of moon
through wooden slits of the fence
that keeps us strangers
in a strip of world we keep.
We turn imprisoned
between a kiss and a hand fallen madly
on a waist, to see how the sweep
of snowy grasses curve in brushstrokes
against the humid lead of the sky.

It is then I promise you a poem
about this moment, for me alone

an instant caught between the anxiety
of romance and the affronting
stillness of the sea, lulled in summer
droning, beneath a humorless scythe of
moon mired in myopic fogs. The only flowerings
are those of pampas grass facsimiles
straying ivory across a night
cracked by five freighters and their lights
in the otherwise buried horizon.

Later, soon,
in the civil hum of the air
conditioned room, we will draw the drapes
against this nature, leashed and unfaithful,
and fall upon each other like rancid
blossoms who have spent their springtime well
and now, their seedwork done,
dance away the thickness
between branch and ground.

The Woman Who Wanted to be Loved

Jayanta Mahapatra

Somewhere, a woman's body knows.
Rain is her mother,
a fitful time of sweat and tears.
Quietly she dies of ghosts of love
she found among the water and grass.

Her dark days cannot be braided into a poem.
But her body wants to escape from greater things.
There was a time when her breath rose up,
a flag to flutter in the wind. It was the hour
when her black hair with its long spears
needed the sacrament of blood.

Seasons pass, and she becomes stone.
Sighs of mango blossoms bring in
the scents of summer, scentless around the bone.
Love can break and still keep its promise.
It can borrow a dawn and haunt it through time.

Hypatia; In No Mood

Rachel Levine

The burning sun is a zero
and though it is the center of the cosmos,
helping things to grow,
you cannot extract ten sheaves of wheat
or a thousand fat geese
or a multitude of loaves and fishes
from nothing. Yea, these things would burn
to cinders, like the eyesight of those
coming up from Plato's cave,
or the purported wax wings of Icarus.
Naturally, the sun is not the father, nor the rest
of the so-called Trinity. No,
the sun is not God, but it is the essence of Good,
is what I said, and the monks shouted that
I must be a witch
as sure as the carnelian beads on my abacus
click, click, click . . .

So today I am a heretic
as the moon visits my body
for the 384th time.
As if a fat goose had been bled
between my legs and I awoke
to the usual blackish-red stain
on white linen, here where Helios
dances lightly on the brackish
reed-whiskered mouth of the Nile,

and I am in no mood
to teach today, since those cursed monks
have been interrupting my lectures
with their shouting from the back of the theater.
Yesterday I gripped the lectern until my knuckles
were white as scrolls and swore
an oath at them . . .

Today I count 16 long white hairs amongst my other black—
one for each year of the flaxen Table Slave from Gaul
who my husband ran off with to Rome—I am certainly
in no mood, though perhaps
I can get some serious work done
now that he's gone . . .

My father taught me to lead
a Pythagorean life; to believe
only in right angles, that everything
would balance, find its true axis,
and he was correct . . . But today I am
in no mood and even the numbers
are irrational, screaming.

Bloodknots

Ami Sands Brodoff

Shana closed her eyes and everything opened, bloomed. Inner swells rose, building speed and height as they rolled through her, breaking heat and emptying in a rush of blood, the space between her legs like a stretched mouth, her mouth and her baby's gaped black in screams. She felt like she was rising from the delivery table, high and helpless in the wake of pure pain and pleasure.

Already a mother, she'd missed this part the first time.

Her baby girl weighed nine-and-a-half pounds, with a tuft of chestnut hair, her eyes squinched shut against this other world. The nurse handed her the baby and Shana held her daughter to her breasts straining to hear her heartbeat. Dr. Zimmer squeezed Shana's hand, her husband David kissed the top of her head, as if she were a child again.

Too many people were all over her, but Shana felt their hovering care only distantly, prickling touches like mosquitoes inching along her skin, as if she had grown huge with this birth. She folded her arms around her new daughter, Ariel's warm weight making its imprint onto her emptied belly.

During delivery, David had stood at her shoulder watching the white wall, confirming Shana's sense that childbirth was at its core exquisitely solitary—she was alone, the baby was alone in its passage from darkness to light—one by one, they all left the room, even Ariel, whisked away by a nurse to be sponged clean.

Shana's room was washed with white silences and sunlight, deep shadowed snow and glittering pines just outside the window. This winter had held on. Already it was the last day of March, soon the weather would turn. Looking out, Shana thought of her little boy Azul, picturing her husband's and son's limbs entwined in sleep as they would be that night, just like most nights during her five months of enforced bed rest, her growing belly like a great swelling shield forcing them into a shared space of their own. Shana felt her eyes smart, she couldn't cry.

Aretha sang "Spirit in the Dark" and Shana moved to her voice, lying down. She called family and friends, arranging the dried flowers David had picked in her favorite colors. Plundering through the wicker basket he and Azul had packed with fresh fruit, cheese and chocolate, she unearthed the plastic button Azul must have buried in there with the food: a photograph of the two of them taken on their last outing before her confinement. Azul sits sideways on her lap, her hand spanning his sinewy brown thighs. Their cheeks touch full-length as Azul slips a treasure into her pocket, a pebble he'd found glinting from the dirt switchbacks leading down to the sea near their summer cabin.

At three-and-a-half, he was still transfixed by his own image. Shana remembered him gravely leafing through the glossy brochure at Penney's, examining all the objects you could acquire to keep a loved one close—frozen in time, fixed in space—buttons and lockets, key chains and keepsake boxes. Azul chose two of the same brightly colored buttons, each a hair smaller than a half-dollar, a matched set. Throughout her pregnancy, he refused to take the thing off, even to sleep, cherishing this miniature of reality, this bit and piece, and she couldn't help thinking that people expelled from their own pasts became the most fervent picture-takers and collectors.

Running her finger over the button's shiny surface, she phoned her older brother Josh who was watching Azul. Her son was napping and an uneasy relief filled her, not having to face him yet. She knew she should rest but felt high, wired. Blasting Aretha to the hilt, she wrapped a robe around her stained hospital gown and staggered barefoot into the hall.

The shiny hospital linoleum was spongy under Shana's feet, her body suddenly light, buoyant. She needed to feel it move and twirled down the corridor to "Natural Woman," a take on the number her students would be performing for the spring recital. When she and her sister founded the Auerbach School of Dance a decade ago, the kids she taught in class were her only children. Back then, David would stop by between patients and watch her teach; no longer a performer, she liked being watched, his dark presence an anchor in the back of the room. Once, on a sweltering August evening, the sky an unearthly violet-gold streaked with black, they'd gone up to the roof where it was cooler to watch the sky change. He'd had a God-awful day with patients, absorbing the marshy mire of their minds, and she'd promised to cheer him up. "I dare you," she started. "I dare you to dare me."

"Okay." He pondered far too long. "Walk all the way across. On your hands. Naked."

She peeled away her sweaty leotard and tights, tossing them in a ball on the tarpaper, the air cooler on skin. Flipping to palms, she made the diagonal, back arched, the tarpaper hot and sticky to touch, David in tow, laughing low in his throat. Touching her palm to his cheek, she said in her best British, "How could I ever marry so cautious a man?"

"To make him uncautious."

She patted the flat brick wall encircling the rooftop, which reached her hip. "Right here."

David hesitated again, then lifted her onto the parapet. With her legs wrapped high around his back, she leaned into boundless space as he entered her, moving further and further out as he moved, the pressure of his palms against the small of her back. That's what she wanted, to go to a place she'd never been . . . but when the storm broke, he pulled her in tight against his chest, so her feet touched ground.

Dynamite blasts of water streamed warm and hard against her neck and shoulders, plastering his black and silver hair, heavy and dripping. He'd take her to another place and they would always return again. That was her worst dread, but worse things could happen.

Soon the rain thinned to slanting drops, sun straining through clouds in veins of light. They sat on the parapet, the sandy rasp of mortar against her skin till the rain stopped, the sun went down, talking in desultory drifts about the children they'd have, the trip they'd make to the Isle of Skye, what they'd cook for dinner that night. She knew then that she would marry him. He would take her to a new place and the going would be everything. Now, she wished she could travel in her own past, as if the road went both ways.

Shana whirled around the corner of the hospital corridor, drunk with the newness of motion, each cell alive and particular as a woman's voice rang out behind her, "You best be doing that dancing lying down," and a dark glittering wave shuddered through her falling body, caught by a net of arms and hands. Someone lifted her, propped her to standing. Turning, Shana faced a tall, skinny man with black, matted hair, a milky substance crusted on his shabby sweater, Ariel's bassinet beside him. A nurse clipped past, craning her neck to watch. "Now me," the man said, feigning a swoon. "Hey, I know that game." Swaddled in white flannel, Ariel was sleeping, her lower lip thrust out.

"I was coming to see you about your daughter, Ariel," the man said. "Hey, I like that . . . from the Bible, some kind of flame, right? Or a horse? No—I know—it's a flaming horse! I thought about it for a girl, a super different-type name." He spoke in a rush, his thin voice quavery.

Shana reached for Ariel's bassinet, squeezing the clear plastic handle till her knuckles whitened. No nurses in sight. *Where the hell was David?* She breathed out, a sudden nausea clotting the back of her throat. "Who *are* you?"

The man sucked in his stomach as if he'd been punched, then chewed his lower lip, squinting through blue eyes shaded by deep purplish shadows.

"Dr. Mauro," he said, extending his hand.

He had a wide, mobile mouth. His hair was dirty, his teeth bad. Around his neck and wrist dangled brightly colored paper jewelry, gum chains like the ones she'd woven as a little girl in summer camp. His face was round, soft-featured, pale. When she extended her hand, he clasped it firmly and held on. His hand was warm and slightly damp, so large it enfolded hers.

"Come," he said, one hand on her shoulder, the other propelling Ariel's bassinet down the hall, its wheels clattering on hospital linoleum, "we'll talk about your daughter."

In her room, he loped over and sat on the bed where Shana had collapsed. Drawing her dressing gown around her throat, she reached for the buzzer on the bed rail, blocked now by his narrow, hunched back.

"You don't look like a doctor," she whispered half to herself.

He smiled at her with his whole face, a wide-open loopy grin, unnervingly like a baby's first smile.

"You a mother? *You* look like a *mother!*"

He laughed, then rolled up the sleeves of his mangy sweater. Shana looked at the thin bare arms, a blue-veined strength about them, his hands, one flat on the bed sheet, the other in his lap, graceful and long-fingered, the curved nails short and scrubbed.

"Where's Dr. Levine? Dr. Levine is our pediatrician." Shana scooted to the edge of the bed and went to the window, as if Ernest William Levine, M.D. might materialize there.

"Yeah sure. Well, I'm covering for E.W."

Ariel whimpered from her bassinet, then let out high, warbling screams. Dr. Mauro stood; they reached for Ariel at the same time and blood gushed from her, leaving dark red drops the size of quarters in a trail across the floor. The room browned, a cottony rush clouding both ears. Shana started to say something; felt her mouth open, but nothing come out. Within the vortex of seasound, she heard the man say, "Come here," and felt the gentle pressure of his hand at her shoulder, his other arm in a shepherding sweep around her waist. Outside the winter winds were howling with a sound almost human. She made a great effort to open her eyes, to see. The man's face was close to hers, his eyes thick lashed and fluttering. They were wide and dark blue, like the hearts of small fires.

A stooped gray-haired nurse with tired, kindly eyes rested a tray of food across Shana's lap. "Your husband, he was singing to the baby. He have a nice voice." Shana recognized her voice from the hall. "You got to eat," she added, lifting the cover from a plate of soup, steam spiraling with a rich salty smell. David made the best soups and Shana missed him; his pensive face and meditative thoughts had a way of enfolding her.

"Where is my husband?" she asked, spotting a note on the night table scrawled on a prescription pad for *Xanax*. During her immobility, his calm which had always drawn her turned grim; David's carefully modulated speech weighed her down, his long pauses were absences, chasms she fell into. (Maybe she'd needed a prankster with a clown nose, blowing horns, banging cymbals.) "Where is my goddamn husband?"

"No need to swear, now. He went home to get your boy, that's what he said," the nurse went on, as a blonde aide wheeled Ariel in from the nursery. Shana wondered if she'd imagined the tall skinny intruder, if he were part of some post-delivery dream. "I've lost track of time," she said to no one in particular, lifting Ariel into her arms. Her daughter felt warm and plush, a pink cast to her skin, still splotched here and there with a cheesy coating. Her pale hair was sparse, her head unbearably soft and warm, the pulse visible through fontanelles. She had a downy fuzz on her shoulders, back and bottom, her plump legs crossed at the ankle, one hand, almost coquettish behind her ear, the other at her chin. Her eyes were teal-colored and tearing.

"Has Dr. Levine been in to see my baby?" Shana asked the older nurse who stood close, admiring Ariel.

"Dr. Mauro, he come in to see you?"

"That man was a doctor."

The nurse laughed, deep and secretive, covering her mouth. "Gabriel Mauro, he's temporary in the group. Windsor Plains Pediatrics, right?"

Shana nodded slowly.

"Well, they trying him out."

"Ah, that's comforting."

The nurse laughed again, louder this time. "Some ask for him."

Shana was trying to breast-feed Ariel when Dr. Mauro settled his long frame into the floral covered rocker. "If I scared you before, hey sorry." His head bobbed like a toy with a coiled spring neck. "I have that effect on people."

As he fixed his eyes on her, Shana draped her exposed breast with a burping cloth she'd slung over the bed rail. She scarcely recognized this body of hers. Her breasts were tender, throbbing and lumpy, the swelling extending nearly to her armpit; nipples and areolae were double their size, the shade of blackened plums. Ariel nuzzled Shana's breast with a pathetic sputtering. Frantic, Shana tried the cross-cuddle hold, the side-lying position, the football hold—positions she'd studied from the manuals she'd armed herself with—moving Ariel about like a sack of goods. The baby's head wagged, her mouth zoomed in with a life all its own, a line of spit glimmering. Sputtering off, her screams spiraled; the cloth slipped from Shana's shoulder, crumpling in her lap.

"Nursing's hard," Dr. Mauro said, nodding. "Nobody tells you, not those lunatics from *La Leche*—where are they when you need them—anyway, she's doing fine. Color's good, lots of activity, lusty cry." He double-crossed his legs, tucking his foot inside the ankle.

In a moment of inspiration, Shana stuck her pinkie into Ariel's mouth and the baby took it with a sudden grab. Shana's breath came raggedly, sweat beading from her pores. "So . . . she's fine?"

"Her bili levels are a little high, borderline. But not to worry, I don't want you to worry about anything."

"Translation?"

"We'll have to watch her for jaundice. Right now, she's producing more bilirubin than she can handle . . . if it builds up, we'll put her under the lights till we get her levels down. Then you both go home and really get to know each other. Sound good?"

Shana nodded, reassured by his official medical explanation, the sprinkling of clinical jargon, the fact that he sounded somewhat like a real doctor, now. "As long as it's not serious."

He glanced down at her chart. "You had a rough pregnancy."

Shana laughed, more of a gasp. "Yeah, right. After sixteen weeks, she wanted out."

Ariel sucked furiously, kicking her legs, as if the force of her lips might bring forth food from Shana's finger. Feeling the rhythmic squeeze of her lips, the soft pummeling of her legs, Shana thought of her and David's astonished joy at this surprise baby after so many years of trying, then the precariousness—of the forming fetus, of her body as a safe house—the very real possibility that this longed for child might be born and die, in the same moment.

"Bleeding, some premature labor—"

"I was teaching a jazz class," Shana broke in, "it was the end of my fourth month—I was starting to feel really good—you know how you do." She moved her finger around in Ariel's mouth feeling the firm pink gums, the hard spots where teeth buds were already forming under the skin. "I did a split—and this knife plunged into my gut—Zimmer put me in the hospital on an IV." Shana stroked Ariel's head. "After that, if I tried to go to the bathroom, she assumed it was time."

Though Shana's tone was light, a burst of her old terror returned. She listened to Ariel's heartbeat, high, quick and strong, the curled cushiony body rising and falling as she sucked.

"—Well, we made it. Anyway, it's easier this time."

Dr. Mauro shook his head, eyes narrowing. "So you had an even tougher time with—"

"Azul," Shana murmured, remembering the years of waiting, casual lovemaking gone purposeful and joyless, a sperm test for David, dye shot through fallopian tubes for her, fertility drugs, Chinese herbs. And then there was the waiting: as they decided on foreign adoption, selected an agency, prepared their documentation and met criteria for suitability; the waiting after home study and documentation were complete; the waiting for a child to be located for them; the waiting while legal procedures were completed and arrangements made.

At last a baby boy lost and found. From Columbia. Next to nothing known about his parents' or their medical histories, his exact age not even known.

Shana heard the baby before she saw him, before she felt his dense compact weight within the warm flannel swaddling. His cry went right through her, palpable as a tensile hand, reaching. She learned to know him through his cry. When he was hungry, he howled. When he was wet or soiled, he bellowed. When he wanted to be held, he keened. And when he was misunderstood or ignored, he roared. His cry etched a channel in her heart. She knew he would survive.

And so she tried to nurse Azul, forging the physical connection they'd missed. Yes, you could breastfeed an adopted baby with a will and a way. His suck would stimulate her milk production. For three months, she wore a feeding bottle around her neck, slim tubes leading from the bottle taped down her breasts extending slightly past the nipples, the bottle filled with soy formula. As Azul nursed at her breast, he took formula from the tube until she produced enough milk to give up the supplementary nutrition system. That was the theory.

Her body said, No. Shana tore the apparatus from her neck and the baby took the rubber nipple into his mouth with a greedy snatch.

Now, Ariel pulled off her pinkie, crying out. Stooping slightly, Dr. Mauro walked over to the bed, a dip in each gangling step. He brushed past her and put a pillow behind her back, another in her lap. Shana cradled Ariel in her arm, tummy to tummy, the baby's head resting in the bend of her elbow. Shana lifted her swollen and marbled breast to her daughter's mouth and pulled her in close. She heard Ariel's gasp, as she seized the nipple in a life-or-death clench, heard her sucking and swallowing, a warmth spreading through her from the baby's mouth, from her soft body. Dr. Mauro's eyes were on her and her new daughter. Shana reached out her hand blindly and he took it, her fingers curling into his.

That afternoon, Shana heard Azul's voice, urgent and feverish, from down in the parking lot. Single words floated up—*Mama, magic, luck*— and she rushed into the hall as he careened toward her wheeling a red plastic suitcase, cradling his stuffed moose in one arm, a mesh sack filled with books, snacks and videos dangling from his wrist. "Mama!" he called out, tripping over the suitcase which snapped open, its contents spilling onto the floor: a shiny foil star dangling from a wooden stick, red dice, a lava lamp; colored rocks and shells; a pad labeled, "My Magic Book," and a drum fashioned from a tin can and piece of rubber stretched over its lid . . . "Mama," he said, "I have so much luggage."

As she lifted him into her arms, he wrapped his legs around her waist and she saw the button pinned to his red sweatshirt, thankful that she remembered to pin hers to her dressing gown. His sweatshirt was adorned with two snap-on frogs; he'd strung ropes of her beads around his neck, smelled of her perfume, and wore David's tie as a belt. For a moment, they held each other, searching for the place they'd found together, then lost, like a treasure hidden in a secret place in deep wood. Azul's head burrowed into her chest, his legs swam seeking bottom. His body was very thin, but strong: fibrous and elastic as rope. His hair fell across her cheek, coarse and sweet-smelling. She whirled in a circle holding him, first one way, then the other. One of his sneakers fell to the floor. They were still and she whispered to him, "Put your head down, Az, put your head down on Mama," and he laid his head against her breast as he'd done as a baby, and for a moment, everything was right in their world.

David wrapped his arms around their backs, enfolding all three in a family huddle. "At last," he said, kissing her. "Finally."

"I got a idea," said Azul, "a magic star on a stick."

"And what can you do with it, Az?" She swiveled him sideways, holding and rocking him like a baby; Azul squirmed, jumping down. Holding the foil star aloft, he whirled it faster and faster above his head. "I can make anything I want. Come or go away."

Shana and David looked at each other, then gathered Azul's toys, so they could have some privacy in Shana's room. Barely a second later, a sullen nurse deposited Ariel in the room and said, accusingly, "She's hungry," leaving abruptly. Ariel mewled from her bassinet, at first intermittently, soon in a steady grumbling.

"Pick me up, pick me up!" Azul ordered, and Shana encircled his waist with one arm and lifted him, scooping Ariel up from her bassinet with her other arm, the baby's head wobbling, unsupported.

"Here," David offered, sliding Ariel from her arms, deftly supporting the baby's head with a broad, splayed hand. Shana watched him as he held the baby close against his chest, rocking her in a vertical motion. He glanced up, watching her watch him. Azul said, "There's a yuk smell."

"Maybe the baby needs a change," Shana answered.

"No!" shouted Azul. "A bear in the woods after bad men shooted him. It's you, Mama, your body." He put a yard of space between them. "I'll stand here."

Shana folded her arms across her chest. There were moments, since delivery, when her own smell wafted toward her, fluids separate yet a part of her—her and Ariel—all that was contained now spilling, her insides turned out.

Ariel's mewling escalated into cries. David rocked her faster, up and down.

"Hey," Shana said, "watch her head."

Azul stomped up to Shana from behind and shoved her with all his strength.

"Stop it!" She reeled around. "Give me her," Shana said to David, taking the baby. With one hand, she hauled out her breast; she nursed Ariel standing up, circling the periphery of the room.

"I'm hungry," Azul said, beating the toy drum with a colored rock, then the moose's head.

"Here Bud," David said, laying out a juice box and package of cookies. "You can have a picnic."

"I want pancakes," Azul said. "Chocolate chip pancakes."

"When we get home," David pleaded.

"No, now!"

"Indoor voice." That was David. "Remember, Az. Indoor voice?"

"Not my indoor voice!" Azul grabbed one of her arms that was holding the baby, breaking Ariel's suction on her breast.

"Your mother's got to feed her," David said.

Azul backed away like a bull, then rammed into Shana's stomach. He did it again. And again.

David grabbed Azul from behind, wrapping his arms around his back confining and containing him. "You stop it. Now."

"When is her Mommy coming?" Azul asked. "So for she can go back into the egg."

All through the pregnancy, he'd asked them, "How does a person make a person?" They'd tried to prepare him, but the notion of pregnancy and birth was a goulash of horticultural imagery of seeds planted in earth, the growing baby in her belly showered with hot soup and pizza, and eggs hatching, like the baby chicks he'd seen on a neighbor's farm.

"I *am* her Mommy and I'm your Mommy, too," Shana said, her voice so thin and taut, she was almost singing.

"Don't say anything." Azul covered his eyes with both hands. "I don't want to see you."

Shana saw the button with the photo of the two of them hanging on his sweatshirt from a thread. She went to him while holding Ariel who in a private world of simple survival was still sucking. While Shana held the baby, Azul burrowed into the space between her legs falling into the heavy folds of her dressing gown. Shana handed Ariel to David. "Burp her," she said, lifting Azul into her arms, holding him tight. All seemed okay for a moment, then he butt his head against her chest, pummeled her back with fists, kicked her shins with his feet, belting out guttural cries. Shana planted Azul on the floor, then grabbed him by his arm, so hard he spun around. Her hand was raised, trembling, heat flashed through her and the room turned harsh, its colors too bright, the outlines of objects black and menacing. She knew if she smacked him, she might never stop. The space between them was charged, a magnetic force field.

Azul looked at her as if he were trying to find her through a many-layered mask. "Mama?"

She couldn't speak for a while. "You know, I'm a person too," she said finally.

"No. You're my Mommy."

Shana looked at Azul, then David. The baby's mouth was open, her head wagging, rooting at David's broad chest.

"Maybe I better give her a bottle of formula," he said.

All the air punched out of her chest.

David handed Shana their daughter and took Azul's hand. "C'mon Bud," he said, "let's explore." Azul crumpled into David's side and out they went.

*

A half-hour later, Shana walked Ariel back to the nursery and found David, Azul and Dr. Mauro in the patient lounge. None of them seemed to belong there. It was a bare room with a green plastic rug made to look like lawn, a large television, a coffee pot, a few tattered Dr. Seuss books, a video on making friends, and two wicker bowls, one filled with saltines, the other with tea bags and packets of instant coffee, cocoa and creamer.

This Dr. Mauro seemed to have all the time in the world. The hospital was pretty quiet; still, Shana was used to Dr. Levine rushing around on a schedule timed on split-seconds. She smiled to herself, wondering how long Dr. Mauro would last, as he unraveled a length of rope from the neck of Azul's stuffed moose. With complete absorption, he began tying knots, for Azul's entertainment. He was deft, his hands quick and graceful. His arms had a white tensile beauty, their strength and fluidity reminding her of the motion of plants undersea. He made figure-eights and sheet bends, clove hitches, butterflies and cat's-paws, weaver and water knots.

"Cavemen tied knots," he told Azul. "So did the Indians and Eskimos."

"Did they make magic? *You* make magic," ordered Azul.

"What kind of magic do you want me to make?" Dr. Mauro asked, his hands never stopping their fluid motion.

"Make knots go away."

Loosely and with great deliberation, he tied a square knot. While Azul watched, he interwove and tucked the working ends even more "to make it really secure." Pulling slowly on the ends, the knot fell apart, leaving bare smooth rope.

Azul ran his hand along the rope to make sure the knot was really gone, not hidden.

"Is there somebody you want to keep captive? Your own special prisoner?" Dr. Mauro asked.

Azul looked at the ceiling. "Daddy!"

Working quickly with the rope, hand-over-hand, Dr. Mauro linked David and Azul together in a set of interlocking rope handcuffs. Azul climbed in and out of the large slack loops linking the handcuffs which tied him to David; laughing, he turned somersaults through David's arms in an effort to get free. After watching the captives for awhile, Dr. Mauro passed the slack length of rope under Azul's wrist loop and then over his hand, releasing them both.

Azul clapped his hands together. "Look!"

"Ever have something—or some*one*—you want to tie to a rope—"started Dr. Mauro.

"Something giant big?"

"Yeah, something giant big and heavy where you don't want your line to ever break?"

"Like a giant big fish I could eat till I got big and exploded in Heaven?"

Working faster and faster with the rope, Dr. Mauro tucked the working end through its own loop, two, three, four times, making loop after loop after loop.

Shana watched, Azul and David stood transfixed. "Bloodknots," Dr. Mauro said, "they'll never break. Not ever."

Azul glanced over at the doorway. "Look Mama!" he called out in his outdoor voice. "Bloodknots. For so they never break."

Soon Shana kissed her husband and son goodbye, lingering for awhile with Dr. Mauro in the lounge. "How'd you learn all that?" she asked him.

He twined the length of rope around his fingers, handing it back to her to return to Azul. They picked up a book he'd left behind, one of the snap-on frogs that had popped off his shirt, crumpling cookie wrappers and juice boxes and putting them in the garbage. "So," she pressed, "are you an angler? Or a sailorman?"

He smiled a slow secret smile. Though his face was round and soft, like a person not fully formed, there was a stubborn definition to his ridged chin and full mouth. His eyes were both dreamy and intense, a quickfire play between his private world and the outer one. "I just like to play around with rope."

"Rope, eh?"

She bent to pick up a few strewn toys, gathering them to her chest, as if they were alive. Every day at about this time, she used to pick up Azul's toys with him, make a game of it—one of the simple daily chores that had been off-limits during her pregnancy—each in its smallness and dailiness unimportant, but the cumulative mass, the foundation of their life together as mother and son.

A sound from deep within the body escaped her throat, involuntary and private.

Dr. Mauro reached for the collection of toys she held awkwardly against her chest. "He'll be back."

Shana still hurt all over, exhausted and bewildered from the birth.

"You don't know what it's like, hey, I was flat on my back from November to now, Thanksgiving through Christmas, New Year's and Valentine's Day and David's birthday—that's five months—I mean, shit!—149 days."

She watched him let her words settle like sediment. He stood very still, just listening, then began to pack Azul's toys into a plastic grocery bag someone had left behind that said *With Love From King's* in green block-print. A nurse paged Dr. Mauro over the P.A. system and he slung the absurd bag over her wrist, holding her shoulders for a moment, as if to steady her before slouching into the hall.

Shana stood in the lounge within the fixed urgency of a trance, remembering the immense loneliness of immobility, lying in bed, heavy and isolated. Hearing David's deep, soft voice interlaced with Azul's loud, insistent one, across a great distance though they moved only one room away. For the first time, she was lonely when she was with them, a loneliness immense and unsettling. Her husband and son waiting on her, bringing meals on a tray, letting her rest and rest again. Their solicitude, the bloodless politesse, as if she were an expensive house filled with breakable priceless furniture; they could look but not touch, they could not inhabit her.

All motion and growth were within, invisible, except for the rising opaque mass of her belly, a mountain landscape neither she nor David nor Azul had complete access to. Shana turned inward.

When the baby kicked, she shaded in the plump blunt toes, the network of thread-thin lines on the sole of her unborn daughter's foot. Sometimes an arm swam up into her rib cage and Shana imagined the cupped hand, its webbed fingers. When she stood to go to the bathroom, there was the sensation of a hard black ball dropping, and then Shana imagined the developing brain crackle, long wiry cells, staccato bursts of electricity, pulsing waves like currents shifting sand on the sea floor. She'd read about a baby's brain at birth—as many nerve cells as stars in the Milky Way—she was still. And waited.

The inner landscape was roiled, alive. Shana existed in an erotic haze, a heavy pent-up tingling inside swollen breasts, the pit of her belly, between her legs, like criss-crossed electrical wires, tightly wound, compressed into a ball. Wakeful, she felt David's immense weight beside her, his careful lumbering movements jostling the bed, his touches gentle and too tender and solicitous—made her want to bite, scratch and scream—anything, to pull him back to her, but this, too, could bring on labor. Night after night, she lay awake tumbling into the hollow he made in the sheets, only touching when they bumped, got in each other's way. Until Azul cried out for David . . .

Wandering slowly back to her hospital room, Shana wasn't sure if she became more dense and compact—self-sufficient—in that monstrously heavy and immobilized pregnancy or had grown hollow. Some days, she wondered who she was, if she would ever find her way back to herself, to Azul and David.

Dr. Mauro fell into step with her as she approached her room.

"It's amazing what you feel," she said, still in her own world.

He shook his head fast, almost a tremor. "I mean, to have them inside you—"

She saw him in his clean but cluttered office, dressed in a pale pink shirt and cartoon-character tie, the well-appointed glossy photos of the wife and three or four kids. "So, how many do you have?"

He formed an empty circle with thumb and forefinger.

"I'm surprised," Shana said, as they stood together in the doorway of her room, half in, half out. She wanted to ask why, to find out more about him, but didn't know how or where to begin. "It's scary to think—" she went on, picturing cavemen eating the still-bloody hearts of rival tribesmen, devouring and ingesting and holding onto their souls. She was losing hold; quickly, she glanced into the room at the wood paneling concealing emergency equipment—gas, oxygen— "I think I'm going nuts," she confessed.

"That's common," he said, nodding. "After a birth."

Her face must have shown her disappointment.

"I mean," he reassured, "I'm sure you'll do it in your own special way."

They lingered a moment in the doorway. Shana had a sudden urge to touch him, to caress his face. Taken off guard, she turned abruptly and went into her room.

The sky was a pearlized gray, the bare winter trees dusky silhouettes; opening her eyes, Shana wondered if it was late-morning or afternoon. Her Early Music CD was still playing, the voices ribboning into the silent room. She'd had a stream of visitors, then unplugged the phone so she could nap. It seemed as if she'd been in the hospital for a very long while, but when she glanced at her watch, she saw it was just her second day.

Ariel lay asleep beside her and she lifted her daughter's curled form, still soft and heavy with sleep, moving to the rocker, singing to her. At birth, her skin had been ruddy, then lightened to a lovely rose; now it was paler, a yellowish cast to her cheeks and chin. She heard Dr. Mauro's voice a moment before he stepped into the room.

"I think we'll keep her, baby girl's got to spend some time under the bili-lights." He walked around and stroked Ariel's sparse hair, his long slender fingers nearly enfolding her head. "I'll talk to Zimmer, see if we can't get you signed in here couple more days."

A gift, that's what this was: the promise of several more days in the hospital, alone with Ariel. Shana felt a sudden spasm of guilt, thinking of Azul.

"Right," Dr. Mauro said, out of nowhere, folding his long arms across his chest. He was dressed more or less like a real doctor now, in a white coat with a pale blue T-shirt underneath. The gum chains were under the T-shirt like an intimate piece of jewelry with great sentimental value. His hair was cleaner, his shoes polished. A nurse walked in, depositing a pink wad of telephone messages. Glancing at the phone, she clucked her tongue. "I always did want to be a personal secretary," she said, walking out.

Dr. Mauro shut his eyes, as if imagining something, as Shana leaned over to plug in the phone. Immediately it rang. As she picked up, Ariel let out staccato shrieks, then an angry cry full of vibrato. Shana found herself looking to Dr. Mauro, and without saying anything, he took the baby from her threading his slender forearm through her legs, his open hand against her belly as he flew her through the air, whistling.

"He's on strike," David said, and a muscle clenched inside Shana's stomach. "Won't eat. I mean, anything."

"Let me talk to him." Azul was too thin, fussy about food; some days, he lived on air. Shana heard a muffled squeak as the phone changed hands.

"Mama, when you coming home?"

"Azul, you've got to eat."

"Mama, what you said?"

Ariel started crying, her chin quivering, and Dr. Mauro handed her back to Shana. Nodding toward the door, he approached it, but didn't leave. The baby took a sharp intake of air and began nursing ferociously, her sucking and swallowing clearly audible and Shana relaxed within the tingling hot needles, the shivering sensation, as her milk let down and her full breast softened, emptying as the baby nursed.

"Honey—"

"Mama, can you see me through the phone?"

"No, Sweetie, I—"

"I can see you through the phone, Mama. In my imagination."

"I see you in mine, too, in my mind's eye. So. Why aren't you eating, Azul?"

"I eat," Azul said, "dust from my magic star, so for I can go to heaven."

The baby sucked, pausing and trembling with the effort, which seemed to exhaust her. What Azul said took a moment to register, settling like a black iron hand against her chest.

"What you doing, Mama?" Azul asked.

"Resting . . . Az, if you could eat anything in the whole wide world—"

"A banana strawberry milk shake."

She breathed out sharply, as the baby sucked on and on.

"*You* make it, Mama."

"Okay, we'll make it together. You down in the kitchen?"

"You're a hundred-percent right," he said. "You Sunday driver!"

"Take out milk, pour a big cup into the blender." The phone crashed to the floor. She heard him opening the fridge, a clattering of objects on the counter. Azul picked up the phone and she went on with her directions. He put the phone down again and Shana heard water running in a hard fast stream. Soon there was the roar of the blender and the welcome sound of Azul drinking the cold, rich shake.

She just listened to her son drinking, as her daughter nursed.

Glancing up, she saw Dr. Mauro still standing in the doorway; when she looked up at him, he slipped out. On the other end of the line, Shana heard the metallic clink of metal against glass, a crash in her ear as the phone dropped to the floor, then the sudden cut-off.

All evening, she tried to get back through. Frantic, she sent her sister over to the house. No one was home. In thoughtless panic, Shana threw on her coat and started walking down the hall out of the hospital with Ariel in her arms, but a nurse intercepted her and led her back to her room. She lay down on the bed and wept, the nurse trying to comfort her, assuming it was a bad case of post-partem blues. Finally, Shana asked her to leave. That was midnight.

David called her two hours later. "I don't know how to tell you this," he started. "When you were making that milkshake, Az dropped in the button, swallowed it, pin and all."

Shana's mind went white.

"We're at Saint Joe's," David went on. "Got the best pediatric G.I. guy around. Azul is out of danger, Shana. The metal pin showed up on Xray. The button made it into his stomach, but it was too big to pass out. They went in with an endoscope, this miniature TV camera, and they pulled the thing out with a snare."

"I've got to see him—David, I've got to get out of here."

"He wouldn't know if you were here."

She was suddenly so scared, she couldn't think or speak.

"Shana, I told you, they gave him a sedative. Look. Zimmer doesn't want you leaving the hospital, yet. It's not safe—for you or Ariel—we'll all be home soon. Together. Everything'll be okay. Okay?"

She felt hollow, mute. David waited on the phone until she said something. Shana made him promise to call back in an hour, sooner; then she eased the phone noiselessly back into its cradle. And waited for it to ring again.

Her last night in the hospital, Shana walked down to the nursery to check on Ariel. Her baby daughter lay on her back, a black mask over her eyes, a smile on her full lips, basking in the heat and light of the bililamps. She'd been in close touch with Azul; he was home now, nearly recovered, but she felt responsible for what had happened.

Shana paced the halls, then returned to her room; her belongings were spread out in disarray—she knew she should pack, get ready to go home—but couldn't bring herself to start. Finally, she forced herself to try on her going-home outfit, a loose plaid flannel dress, all grays, greens and blues—it pulled across the chest but was otherwise okay. Her ankles and feet were still swollen from the birth, so she slipped on her fuchsia driving moccasins.

Outside, Shana saw the movement of the breeze stirring the pines, the bare oak trees' dripping, and imagined the feel of cool wet earth under her feet, the soft mulch of brown leaves. She went to open the window, but it was sealed.

On her night table stood the two celebratory bottles, *Nuits-St. George* and *Pol Roger,* unopened. Shana imagined into the following morning, David and Azul coming for her, as she snapped Ariel into her newborn layers and broke out in a sweat, suddenly horribly frightened. It was as if she stood on a ledge and could not go forward or back; she had no idea what would happen next. Stepping into the hall, she saw Gabriel Mauro dressed in his coat and an olive green hunting cap, its lamb's wool flaps tied above his ears with a leather thong, faintly ridiculous. She called out to him.

He turned and walked back toward her room. She was prepared with some spurious question about the baby, Ariel's jaundice, but dismissed it and asked him if he'd like a glass of burgundy, taking the corkscrew from her suitcase.

"I need to get out of here," she murmured with whispered force, each word under pressure. "A walk outside."

He opened the closet, reaching for her coat. As he held it open for her, Shana slid the bottle of burgundy and the corkscrew into the deep inside pocket, then the paper-wrapped plastic glass from the bathroom.

They walked down the hall, Shana behind Dr. Mauro, turning in the same moment to glance back at the nursery. A nurse said goodnight to Dr. Mauro without looking up. They walked out the front entrance of the hospital into the early evening.

Once outside, Gabriel Mauro wrapped his arm loosely around Shana, his palm at the small of her back, guiding her to a wooded path behind the hospital grounds which ran alongside a canal, risen with rainwater and melted snow. The evening was fresh and mild, a different season from the one she'd left just days before. They walked slowly along the muddy trail, the mulchy leaves and earth pulpy under their feet, ambled without speaking, the bottle of wine heavy against Shana's hip. She felt the evening breeze lift her hair from her neck and billow the hem of her coat as it purled the river's surface, a mild breeze with an underside of winter. Thin, pearly clouds scudded across the dark blue sky, one lone star burning white above them. She walked close to the motion around her and was part of it.

"They're trying me out," Dr. Mauro said abruptly. "See if I make out."

Shana smiled, a little uneasy.

He shrugged thin shoulders. "I'll just take off maybe, go to China. Adopt one of those throwaway baby girls . . ."

He suddenly seemed very young to her. "Really."

"I'm contemplating an asexual existence. Nothing adheres, you know? My last three . . . bonds? Liaisons. *Relationships*! Well, they ended badly."

She nodded slowly, uncertain how to respond.

"I mean, I'm not from column A and I'm not from column B."

"What do you mean?"

He didn't answer right away and they kept walking along the towpath. Shana looked at him, his head bowed to the ground. She thought of him deftly tying knots: how quickly he made them; quicker still, his knots dissolved.

"You know when you're born, right?" he said finally, "you just come out. They give you a name . . . but that's not you, it sounds strange in

142

your own ears. You grow up, go here and then there, do this, maybe that. You look around, try to find a space to open up so you can squeeze yourself in but this niche never comes, never quite holds you . . ."

He glanced at her and Shana felt warm, drawn to his misshapenness.

Along the trail they saw a blue heron wading in the marshy bank, tottering on its spindly legs, its long tapered bill parted in a hoarse cry. A while later, a flock of geese rose from the water in a V shape. They walked until the sky turned from blue to black, the lacy silhouettes of the trees blacker still. When she needed to rest, they sat in a mossy clearing on a small rise above the water. Shana eased off her coat and spread it on the ground, so they'd have a dry place to sit, then scrambled to the edge of the river, reaching her hand into the current, the water so cold it made her bones ache. She pulled out the bottle of burgundy and opened it, remembering the plastic glass, its paper making a loud crinkling in the quiet of the woods. She filled the glass and they passed it back and forth.

"Do you go by Gabriel or Gabe?" she asked, thinking how much she loved that name. It might have been Azul's. Gabriel was feminine, all air and light, Gabe, pure earth. She was puzzled about him. "So. Gabriel or Gabe?"

"I don't know anymore," he said. "You pick."

The wine warmed her insides, but there was a place it couldn't reach. Shana leaned back against her elbows, her knees up, feet pulled in, listening to the rush of the river.

"What does it feel like," Gabriel asked lightly touching her belly, which was surprisingly flat when she lay down, but loose and boggy, "here?"

His hand sank into the soft flesh, like a print in wet sand.

"Empty." His face above her disappeared. Shana looked into the water, kept looking.

"And here?" He lay his hand across her breasts and she thought of how much she loved nursing, nourishing herself as the baby suckled, reinhabiting her body through Ariel's lips, stroking her soft warm head and dimpled back. Motherhood filled a yearning empty space inside but opened another place, hollow and aching, like hunger, fear. He rested his head between her breasts and she threaded her fingers through his thick matted hair to the scalp. He closed his eyes and she imagined him imagining the birth.

"I can feel the place where she came out," Shana said, "like a ring of fire."

"I'll never have a child," he said.

"Maybe—you can, you *will*."

"Not a child inside me, growing."

She turned, turning him with her, so they were side by side facing each other. Shana thought of Ariel growing inside of her and coming out and Azul appearing outside of her and coming in, remembering the escort from *Casa del Mundo*, her bright smile pulsing and spinning, red as an emergency bulb, as she strode off the plane and passed the swaddled bundle from her arms into Shana's and said, "Here is your son."

Everycolor balloons rose into the air next to the baggage carousel, the crowd from her synagogue cheered, bumping into cartons filled with mittens, hats, bunting. Shana fumbled as she took the white swaddled bundle, holding it far enough away to see into the child's face. He looked at her with narrow, dark eyes, then squeezed them shut in fury, pain and screaming.

And now her own terror was back, like vibration before it makes sound. She moved to turn, to get up and Gabriel held her, in his arms the electricity of tension and want, as if a space had opened within him to take in her raw draining places. His thin chest against hers, she felt the tingling deep inside her breasts and the milk let down, warm, soaking her dress. Her empty womb contracted and she gasped with the pure white blade of pain, as the fluids that had cushioned her daughter, cushioned them both, emptied, rushing down between her legs. He ran his hand slowly across her inner thigh, then his lips. He licked and swallowed.

Summer Party

Patricia Lear

All outside was a priceless summery jewel on this summer Saturday morning. The neighborhood was fancy with big houses that were almost like mansions, at least in size though a few of them had kind of seen better days. Some were more renovated than others, had more things done to them, verged on being pristine—actually most of them were like that.

The morning sun was preheating diligently in the sky, virtually ticking like an oven, and it, mixing with the raining and misting sprinklers that were everywhere, gave the neighborhood a humidified, steamy lushness. It was quite a thing, really, the way the crummier seasons had trudged along throughout the year to culminate in this day.

Recently Mr. Cool had moved back home, back into the neighborhood's epicenter, back into his mom's house, right back into his old, rock-postered bedroom actually. He had been out late the night before working his waitering job at the Mexican restaurant, and on this summer Saturday morning he and his mom were up early and had edged themselves over by the row of windows in their TV room so they could better see what the new neighbors next door were up to.

Over there had been going on for hours. It was action central over there where in recent months the house had been gutted and rehabbed and put in perfect condition before the new owners had moved in one single lamp. Then they moved in everything, absolutely everything.

Now, on this Saturday, there were cars crunching forwards and backwards on the gravel driveway, people going in and out the sliding glass doors in the back of the house, others milling about the lawns and up on the terraces. There were little charged-up neighborhood girls tied together at the waists with ropes whinnying and tearing-ass around playing galloping horse herd. There was a lawn crew—Latino radio station blasting from one of their trucks—winding down from a full court press on the grounds with their lawnmowers and leaf blower machines.

No matter where Mr. Cool and his mom were in their house—and they had been all over by then, and even out back on their flagstone terrace and even out front on their screened-in front porch—they could hear voices from the neighbors shrieking things like, "I could just pinch myself!" and "Oh, darling, I hope this weather holds!"

"Now look, what's this thing?" said Mr. Cool.

Outside a truck that said Indestructo Tents on its side was trying to back into the gravel driveway. It was making a high beeping warning sound.

"Whew! What a deal!" said the mom.

"My oh my, but isn't Jackie O blowing some major bucks," said Mr. Cool for about the tenth time that morning.

"You mean Ethel," said the mom, passing Mr. Cool's cigarette back to him after taking a little drag. "At least I'll never have to worry about doing all that again."

"Why Ethel? We just agreed she looks like Jackie O. All those little shift dresses."

"I was thinking she has too many babies to be Jackie O. Ethel had all the babies," said the mom.

"Jackie O's way too good looking to be any Ethel," said Mr. Cool, squinting up his eyes . . . same eyes his mom had, but younger, then he took a real smoker's drag on his cigarette with her studying him closely. "Where is she anyway? I see her and then I don't see her. She's flitting around all over the place."

Standing with the sun pouring in through the window, Mr. Cool was dressed like from the night before in his waiter pants that rose high and bull-fighter-like. He had his hair stuffed back into a bushy ponytail. His mom was one of those youthful '60s moms who had had her kids early. Aging was just beginning to tongue her a little but it hadn't eaten her up yet.

This Saturday morning she was still wrapped up in her scalloped-edged terry cloth robe and had her hair twisted around on top of her head and stapled there with a single barrette. The ends stuck up and waved like the ivy that backbended out of the pots of geraniums that were sitting on everybody's terraces all over outside. She and Mr. Cool both were wearing rubber flip-flops.

"You look like your Uncle Peter who, did you know, just moved to El Paso. Just the way you looked then," said the mom.

"So I've heard all of my life," he said, studying her back, her skin shiny from some face cream.

"Maybe I will go down there and see everybody," she said.

"I think you had better stay planted here and deal with your shit," said Mr. Cool.

"Isn't this fantabulous!" someone shouted from outside.

"You know I have decent enough memories of all this. My goal is to kind of slip away from here, maybe leaving some decent memories for people to remember us by. All this was sweet to us. It's just time—"

"—to be someplace else," said Mr. Cool.

They were each drinking big travel mugs that said Starbucks on the sides. There was a paper towel with a couple of the muffins Mr. Cool had whisked together late the night before in his mom's cutting-edge state-of-the-art kitchen, which had everything—Viking 6-burner stove, chopping block table in the middle, granite counter space galore, every pot and pan made by All-Clad hanging from a pot rack in the ceiling—after he had come in late at night from his waiter job at the Mexican restaurant. He loved his nocturnal cooking—practicing muffin recipes for the coffee house he wanted them all to open—along with the wine sipping, the big-thought thinking, the cappuccino drinking, the dope smoking, and the CD listening that went along with the nocturnal cooking.

"These are good. These are really, really, very, very good," said the mom taking a bite of one of the muffins. "Man, you are getting good. So that's how you see it? I am going to reinvent myself as a bohemian coffee house owner?"

"And reinvent us along with you. We'll all reinvent ourselves together," said Mr. Cool.

"Gee, and I had been thinking travel or real estate agent or even decorating."

"You got to get your mind to quit turning to all the usual little shit," said Mr. Cool. "It's like a horse returning to the barn. Bust loose, Mom."

"I think I am my own worst enemy," said the mom.

"You are," said Mr. Cool.

Just then, Missy, Mr. Cool's younger sister, along with the old childhood dog creaking along, came barefoot into where they were. She was wearing a white T-shirt big enough to come down and cover her underpants. The dog was all joints and skimpy fur. Missy had been upstairs sleeping late sleeping off a cold. She had recently gained a little weight—her face was a little rounder, her boobs were bigger, and she had hips.

"Aww, it's the Fluffy Princess," said Mr. Cool folding his hands together Chinese style in front of his chest and bowing slightly.

As they watched she went over to the leather couch and wrapped herself up in the mohair throw that was always there. She clicked the TV clicker to turn on the TV. Now everybody had to yell over the TV.

"How are you feeling, baby?" said the mom, being all motherly-like because of Missy's cold.

Missy wedged herself deeper into the couch, knees to chin, then kind of leaned over onto some pillows. The old dog circled around three times and dropped onto the floor. On the TV were super models, the Care Unit, Matsuda, black back-up singers.

This happened all the time to the mom—the kids turning up like Missy had done yesterday, or Mr. Cool the month before. It happened when they had a cold or the flu or when they were just short of funds, or because of some event in their chaotic love lives, or just when the world got to be such that MOM & HOME and their OLD BEDROOMS started looking pretty good. Officially though they had their own lives, jobs, apartments, roommates, even sometime live-in loves.

Just then there was a new commotion outside. The caterer's Lexus, metallicy, throwing off sun swords, was pulling into the neighbor's gravel driveway.

"Hey, the Bountiful Basket's here," said Mr. Cool from over by the windows where he was rebunching his hair up into a fresh ponytail. "I think that's what it says out there. Doesn't that say 'The Bountiful Basket'?"

"Are my girls here yet," the caterer was yelling to a group up on the terrace. Mr. Cool watched as she popped the trunk of her car and began pulling out stacks of trays and baskets and Tupperware.

"I can't believe that's the caterer," said the mom coming over to stand beside him. "*That's* the caterer? Does it really say 'The Bountiful Basket' out there?"

"Yes, I'd say it sure does. Why?" said Mr. Cool, masterfully twisting the rubber band around and around in his hair.

"You couldn't spend more! I don't know anyone who would use that caterer. They're over there burning money."

"Maybe I should go over there and show them my muffins," said Mr. Cool.

"Even me in my heyday—" said the mom.

As staff ran out of the house to begin helping her lug things in, the caterer began ordering them around, saying do this, do that. "What a stupendous day! Isn't this great!" everyone was jubilating.

"Boy, out with the old—us—and in with the new—them," said the mom.

They watched for a while. The mom reached her arms over her head and then behind her back stretching out her shoulders.

"Now, she looks like she has a good life. Maybe I should be a caterer," said the mom.

"Maybe you should be a coffee house owner. That other stuff is always going to be there," said Mr. Cool.

"Oh look, here come the flowers. Boy, when you're into that kind of thing, you're really into it, that's all I can say. What is that? A whole truckload of flowers?"

"I need coffee," said Missy weakly from where she was curled up over on the couch. "Somebody get me some coffee and somebody else describe to me what's going on out there." She sneezed three times while blindly fumbling around on the coffee table for the Kleenex.

"Look for yourself, dumbass," said Mr. Cool, heading out to the kitchen to make another pot of coffee.

Missy lay there eye-level with the TV. A band was playing on a beach. Next they were following a young lovely in a filmy dress who was walking out into some foamy water. Missy fumbled around with getting her arms under her and then lifted herself up to a sitting position on the couch. She then stretched the hem of her T-shirt down over her knees. "Okay, dumbass, I will," she said.

"Is the Fluffy Princess waking up? Is that the Fluffy Princess that we know and love?" said Mr. Cool, coming back in with a new plate of muffins. "Fresh coffee's coming, darling."

"What is it? The Cirque de Soleil?" said Missy looking outside.

"Big basheroo next door with the new neighbors," said the mom. "You going to work? Either of you?"

"No," said Missy.

"Yes," said Mr. Cool.

"You know, I've been thinking maybe we should have done more of that," said the mom suddenly reaching over and picking up a microwave popcorn bag that was on the floor. "Sometimes I don't know if I want to go forward or want to go backwards. I mean what are they doing but just celebrating."

"I'm sure we'll find many new ways to celebrate," said Mr. Cool. "We're all going out into the big world." He leaned his forehead up against the cool glass pane of the window. "Somehow all the hoopla outside makes me think of our old next door neighbors—the good old plain old what-were-their-names? Where'd they go off to anyway?"

"Good grief! Does it all evaporate that fast? They divorced and downsized. Like me—us," said the mom fussing around with straightening up some video cassettes here and wadding up the old Microwave popcorn bag there.

"What were their names?"

"The Johnsons! The Johnsons! Jamie Johnson, Joan Johnson, Pedie Johnson, Vic Johnson, Melinda, and Ralphie and Woofer Johnson."

"God, they were boring."

"Hey, looks like they're going to have a dance floor," said Missy. "Looks like one, maybe two, maybe even three tents are going up."

"It really is a beautiful day for all this," said the mom, standing up with her arms full of clutter. "They're lucky with the weather. I really can't believe that you didn't remember the Johnson's name."

"You going?" said Missy.

"Nope," said the mom.

"Come on, Mom," said Mr. Cool pulling himself up and adjusting his waiter pants squarely on his hipbones. "I can't stand this. You want some more reasons? You need some more reasons? I don't want to lose you now."

"Shoot," she said. "Give me some more muscle. Pump me up."

"It would get you out of your bathrobe in the mornings. It would give you someplace to go every day. It would keep you hip. You could hold court. Your friends could come by. You would meet men. You would find love. You don't want real estate school or travel agent school. Man, you can do whatever you want now. You have this little window of choice."

"I am with you," said the mom nodding along with him.

"No, seriously, you have the money—when this place sells. You've cut it one way for half your life. Try cutting it another way for the second half. We can all open this thing together. We'll be right there with you, all of us," said Mr. Cool. "Look over there. Blat. Double blat."

At dawn, when over next door had begun with the lawn crew, the mom was already up. All the noise they were making with their caravan of rickety trucks didn't much matter to her, as far as sleeping went anyway. Truthfully, she had been up so long she could have gotten the whole lawn crew up. She had been pacing around the house, going in and out of rooms plotting what she would do next to get the house to sell.

As she drifted by Missy's childhood girlie bedroom, she saw Missy snug asleep under her down comforter, her hot feet sticking out, sleeping spoon-style around the old dog. There were things jumbled all over, towels hung on two of the bedposts. The old dog lifted his head and said, go away.

She went downstairs and surveyed the disaster of the kitchen from Mr. Cool's nocturnal muffin trials of the night before. She shoved things around a little and made a pot of coffee.

She was thinking as she wandered out to the front porch—where the palest, gentlest air of the early morning chiffoned over her shoulders— that since the house was on the market, her life was even more a constant battle with chaos then it had been before. Even with the maid coming twice a week, when it was just her rattling around by herself in the big dinosaur of a house with the dog and with no kids and with nothing to do but figure out a new life for herself, it was hard.

Wow, what a thought, she thought, that doing almost nothing could be so hard.

She sat on the front steps stuffing her terry cloth robe up behind her knees so that she would not be throwing any crotch shots to the world, watching the lawn crew combing all over the lawns next door. They had their jet-engine propelled leaf-blower machines going, which made her teeth feel like they were rattling against her coffee cup.

She had many issues to struggle with, lots of reasons to not be asleep. Issues like being alone, not really being alone because the kids were there. But shouldn't the kids be out in the world, living their own lives? And sex? What about sex?

Maybe she would put tubs of petunias around the corners of her lawn, and maybe get Mr. Cool to string some fluttery colorful flags from the For Sale sign right up to the eaves of the third floor, like they did at gas stations in places like El Paso, where her brother had just moved, which the sight of the Latino lawn crew over there next door was more and more reminding her of.

Maybe if tonight she sat out in her front lawn in a lawn chair, maybe someone from the party would mambo through the old split in the hedge, where they used to mix it up with the Johnsons during the kids growing up years, and put in a bid on her house. Then that, of course, made her think of all those family times they had with the Johnsons.

"I'll see you next door!" they would say banging on the bathroom door to whoever was still in there. "Partying hardy next door," they would say as they went out the door with maybe leaving a note in the kitchen for whoever might not be home yet from errands or the beach. They would head over through that old enduring split in the hedge for barbecue, cocktails, maybe a birthday celebration for somebody—or for the gentle sweetness of just hanging out on the terrace and looking up at the stars at night—the men discussing the stock market, the latest tax regulations, the moms hashing out their lives, their marriages, their kids' lives—the kids racing around on the grass, up and down on the jungle gym, swinging on the swing set, running through the evening sprinklers, playing Marco Polo out on the quiet curving streetlit street until the bottoms of their callused feet were black with ground-in dirt.

They went from the granite-countered kitchen where they made yet another pot of coffee to the antique wicker rockers on the front porch, then to the froofy, pastel little sitting room with the fireplace off what used to be the mom's and dad's bedroom, then on outside out back to the multileveled flagstone terrace, all three of them settling into the two-ton wrought-iron furniture mixed around with scattered terra cotta pots of geraniums and ivy.

Sitting in a chaise longue, the mom inhaled deeply. The gardens and lawns of the neighborhood with their sprinkler-jeweled blades of just-cut grass invaded her senses, made her almost gasp. Latino radio music Mexican-restauranted its way through the hedge. Veiled in flickering green and gold from leaves and from sunlight, she could see the lawn crew through the hedge sprawled out amongst a stand of weeping willows, drinking Tropicana from cardboard cartons and looking to be heading towards siesta mode.

"Buenos dias," several of the men murmured and nodded their heads through the hedge.

"Buenos dias," Mr. Cool, the mom, and Missy murmured back.

"I like those guys," said Mr. Cool. "You two are not going to believe what happened to me this morning with those dudes."

"No matter what, no matter how boring you think it was, we really did have some nice times over there with the Johnsons. I have been thinking about it," said the mom, suddenly sitting up straight in her chaise longue. She looked over at Mr. Cool. Sunlit tendrils wired out from around his head. "There are worse places to grow up, far worse places. We were a great family."

From through the hedge a hysterical announcer speaking in machine-gun Spanish came on the lawn crew's radio.

"It wasn't all that boring," she said. "Okay, what happened with the Mexicans? I just had to get that off my chest. It had been working on me."

"Now I'm not in the mood," said Mr. Cool. "Give me a minute to regroup."

They lay back quietly in their chaise longues listening to the voices and music from next door. They each just thought their own thoughts. Nobody said anything.

"Boy," said the mom finally breaking the silence, "I am just glad I am not one of those parents who has to explain everything to my kids now that you guys are grown. You know, why we did this, why we did that. I don't want to have spent half my adult life raising you and then the second half explaining about why I did something, what was right, what was wrong."

"She sure is working through a lot of shit today, isn't she?" said Missy.

Mr. Cool nodded and yawned so that his jaws cracked.

"Why are you so tired?" said the mom.

"Work, work. I go to work," he said.

"You kids have got to know that I have friends, and now that their kids are grown, that's all they talk about with them. They have to defend every little thing that they did, to explain themselves day and night until they are blue in the face."

"I'm sure we can dredge up some stuff. It would take about a millisecond," said Missy.

"I have friends that get scared when the phone rings thinking maybe it's going to be one of their adult children just back from the paid-for-by-them therapist full of fresh insights on their childhoods," said the mom.

"We already went to the therapist. Wasn't I about ten?" said Mr. Cool.

"What's making you think of all this?" said Missy.

"It was my job. It was my job. You know, did I do it all right? I think about these things more now that we are doing a wrap-up here, breaking camp. I am thinking of everything. My mind never stops."

"Let's go sit inside again," said the mom. It was getting too hot out there with the sun, even after trying a stint of moving their furniture over under the shade trees where the dog already was, so back they went through the kitchen to the TV room. Mr. Cool scooped up the dog in his arms and carried him.

Missy settled back on the leather couch with the mohair throw. Mr. Cool put the dog in her arms where she had made a little nest for him. Back on went the TV.

"Okay. I'm going to tell you now. You ready?" said Mr. Cool fiddling with a bandanna he had found in the kitchen junk drawer.

"What?" said the Mom.

"Me and the Mexicans," said Mr. Cool.

"Oh," said the mom.

"Is this going to be good?" said Missy, sitting up a little straighter.

"I was dead asleep. Then all this noise happened and so I start dreaming the Concorde was landing—you know to fit the noise into my sleep. Then I dream it's landing on top of me. Then I wake up, boom!" said Mr. Cool.

"That's it?" said the mom.

"It's those leaf blower machines."

"What are you talking about?"

"Okay, I think, fuck this shit. No one can sleep. I am dead tired from work and all, and I hear Mom walking around downstairs so obviously you can't sleep. Something is not right here, and I am a man of action, so I make the crucial decision and go on over there and we have us a little talk. I speak-a my kitchen Spanish to them, and I bring-a them a six-pack."

"You went over there?" said the mom.

Mr. Cool continued, "I say, hey compadre! to the one with the cowboy hat?"

They looked over there.

"Turns out—imagine this—he's the boss-dude of the whole shebang, and I say to him, Dude, I work-a all night in a restaurant and I work-a hard like you, and you-a waking me up, man, and I'm-a tired. My mom and my sister are tired and they strung out with problems, too."

"You went over there?" said the mom.

"I say, You guys-a driving me-a crazy. Shut-a up-a, please. And he comes back like-a all sweetness and light and all polite, and he says, The Missus say we got to be done early. He say that the hot, young Missus who lives there with her husband and their many niños has said to him that the lawn and gardens had to be done early, really early, because the tents have to go up, so that the dance floor can be put down, so that the tables can be set up with the tableware and the pink-a cloths, so that the flower ladies can get in to weave their flowery magic on the tables, so that the food ladies could get in and set all the places up, set up all the things they need to set up, so they can really fuckin' gild up the lily to fuckin' impress whoever they're trying to impress with this bullshit tonight."

"No more joking, dude. What'd you really do?"

"Then Jackie O comes out and says in this breathy little voice, sorry, so sorry about all the noise, what's going on and all, please, please tell your mother I am sorry, please tell her. Please tell her we would love to have her come tonight, and Missy and I come tonight and whoever else might be staying here come tonight too. The dude in the cowboy hat, he gets a big erection. I get a big erection. We both are standing there with boners in front of Jackie O."

"Well, I want you to know that I am beyond horror, simply beyond horror," said the mom. "They must think we're the biggest bunch of jackasses over here ever."

"And guess what? She's pregnant again."

The mom started working with a butter knife at a black rubber ring left on a window ledge from one of the travel mugs. "This dinosaur can't sell fast enough for me."

Mr. Cool began placing the bandanna across his forehead and fumbled around with trying to work the ends under his hair in the back.

"So then," Mr. Cool says emphasizing *then*, "she leaves and all the Mex's go whoa, whoa, whoa about her, and, I relate, you know what I mean? When I see them up close, and they're poor dudes, working dudes like me, like the guys I work with at the restaurant, and I have this revelation and bolt of lightning and identify and all, and I say, okay, dude, caio, compadre, you got your job to do, man, I understand. I'll sleep next month or something."

"Did they take the six-pack?" said Missy.

"I say, Don't let them work you too hard, man. Stay cool. Hell, yes, they took it."

From outside came, "When you get a second, tell me where you want these tables."

"I like those guys. They're cool dudes." Mr. Cool got the bandanna worked through his hair in back and began tying it up high and tight. "No more white bread city. We have to paddle, Mom. We have to swim."

"Now you're making me feel bad. You're just making me depressed. Here's what I have to do today before I open this coffee house," said the mom standing up out of her chair.

"Sounds like at least the start of a plan to me," said Mr. Cool.

"You're throwing off sparks now, Mom," said Missy.

"I have to sell the house. I have to keep the house perfect so I can sell the house. I have to lose 25 pounds, get divorced, find somebody to come and take all the stuff that is in the basement, get someone in to redo the water damage in the basement, put ads in the paper about our house sale, put tags on everything for the house sale, go buy the tags, find a housekeeper for grandma, take my car in for its 30,000 mile tune-up, find health insurance for myself, have my impacted lower wisdom teeth out before I am off Dad's health plan. I have to seriously figure out how I am going to support myself. That's all I can think of off the top of my head for today. Do you want me to go and get my list so you can hear the rest?"

The mom was pacing around the room.

Mr. Cool yawned. "All I'm saying is you can have a better life. So what is it going to be is all I'm saying."

"Look," said the mom, suddenly stopping in front of the window. Waving Mr. Cool over, she said, "Come over here, quick, over this way."

"I got to go to work," said Mr. Cool getting up and walking over there anyway.

"Oh, there she is," said the Mom, "There she is. She's up on the terrace."

Mr. Cool put both of his hands on the sill and leaned close to the window looking. "See what I mean?" he said. "She really does have that kind of Jackie-O-wifey sort of look about her, doesn't she? I find her incredibly desirable."

"Okay, Mom, I can see we're going to have to get you through this thing," said Missy.

The mom was standing with her arms crossed over her chest staring out at the neighbor's lawns taking in the final party preparations. It was twilight, a velvety, hushed twilight with lit candles flickering out there, yet still day, bright and sparkly, somewhere off somewhere through the trees. She had rolled the sleeves of her robe loosely up to the elbows, and her hair had completely escaped it's barrette and was hanging down her back.

Missy was padding through the dining room in Mr. Cool's flip-flops heading out towards the kitchen. "Food could be the answer, Mom. Should we order in? Want to cook something? You want to go out? Go to a movie? Why don't you go and get in the shower? Let's start with the basics."

"I wouldn't leave here right now for all the tea in China," said the mom. "I feel like I am throwing that party myself I have been watching it so long."

The neighborhood cicadas were in full swing. Ice was being brought out for the bars. A few waiters in black tie were standing in a small clump talking. A combo was warming up, doing bright little squiggly riffs. A car was slowly crunching up the driveway.

"Come on, girl, get yourself away from that window," said Missy standing in the kitchen doorway stamping her flip-flop. "No good can come of you sitting in that window all night. Want to go down in the basement and start going through stuff? Remember—the house sale?" said Missy propping open the swinging kitchen door.

"Get real," said the mom, tucking some of her hair behind her ear. "I have to see this through. I'm getting close to something. I have this feeling."

"Praise the Lord for that," said Missy. "I am going to open a bottle of wine. It'll be good for my cold anyway."

"Oh, okay, open a nice bottle of red. Okay, I'm going to go take a shower. Could you let the dog out, Sweetheart?"

Later, Missy and the mom were sitting on the couch sharing the mohair throw. On the coffee table was a bottle of red wine and a couple of smeary wine glasses and Missy's Kleenex box. The mom was wearing a pair of jeans and had her hair combed back and twisted up on top of her head. She wore a pair of dangly earrings Missy had left on the sink in the bathroom upstairs. They had found the movie *Paris, Texas* on TV, and in between, while the commercials were on, Missy would flip around through all the channels. The sound was turned up loud because of all the party noise that was going on outside.

On the TV, Harry Dean Stanton was walking and trudging and stumbling across the dusty desert. He was wearing a dust covered black suit. He looked crazy, glum, out of it, yet weirdly intent.

"See, he's driven by love," said the mom. "Dad and I saw this years ago. His wife that he loves passionately disappeared with his child and is now a pay-per-view peep show dancer, but he doesn't know that yet—"

"No, she disappeared but left the child and his brother and his wife are raising it because Harry Dean went off to the nuthouse," said Missy. "I saw it too."

"Okay, yeah, you're right. Time yet for another party report?" said the mom slapping her hands down on her thighs as another commercial came on.

"You want some more pizza? I put the leftover in the oven," said Missy squirming her legs around to disentangle herself from the mohair so she could get up from the couch.

"Okay, what's he doing? Tell me everything. Give me an update," said the mom.

Missy went over by the windows to look out. "I don't see him. I can't find him," she said. "Oh there he is. He's talking to Mrs. Arnold. He's waving his arms around."

"That's him being emphatic."

"Now he's going over by the bar. He's probably getting Mrs. Arnold a drink. He's in line at the bar. Mr. Miller is coming up to him. They're just talking. He's just in line. He's waving his arms around. I wish he would stop that. It's irritating."

"Irritation is what ends marriages," said the mom reaching over on the coffee table for a piece of pizza crust. "Is every single one of my friends there?"

"Hey, now look. The dog's out there wandering blindly about. Wait until Dad notices the dog. No, not every single one."

"I'm coming over there," said the mom, trying to disentangle her legs from the mohair throw.

"Hold that thought," said Missy coming over and pushing her mom back down on the couch. "Here's the movie. Stay in your seat, Mom. He's not doing anything except hobnobbing around. He's just at a party. There are zero signs of anything really interesting going on."

"You'll tell me if there is anything interesting, won't you?"

"If you insist," said Missy.

The movie came back on. Harry Dean had been found in the desert and taken off to the nuthouse. His brother was just coming to fetch him. The mom and Missy watched for a while. Music played softly outside plus there was the sound of talking and plates being served by the staff.

"I wish we had some ice cream," said Missy. "We could make our hot fudge sauce. What do you think they're having for dessert over there?"

"Why don't you phone over there and find out. Think about this. You know how hard love is? Look at your relationships. It's no different with us oldies. Just imagine the last boyfriend you broke up with. Now just imagine that when you decided it was over, really over, that you were legally tied to this guy and no matter how bad it got or he wouldn't listen to you or everything he did irritated you, you were married and couldn't get out so easy and so you stuck with the deal for 20 more years," said the mom.

"That is the most awful thought," said Missy. "I hope nobody in this room does that."

"Yeah, well," said the mom.

The mom got up from the couch and headed upstairs. After she went to the bathroom, she brushed her teeth, and then went into Mr. Cool's room to rummage around for some cigarettes. On the floor by his bed, she found a squashed-up pack and took them and some matches outside to sit in the dark on the front steps. The band next door had segued into blasting rock and roll. She lit up a cigarette and blew out a long stream of smoke. Cars lined the street up and down the block. She sprawled her legs down on the steps. Next door was lit up like Grand Central Station and she could see her For Sale sign faintly visible and lonely down on the lawn.

She started thinking that you have to take the bad with the good, that life is a hard bargain sometimes, and that she had never known that smoking was so soothing. She thought about if she wanted to be at that party or not and decided not.

All of a sudden she heard a rustling in the bushes that made up the hedge that separated the two houses. First the old dog burst through and right behind him came her husband brushing off leaves from the arms and shoulders of his tux. He was heading right for her but couldn't see her because of the dark. It was too late for her to get away. When he was on top of her, she said, "Hi."

"Yikes! What are you doing here?" he said. "Hey look, this dog is in the middle of everything over there. You scared the shit out of me, Marcy."

"Okay, well, put him inside if he's too much," she said.

"I thought you'd be out," he said.

"Missy and I are watching the tube. Can't you see the flickering light from the TV in the back of the house from over there?" she said. He shook his head and ran his hands through his hair smoothing it back. Then he reached down and grabbed the dog by the collar.

"What brings you here?" she said, hiding the pack of cigarettes behind her so they would be out of sight.

"None of your beeswax," he said.

"No, seriously," she said, feeling in the back of her throat how much she hated it when he said "none of your beeswax."

"I'm just coming over to use the bathroom. It's easier than over there," he said starting up the steps with the dog.

"Hey, I got to talk to you about some things."

He turned around and looked at her for a second, sighed, then sat down on the steps and started rubbing the dog behind his ears.

"You've been coming over here all night, haven't you?"

"Once or twice. House wasn't locked—as usual."

"How's the party?"

"I like parties."

"What are they having for dessert?" She sat up straight and pulled her knees up close to her chest.

"Look, Marcy, what do you want to talk to me about?"

"I just want to know what you're having for dessert over there? Missy and I were wondering."

"You guys want some? Nobody's eating theirs at our table. I'll bring you some for the john use. You can see what it is for yourself."

The mom put her head down. Missy's dangly earrings fell forward onto her cheeks. "I can't get the basement cleaned out."

"Get the kids to do it. Tell them to rent a U-Haul or something. They should be doing something."

"There are no bids on the house."

"Houses always sell eventually."

"Are you happy?"

"I'm trying to be."

"I don't want that over there, you know, all that."

"I know you don't. I know that. I really got to take a leak, honey. I'll see if I can smuggle you and Missy some desserts."

"Looks like a real rager out there," said Mr. Cool walking into the TV room unbuttoning and rolling up the sleeves of his shirt. "Cars are parked for blocks out there, man." Surveying the situation with the two of them, he said, "Have you two been here all night? I don't think that's a really good idea for your heads, do you?"

Missy was sitting propped up against some pillows and the mom was leaning up against her, sitting in her arms, covered in the mohair throw and holding a wine glass. She looked like the old dog looked in Missy's bed earlier . . . all snuggled in. Wadded up Kleenexes bloomed all around. On the TV was the Nature Channel. The segment was on how deer live and thrive in suburban neighborhoods. A homeowner was showing a rosebush to the camera that had been stripped clean of roses by deer. There was a piece of pizza upside down in front of the TV and a couple of dead bottles of red wine on the coffee table.

"Mom's been going down for the count," said Missy. "We're getting her back on track though, right Mom? We got her taking some chocolate nourishment here."

"What is that?" said Mr. Cool, working at taking off his little bow tie.

"Dad brought us over these little soufflé-things from next door. He said nobody was touching them at his table. He's going to come back later and get the plates. Look. Limoges."

"Dad's been over here?" said Mr. Cool going over by the window. "Look at those dorks out there. Man, I know I like the Latinos better."

"Yeah, he just comes trucking through the hedge," said the mom. "What do you think about that?"

"Who'd want to go to a party where the people didn't eat dessert?" said Missy patting the mom's arm and rocking her a little.

"Earlier he was dancing with Jackie O," said the mom. "You should have seen them. You would have loved it, dude."

"We were glued to the window," said Missy.

Mr. Cool found the clicker and surfed the channels on the TV a little. Net bodysuits, bongos, super models, stiletto heels, public notices, a train going into a tunnel.

"Dad and Jackie O. Wow. Got to get my head around that one."

It was the next morning. All outside was the same priceless summery jewel it had been the day before. The crummier seasons were still far, far away. The mom was up early. She was sitting out on the front steps with a cup of coffee watching the guys next door dismantling the tents and carrying them to their truck in broken-down pieces.

The mom was in a fog about a dream she had been dreaming lately that had just come from nowhere that she could figure anyway. It was a weird yearning kind of dream, a tugging-on-her-heart dream, arising right out of her—womanhood. She was mulling over this dream which was about someplace like Texas and about being a kid there (which she never was) and the dust and tumbleweeds and spring fields of blue bonnets that must be there, and the long lonely desolate dusty highways and the rusty old gas stations where there were tubs of petunias sitting around outside and where they had strings of those plastic flags she was going to get for the house strung up that fluttered madly even when just a car went by, never mind an actual breeze. This image had somehow settled upon her from somewhere, something like long ago where there were coffee shops and not coffee houses.

What she felt was a yearning to be back in where she had never been. What she wanted was to wear a faded flowered dress—tight over her pregnant belly—to have pale, wan children (wild boys with buzz hair-cuts), to be married to a mean man (though everyone would say he was good), to have wild scary nights in bed doing things he would make her do, to feel you had no choices in life.

These thoughts were crystallizing in her mind as she sat outside, as the paper was thrown from a Jeep up onto her lawn, as the truck next door that said Indestructo Tents rumbled away with the dismantled tents. At least then, she thought, with a mean man, she would have peace of mind. She was thinking of the time, her mother's time, her grandmother's time, of her growing up time, when the worst thing you could say about a woman was that she was not happy. She could be happy in an unhappy situation that was forced upon her. She could be happy with whatever life brought her. Then it would be God's will she was happy with, not her own choices.

"My goodness," she thought, standing up and wandering inside the house and through the halls and on back to the kitchen. Looking around at all the cooking mess from Mr. Cool's muffin trials from the night before, she thought, "Who would I ever tell."

Thin End of the Wedge

William Lychack

She becomes a widow well before his father dies. That's how she man-ages: the mother's a widow before the father dies, the father dies before he's dead, and the boy? The boy's just this boy like any other, nearly ten, an only child, end of story. End of story except that there in this boy's doorway the mother stands without his knowing and watches him until her arms unfold and her throat clears and she hears herself say into the room, "Your father's not going to be home for dinner tonight."

And the boy turns at her, "So?"

And the mother tries to toss that frown of his right back to him, but she can't. Across his room she steps instead and clicks his radio off and pushes the dresser drawers closed until they all lay even. She runs her hand along the wood and faces the wall and stands as remote as the moon to the boy. He can't see her face, but when she does turn to him her mouth folds down and her chin starts going so fast that she couldn't ever have been controlling it. And in his stomach the boy feels what he is watching, feels in his stomach that he has swallowed a bit of metal—a washer or coin—and someone is bringing it back up along his spine with a magnet.

She clocks her tongue and walks head up past him out of the room, the knuckles of her hand brushing the wall as she goes. He listens as she stops in the kitchen and taps aspirin from the bottle. He hears the water run, a glass filled. From that window over the sink she can look out and see the line of trees at the back of the yard, the bulbs coming up, it being spring and warming and the grass going green. The boy can look out his own window and see the same thing, and he hears her walk into the bathroom, the door click closed, and then he hears the toilet flush and refill and her footsteps soft up the stairs to her room over his, where she must stand perfectly still, for he doesn't hear anything, just silence and himself swallowing and breathing and his throat dry.

The mantle clock chimes five from the living room, and the house keeps still as the clock ticks softer, then louder, then softer again. And down again in the kitchen she is beside the cuckoo and he goes to her and they watch the hurried pendulum of the cuckoo race back and forth, a maple leaf, nervous almost, and the pendulum swing is what they watch as the clock warns and then goes off five times. The clock plays Edelweiss and the pine cone weights inch down the flowered wallpaper.

For dinner they drive across town to the old brick train station, a pizza parlor now. At one time this place ranked sixth in all of New England in volume of freight handled, and you can still hear train cars pound through the town at night, but no passenger trains stop in Cargill Falls, Connecticut. None even pass this way of mill towns and dairy farms any longer. And Anna says ten words as they drive home—count them—the boy watching as her eyes follow the sad-luck storefronts and sags of tenement porches along Providence Street past the church and cemetery and Church Street and the brickwork mills along the curve of the river, and his mother saying to smell that as they coast over the bridge over the water below all barrel-brown and filled with chokeweed and carp.

Daniel holds his breath and shifts the warm pizza box on his lap and doesn't know what he can say to any of this, her saying how it's a wonder anyone stays here at all. He looks to her again, and her skin looks chalky and dry in the half-light, and he asks, "Do you know if we have any milk home? Should we stop maybe?"

She shakes her head no, and his shoulders relax when she turns onto their street with its young trees staked straight with cords and its houses set back off the street by small square lawns. At home the house seems to be holding its breath as they eat in front of the TV news, and his mother is leaning forward on the couch, not eating and not breaking her staring at the picture window, the curtains hanging in long folds.

"And where'd you say Dad'd be so late?"

"I don't remember saying anyplace," she says.

He laughs a little—it's the way she sounds to him, he can't stop the bubble of his laugh—and she swings her head round from the window to him and doesn't need to say a word with that look.

He bites his lip and waits and looks over at the television, down at the pizza. And when she turns to the window again, he says, "So then what's the matter?"

"Nothing's the matter," she says, "why?"

"I don't know, you're just acting sort of like a statue."

"And what, pray tell, does a statue act like?"

"I don't know," he says, "you're just staring, I guess."

"What's wrong with that?"

"It's creepy."

"Oh, is it?"

He lets out a deep breath and says, "What the heck, Ma?"

"Don't talk like that," she says, "not to me at least." And her voice has a catch in it, and it gives him that pull in the stomach again, and she smiles quickly and pushes herself up off the couch and looks at the side of his face, musses his hair, and she sets to what would become her endless pacings.

And he follows her that night as she walks the floorboards over his head. She paces the cramped length of her room all hours, back and forth, she paces and only the jump of the phone and its ringing breaks the hiss-scrape of slippers over him. No more than twice—a bell and a half—does it ring before the hall light snaps on and she is hard down the straight flight of stairs. The phone goes on ringing and she stands all shadows in his door frame. Her shadow bends large across the ceiling, and he watches it.

They aren't home tonight, she tells him. Her voice is even and slow over the ringing and she says, "We've gone out." And the rings keep rolling out and in like a snake's tongue slithers out electric and back in and out and in, live as a whip, the ringing phone, and the boy's sitting in bed and he doesn't—he can't—do anything with her there in the doorway in the frame of light, her arms crossed, her weight on one leg, him counting ten, eleven, twenty-five rings, then thirty makes it endless, and is it any miracle who these rings should come to sound like? You could practically hear the belligerence and the dead-cold pitch the man's voice could take.

And when the phone stops, Daniel and his mother brace themselves for the shrill jump of the man to ring again behind her. But the moment passes, and the sound—a hum of bells—lifts.

From the hall, he hears her say, "Sleep," to him.

And the rest of the night he keeps as still as a stone and holds his breathing shallow in his stomach, holds still like the house so that he can hear her moving upstairs. Her voice murmurs down through his ceiling as she talks or sings to herself, he can't tell one from the other, and it's probably both. And rain begins to blow against the windows, and Daniel breathes into the covers to warm himself. And he must fall in and out of sleep, for at odd points in the night he sits up in bed and believes the front door has flown open and that his father's car waits idling in the drive.

In the morning the rain continued. Daniel rolled half-asleep onto his back and stared at the ceiling. The fingerprint smudges over the bed were his own. In the ashen light you could shuttle your eyes from one mark to another to fall back to sleep, if you chose. He turned, as if turning away from that idea, and watched the evergreen branches lash mutely against the wet glass of the window.

He never awoke all at once, as his father did. His father could wake up on a dime, but Daniel woke slow, layer by layer, until he was up out of bed and hugging himself and standing on the balls of his feet on the cold floor. Then he was to the bathroom and then down the hall to the foot of the staircase and leaning forward, hands on the stairs, to hear the running shower. And up the stairs to see their bedroom door standing open and inside the stripped sheets and blankets in a bundle beneath the window and radiator, he saw the suitcases openmouthed near the closet. There were cardboard boxes, and he stepped onto the small rug and looked vaguely at the bed, at the closet door, at the curtained window, at the frosted light fixture on the ceiling . . .

And from behind him she said, "He's not here."

She wore a bathrobe and had a towel turbaned around her head and smelled of powder and hand cream, her skin was red from the hot water. "You're not going to miss your bus now," she said and pushed the towel off her forehead, "are you?"

She called in sick to the department store where she worked downtown, and Anna packed Bob's things into boxes. Sent him packing, she would say, kissed him goodbye.

Had they still lived in the saltbox apartment by the river, she would have dropped everything off the dock into the slow-moving water. But here she could only put his boxes on the street in the rain for the garbage men to take away the next morning. This's better, she told herself. A public decision is more real, more decisive. A river would've just carried it away. That was what rivers did; they forgave.

Anna struggled the mattress over the grass out to the curb. His shirts and pants she hung up into the low branches of the front trees. She stacked files and boxes and trash bags full at the streetside. Anyone could look out their window or drive by and see this and say what-all they pleased, she didn't care. She wanted only to be thorough. She came from a long line of thorough. It was in her blood to change locks and put up heavy curtains and throw away, leave. It all fell easily to her—her whole family prone to this—and she rearranged all the furniture she could physically move. To do more she would have had to knock down walls and hire carpenters.

Just the space of a Friday at school and the house the boy came home to was not the house he had left that morning. His father's pants and shirts hung in the trees and lay draped over the bushes out front. Boxes and papers and shoes and boots sat at the gutter, everything dark and soft with rain. He didn't want to come home to this house, but he didn't know where else to go and cut across the lawn to the back steps.

Through the storm door he saw his mother mopping the kitchen floor. She looked somehow undone: barefoot, her duster half-opened, her hair uncurled. And Daniel opened the screen door just enough to come in and wipe his shoes on the mat. He caught the door as it closed so it wouldn't slam, and his mother lifted the mop into the sink and ran the water and pressed the braids with her hand. She wrung the braids and wiped her hands on her hips and spoke up to the ceiling to him, "And why aren't you at school?"

He had the thought before he answered that she didn't really know who he could be, that he could've been anybody standing behind her. And the chairs sat upside down on the tabletop. There lay a wooden rolling pin on the counter, a paring knife on the cutting board.

"It's three-thirty," he said.

"And you should be out playing. You usually go play, don't you?"

He inched onto the edge of the wet floor and watched her lift the mop from out of the sink and put it down on the floor. Then she turned to him, a black smudge across her nose.

"It's raining," he said.

"So? Play in the rain. Babe Ruth would've played through a little rain."

"Babe Ruth?"

"Whoever," she said, and again she had those target eyes of a statue and she lashed the mop at his sneakers. "I'm busy here," she told him. "So why don't you just go to your room?" she said, and his dirty footprints she wiped a step behind him.

Daniel closed his bedroom door behind him and pushed his desk chair under the knob and sat on the bed and clutched the covers and waited and listened and whistled softly through his teeth to himself. Waited for what, he didn't know, but his heart quit its rushing against his throat and ears. She didn't come to his door the way he had started to hope and expect, she would never really come to his door to explain it all away to him.

Out through his side window he could see his father's blue and brown pants and shirts hanging dull and dreamlike in the trees. In the dark spaces of the trunks, you could see the rain. He watched the margin of street, the wet dark boxes and the other trim houses and sidewalks and trees and the clothes which moved as drowsy versions of the same man, one version hanging out there blue, one green, one brown.

He lifted open the window, the metal screen, and then he curled himself over the sill and outside to the grass. The clothes from the branches he tore down all he could carry. He brought the cold heavy bundles inside to his closet, where he hung them to dry.

Closer to night the deep grumbling of Bob's car idled and stopped in front of the house. She closed the television, quick-checked the locks, and led Daniel upstairs to the attic. On the narrow steps she turned close on him: "Pretend no one's home."

Her breath made him shiver, the way he felt the words cobweb across his face, and he followed her up the stairs and kept quiet in the tindery attic with her. They kept the lights off, and Bob knocked on the side door below, his keys in his fist.

"Anna," he called. "Hey, Anna, c'mon already."

They stayed beside the attic window, kept still, and watched his car idling empty in the street. He yelled for them, his voice uneven and far, and he whistled through his fingers. And from behind the gauze-white curtains they kept watch as downstairs the man knocked and called himself hoarse. He yelled for the boy, called low, "Daniel, you home in there somewhere?" And Daniel and Anna hid and watched the tops of the world from above, all of it to-scale and dusty in this light, a model some boy could reach his hand into and rearrange and set right.

"Anna, would you please?" And Bob hit the door again hard. "I could break this fucken door, Goddamn it!"

He kicked the base of the door and stepped out to the limp cardboard boxes near the street, where Anna and Daniel could see him better. He bent at the waist to pick through his wet letters, books, clothes, shoes, the papers still dry and light-colored underneath the piles. From the sugar maples he took down the rest of the shirts and pants and laid them over the front seat of the car, which still idled at the curbside, the exhaust rising white and pink around the trunk and taillights. Bob lifted garbage bags into the car, carried luggage and boxes to the back seat—a pile of record albums, a case of tools, a burlap sack of emptied drawers full of tangled string, extension cord, fishing tackle, a desk lamp, a caulking gun—and between each trip he would stop and sometimes spit on the grass and glance to the other houses and their unmoving curtains along the street.

From the high angle of the attic, as it grew darker, Bob's shoulders slumped narrow and he had a bald spot. He rested a foot on the fire hydrant and lit another cigarette, all the while watching the house for signs of life. He took his old keys and turned them from his key chain, flipped them like coins into the lawn, and watched the dark windows of the house.

And Anna stared invisibly down on Bob as though he were some errant, trespassing boy, the collar of whose jean jacket nearly glowed round his neck down there in the failing light. And as the man sneezed and looked into his hand and then twisted the wedding band off of his finger and placed it on the bolt on top of the hydrant, Daniel reached slowly to the window. It was all he could do not to rap on the glass and holler down.

"Don't you dare," she said, "don't."

And he didn't.

And with the day coming night and the rain paused and the other houses on the street darkening, Bob drew his coat tight and stood there getting wet, lean as a ghost to them through the gauzy curtain. Daniel stared down and started to shake—from the damp chill of the window and attic and because inside he dared, was daring—and into his hand he gathered the dried wasp husks from the floor in front of him, the light outside falling funny.

Bob gradually faded into the wavering light of a cigarette. And soon he sank into nothing but the triple taillights of his car down the street. Then, for the longest time, there was just the wash of streetlights and rain that the boy and his mother watched.

Fulldark before they found their way down again, Anna led the boy to the stairs, telling him careful as they went. She held his hand and pressed his fingers too tightly and kept saying careful to him. A step behind her, he followed and scattered the dust-hollow wasps into the dark. The last and largest he slipped into his mouth.

The storm picked up that night, and with rain and thunder in rushes to the screens and windows you could at least blame the bursts of lightning and the rain for such sleeplessness. You could go a whole night without sleeping, what with rain and wind coming down like this, your mother pacing above you, school tomorrow, and your father kicking at the door every time you closed your eyes and tried to sleep with the thunder and the scrape of your mother's slippers going over you.

And late in the night, at first like branches itching against the screen and aluminum siding, Bob grew insistent for the boy out there in the storm. The man stood in the dark at the window and like branches he tapped at the wood and then the metal of the frame with his fingertips and then knuckles and then heel of hand, his face close to the glass to try to see inside.

Daniel got up and lifted open the window. The rain fell loud and gusted sideways through the screen with its skillet sound like static. His father stood outside, soaked to the skin and shrunken-down as he pressed his palm to the screen and leaned up close. "Say," whispered Bob, "do me a favor-n-open this up for me."

The boy didn't move. And yet, then again, he did move. His insides all jump and buzz, he moved. Like never before he moved.

"Lemme up," said Bob. His voice sounded sore as he squinted up to the boy and said, "C'mon, how about a towel and some dry clothes for your old man?"

Rain spattered into the room and down to his bare feet the boy glanced because the cold spray burned exactly like sparks, hot and sharp. Bob stood without moving and the storm groaned over the house, flashes of lightning went white inside the clouds, and the thunder tumbled over and away. Then, cocking his arm back, Bob punched the screen with the heel of his palm, pulled back and hit it again harder, and then harder again still. The man jimmied the frame out sideways and dropped it on the lawn behind him. He put his forearms on the sill and started to lift himself into the house.

But the boy closed the window and Bob fell back. Daniel leaned down on the window to close it all the way. He turned the metal lock on top of the sash and kept shaking inside as his father's face contorted through the wet-smeared glass. The man looked up to the boy and stood perfectly still, almost at-attention, blinking the rain out of his eyes. His head tipped to the side slightly, as if he—Robert M. Cussler, a forty-seven-year-old man, this former Marine Sgt, this self-made, self-commanding, self-everything man in the rain—as if he couldn't believe this either, what had happened, what was happening.

Bob raised his face to the rain, and wiped the water from his eyes with his hand. He bent to recover the screen, tapped the grass cuttings from it, made it square again. Then—just before he turned and disappeared into the woods that bordered the back of the yard—Bob replaced the screen in the window as best he could.

He didn't tell her that his father stood there that night in the rain. He wanted to, but he never once said how Bob came back and kept coming back. How his father would pull right up the driveway in broad daylight and then waltz into the house, dressed in nice pants and stiff cotton shirts. That the man had chocolate coins in his pockets. That he produced them from the back of the boy's collar, tickling the nape of his neck.

Mom, I did like we did.

I hid.

I didn't dare.

At least that much of the story had words and the words had legs and lives of their own, lives that existed without him. And Daniel would already picture the words crawling out of his mouth, coughed half-sprung from his throat with their clicking, grasshoppery wings.

But if he didn't say any of it, maybe it didn't happen. If he swore to keep it down, maybe none of it had to have happened for real: the run of the boy to the attic, the heavy footsteps in the kitchen, and the calling out in the living room, his father's voice, "Can you hear me?"

The man walked through the rooms of the house below. "I bet you can, can't you? Loud-n-clear, you hear me, right?" And his father's talking boomed through the walls and floors, and his boot heels hard and heavy, and those heels could have just as easily been walking across the cake-white ceiling the way they came down so clean and stern, room to room to room.

"You watch," called Bob, "there's no out-stubborning me."

And Daniel listened as the man searched the house and called to the boy from every room and closet until at last he found the steps to the attic. He pulled the light on by the long string and began up the stairs—step by slow step, the man's shoes on the stairs—and in front of the window, on an overturned clay pot, Daniel sat with his chin on his knees. The boy stared down at the row of wasps and beetles and broken green flies he had lined in a curve at his feet.

"Not even a hello to Dad?" said Bob.

And he continued to the window and squatted beside the boy. The man's dress boots had bronze-colored zippers up the inside ankles and creases in the leather, dust in the creases. He put his arm over the boy's shoulder, gathered him a little closer.

"How you been?" asked Bob, and his breath smelled sour of coffee and cigarettes and the boy leaned aside so his father's hand would slip off his back. Bob touched the floor behind to catch his balance, and then he went down to one knee and reached to open the curtain. It wouldn't slide on the rod and Bob let go and the light wavered as the curtains knocked against the wall. Someone had sewn nickels and wheat pennies into the hems to weigh them down. And Bob clopped the boy on the back of the head—not hard, but not lightly either—and then he patted down the boy's hair and said, "You don't need to be a pisshead to me, you know, I'm still your old man and all." And Bob stood up and brushed the dust from his knee and waited on the boy. The air in the attic tasted stale, of old dry wood and insulation, and he kicked the blood back into his legs as he stood there waiting on the boy.

And the boy did not offer anything, not a word, and Bob turned on his heels to the dark peak of the roof and the beams which crossed like the ribs of a capsized ship over them. He asked if he wanted to go for a spin for an ice cream or something, and he waited for some sign of love or hate or fear from the boy—a betrayal of something—but Daniel kept his eyes down until his father snapped his fingers and stepped away from the window and back toward the stairs.

"You'd make a mean card player," said Bob, "that's for sure."

Radical Neck

Bob Hicok

A match beaten by frail wind lights the cave
of his hands, lines that jump like the ibex
of Cosquer in the rippling glow of a torch,
the hunting-magic of vanished men. Smoke
weaves through his lungs into blood, ghost
of plants, of the earth returning to his body.
One Camel down, nineteen to go. Another image:
on the train to St. Louis when windows still
opened: when men wore hats like boys now aspire
to tattoos: one hand on his hip, the other
swinging a smoke back and forth, a small
rhythm falling inside the generous rhythm
of the train. He turned and smiled at my mother,
pointed to a red barn falling down, being
absorbed by the horizon. He stood almost
the whole way, giving his glance to the distance,
and returned to our seats larger, puffed
as if he'd become part of land's green wish.

"The skull had a tongue in it, and could sing
once."

Always the question of how to address the dead.
Dear sir. Beloved though rotted man. You

173

who dwell in the scented couch, fabric of walls.
Yet my father remains exact in what he says,

each communiqué encoded in action, something
he did, as if he returns through what I recall.

Visitations, translucent frames, his arms arcing
toward a block of wood, the ax bold in appetite:

the bow his hands made tying shoes, always left
then right, a celestial order: wrist-snap of Zippo

top, the crisp click into place like the settling
of doubt, his fingerprints on the metal case

proof he'd mastered the prophecy of fire. His
advantage: forever happy in these things:

or precisely morose: or bent toward a river's
"slow and mileconsuming clatter" with a face

washed of need or edge, the only moment I saw him
absolved of himself. A crystal will only form

around a speck, an imperfection: in a rush a world
arises, encloses, becomes. Like this he comforts,

intrudes, a twin voice in a restaurant invokes his face,
then slides his laugh and fetid breath into place,

and for a second nothing lives that isn't him:
I've no recourse but to pursue: yet he's done with me.

———

Radical
neck:
dissection and removal of jaw, lymph nodes, tongue.

At the VA they called them half-heads, chop-blocks.

I visited intending to stare like a child,
to covet his words, by then muted by phlegm,
the esophageal churnings of an aborted throat.

But I looked in bursts, seconds before I'd turn
to Williams Pond or the far copse of alders,
hoping wind was caught in the water, in the hair
of trees, that robin or rose would hover as excuse,
a glory requiring my eyes.

No one came close, even staff strayed until
it was time to wheel him in.

All the while he smoked, plumes escaping the tube,
all love given that pursuit, a reflex gone deeper
than life.

————

As a child I loved the smoke because it adored him, clung
to, stroked his face, filled the Valiant with an animal
made of endless shapes. And the packs themselves, smell
of tobacco new, unlit, the music Raleigh, Chesterfield,
Lark, ashtrays shaped as buddhas, crowns and spaceships.
The cough was always there, his second voice, and when
wasn't someone asking him to stop, my mother, then me,
then doctors holding his clubbed fingers, explaining
a man shouldn't pass out getting dressed. The smoke clung,
became his skin. When asked what I wanted done I said
burn him, make him ash: my revenge: his only wish.

Two Poems

Robert Cording

Last Things

His children came as if their own good health could restore
his. He lost a little more each week, the tumor taking
his legs and then the memory of what just happened
moments ago. Still, he made not walking as matter-of-fact
as walking, found jokes in his forgetting. "Hello," he'd say,
picking up the phone, "you've just reached Bob's
Brain Tumor Clinic; leave a message and he may or may not
get back to you." How quickly he learned to help them again,
as if, as their father, there were these last things to do.
When pain flashed in his eyes, then drained away,
his children could see how their wanting him,
even as he was would give them no peace. When he slept,
they watched him move inside his dream as if he were
mapping the whole circumference of the world
he was taking leave of—the newly planted weeping cherry
just outside front door, the crocus and daffodils he forgot
the names of, and further off, the city he loved, bodiless
clouds skimming its horizon of buildings. Near the end,
papers came and went with the daily news, and faces,
each becoming another and another, flowing past him
like leaves on a childhood river. Half in delerium, he'd speak
of someone he couldn't see who kept coming for him.
Before he went, he waited for his children to come and say
goodbye. And when he was gone, they gathered

around him, and looked into his face, and touched the scar
on the back of his head where the tumor grew and grew,
and found they had the strength to lift his head
in their hands one last time, its weight the size of their world.

Moths

I woke to the flutter of all
their wings over the screen
as, slowly, they assembled
themselves out of the dusty
half-light of morning—
thirty-four moths,
their small grey-brown bodies
covering the screen like lichen.
At noon, they basked
in what little sun there was,
the pale September light
resting briefly on wings
that moved hardly at all
yet never stopped moving
until the moths began
to die. Even then they
seemed more composed
than exhausted, taking
the time they needed,
as if they were dreaming
their death into being.
They simply became their end,
death so naturally wrought,
I needed to touch each one
to be certain. Where
I placed my finger, they broke
out of their bodies
in little puffs of dust, leaving
behind an imprint
on the screen. By then
evening had entered
the day, and the sky, dense
with saturated colors,
collapsed in on itself,
the low clouds igniting
in a bonfire of last light.

And I felt suddenly
the slow, irreversible moment
to moment passion
of every thing to keep
moving—and I leaned close
to the screen and blew
my breath on what remained
until nothing was there,
then stood a while listening
to the wind in the leaves
while the plush dark freed
a scattering of stars and the moon
broke clear of the trees.

Six Poems

Fred Dings

The Woman with Gravitas

There's nothing now she wants or needs from us.
A sad and liquid peace has filled her eyes.

The wreckage of her life has massed inside her,
the way the dust of stars now forms the earth.

The weight of her despair outweighs the world,
so all things bend or fall towards her center.

Children climb into the safety of her arms.
Men and women orbit her like moons.

She seldom speaks, but smiles and listens patiently.
She moves inside a weather of her own

like an evening star which seems to grow more bright
the more it grows immersed inside the night.

Claims of the Past

What if we could find a way to sift
the winds for drifting minds to place in bodies
again? Whom would we choose and why? The saviors

and philosopher kings to stop our squabbling? the poor
who choked in obscurity and filth? the nameless
heroes who sacrificed themselves? the murdered,

the stifled, the unfulfilled? the evil to repair
their shame? the children who barely had a chance?
Who, among all the unredeemed

billions swirling like leaves to be reborn,
wouldn't have some claim for living more?
Isn't it better the dead come back as they do,

briefly, when they surface in a stranger's face
or voice or in a scrap of song, or steadily,
when light shafts through a window in an empty room

and the motes of dust almost coalesce,
or suddenly, when memories storm our solitude
in vacant lots or crowds, clouding us

in pain or refreshing us in a rinse of remembrance,
leaving everything shining, veneered with past,
and perhaps valued more because it does not last.

The Unlived

If only he could memorize like a lover
the body of the ordinary, which was already
a dream much larger than all sleep.

He regretted the future—the one he *would* have lived—
the way he regretted the past, the fossil record
of mere fact, the life that died into being

while all the unlived possibilities
echoed into silence among the vaulted
arches and stained glass rosettes of time.

Each day was proof of his failure to flare
into ash at the flashpoint of recognition
or crack ecstatically open in the globed moment,

saving nothing for his next breath. How easily
his imagination yawned and slept, how vision
grew young and frolicked in the shallows of perception.

His mind floated like a sponge in an ocean, soaked
full by a mere palmful of water, immersed
in all that it would never come to know.

The Bodily Beautiful

Ah, the bodily beautiful, how they are envied
for the perfect rhymes of their bodies' moons and stars,
how the world sets sail for the labial latitudes
of their lustrous skin, forgetting the bloody factories

within. But what of their burden? the daily swelter
in the spotlights of lust, the lovesick legions
and crush of attentive puppets, the ceaseless chatter
and charades of mating games, the splatter of night-

frightened moths who fling against their panes.
How hard it must be among fiestas
of permission and satin pillows to practice forbearance
and cleanse the spirit in the deserts of self-denial,

how hard to leave the shallows of sexuality
and immerse in the treacherous waters of love, to glimpse
the skull of time in the mirror's lie and the bones
of honesty inside those sublime impediments of flesh.

Eulogy for a Private Man

He would not arrange his face to please us,
smile on cue or chime with ritual greeting,
would not distill himself into an aperitif,

dance or fence or wrestle with clever speech,
add to the litter of words that silence sweeps.
He was a dry stream, flowing unseen beneath

his arid bed, a social counterweight
to the harlequins of humid revelation.
But sometimes a lean, muscular sentence would stride

before us and cross its arms in a stubborn stance,
then turn away, as if remembering how the flimsy
bridges we fling to span the abyss collapse,

how our strings of meaning unravel as we speak.
He annoyed us and intrigued us, a hieroglyph
of cliff-faced solitude we tried to decipher.

But perhaps such a stern gravity was necessary
to keep his secret wild moons circling,
or perhaps he preferred the untrammelled woods

of his loneliness and reserved it as a private garden
for one who never came, or perhaps some eclipse
of love produced an arctic cold, a sentinel

trusting no one at the gate, or perhaps
he kept a monstrous rage inside his torment
which could not lapse for one mauled moment.

Who knows the terms of another's life? For some
it may be a victory even to achieve
a distant closeness, an intimate alienation.

Two Sketches of Solitude

A Young Man by the Sea

The pulsing surf spreads its scallops
of foaming lather around the young
man's feet and sucks the silken
sand between his toes. Throbbing
breakers claw and souse the cliff
while lean white wings hover
low and knife against the wind.
Tangles of kelp clump in knots,
and the necklace of shells and bones he kicks
clatter like dice. Polished logs
choke the beach like crossed legs,
and he snuffs the pungent brine and thinks
of swimming out among the rock
stacks wrapped in shawls of mist
thrusting through the waves. Clouds
strew their flaring pastel hues
like lingerie tossed across the sky.
The moon, a molten pearl, laves
the undulant dunes with emollient light,
while grasses comb backwards in the breeze
and whisper from seclusions in the night.

An Old Man by the Sea

The collapsing surf gasps and fans its milky
spittle around the old man's legs
and shifts the sodden sand beneath his feet.
Breakers gnaw at the cliff's battered face
while he treads the wrackline, threading among debris
and stitching a seam which erases in the brine.
Around him shrieking gulls scavenge the bier

of sand, pecking at shards of crabs and clams
among tangled and gangrenous sinews of kelp.
Sun-bleached trees, like bones disgorged
from the maws of storms, lie stranded on the beach.
The stench of eons bleeds into the air
from wind-guttered clumps of feathers and fish,
and the eroded land's last stubborn hunches
stand like gravestones in the scything sea,
encircled sentinels cloaked in mantles of mist.
Among the broken edges of the ashen clouds,
the moon's shell rises like the ghost of the sun,
while lapping waves lull and drone beneath,
beside the unkempt cemetery mounds of sand
and the hollow stalks that clatter in the wind.

The Impossibility of Language

Beth Ann Fennelly

1.
"Blackberries," says one, rolling it in the barrel
of the mouth. "Yes," says the other, "oak."
"Well aged, aroma of truffles," adds the third.
They nod. Roll it and roll it, the way God
must have packed the earth in his palms.
Discuss the legs of it running down the glass.
They bring the valley into it. And color: "The light
staining the glass at Sainte Chapelle." Back to taste:
"Earthy. A finish of clove." They leave nodding—
such faith in the opaque bottles of their words.

2. How I Became a Nature Lover

Suppose I said, "Honeysuckle, "
meaning stickysweet stamen,
the hidden core you taught me,
a city girl, to find. How I crave
the moment I coax it from calyx,
tongue under the bulbed tip
of glistening stalk, like an altar boy
raising the salver under blessed bread
the long Sundays of my girlhood,
suppose my tongue caught that mystery
the   single   swollen   drop
                    O
               honey-
               suckle

The irony of metaphor:
you are closest to something
when naming what it's not.

3.
1934: Imagine Mandelstam, who loved
words too much, with his poet friends,
how they passed the bottle of slivovic.
"Osip," they pleaded, "chitáy, chitáy."
And so he did read about Stalin,
"the Kremlin mountaineer," with "laughing
cockroaches on his top lip," who rolled
"executions on his tongue like berries."
How could Mandelstam have known
one man fisting the table in laughter
would quote the poem to the mountaineer?

Think of Mandelstam in winter: the water
freezes in the water jug. In summer:
the prison mattress shimmies lice.
But Nadezhda visits him. They do not speak
of hope or love or death. He recites his poems
in a whisper that she memorizes. Even in his cell,
"this shoe-size in earth with bars around it,"
as long as he has lips, he has a weapon.

Imagine how much each word weighs
on Nadezhda's tongue. She bears
them home like eggs in that time of no eggs.
She nests them deep inside the secret book.
He dies, committed to her memory.

4.
"I ask you to cinema, coffee, wine,
          you say me, 'no.' You gave my heart
the fire, and now you give me the heart
          burn. Why, when eyes of you
are sympathetic like some fox?"
          We speak barest when we barely
speak—love letters from the foreigner
          before the invention of cliché.

Teaching immigrants English,
      I gave them crayons to draw families,
taught them words for each brown,
      orange, tan face. Guillermo's page
was blank. "I am alonesome," he wrote.

5.
Meaning? Language can so not.

The government releases
films of nuclear testing
from the fifties.
A plane bellies over
an atoll in the Pacific.
It drops a bomb.
The camera,
at a "safe distance"
some dozen islands away,
flips over. The sky
falls. The narrator surmises,
"at this juncture
of maturation,
premature impactaction
necessitates further study."
The mushroom cloud
is a balloon caption
for which earth can't
find words.

6.
Is the ear bereft if an alphabet dies
that it has never heard?

      The latest extinction of language
      occurred last month with the death
      of the lone speaker of Northern Pomo,
      a woman in her eighties.

Are we weaker without the word
in Northern Pomo for begonia?
Does the inner hammer numbly

strike its drum? Does it grow dumb
mourning sounds that it will never hear?

7. Unfinished Poems

rise
from trashcans
sewers & pulp mills
& bind themselves under
elaborate covers
for the endless library
of the unborn
who climb mahogany
ladders to finger
thick volumes
& with vague lips
sound out what's there
& what's not

8.
Synonyms are lies. Answer the question
with *stones* or *rocks*:

Q. When Virginia Woolf, on the banks
of the Ouse, walked into the water,
swallowing her words, with what objects
had she loaded the pockets of her dress?

A. *Stones.* *Rocks* is wrong, as in
"She took her life for granite."

9. The Myth of Translation

Try a simple sentence: "I am hungover."
For Japanese, "I suffer the two-day dizzies."
In Czech, "The monkeys swing inside my head."
Italians say, "Today, I'm out of tune."
Languages aren't codes that correspond—
in Arabic, there's no word for "hungover."

Does the Innuit woman, kept on ice all winter,
sucking fat from ducks for her hunter's leggings,
not divine the boredom her language doesn't name?
Or would the word's birth crack the ice for miles,
drowning the hunter who crouches with a spear
beside the ice hole for the bearded seal? She sucks
the fat slowly, careful not to quill her throat
with feathers. She grows heavy. It is, as it was
from the beginning, a question of knowledge.
If she bites into the word, she'll be alonesome.

Three Poems

Alan Michael Parker

The Butter Knife God

Askew, aslant, awry,
Becalmed, besmirched, belied,

The Butter Knife God practices his A,B,C's.
Full of pronouncements, destitute

With privilege,
He waves himself above

The mesclun and Chilean wine,
As he asks the missing poor and needy,

What kind of god am I?
Or you? he points.

Or you? Or you? Or you?
He shuts his eyes.

He turns them on his heart, practices
His 1, 2, 3's, his A,B,C's,

(Ludicrous, listless, lithe,
Monocled, mountebank, mistake),

All the while—*Hell!*—
Sawing at his heart

With the butter knife
Of the Butter Knife God.

The God of Pepper

In her best gingham dress, teased hair
And Odalisque #3, the God of Pepper

Descends, makes an entrance
Down the stairs

Into the church basement, one
Slender ankle then

Another
Slender

Ankle.
Pot luck! And hers is the Ambrosia,

The gelid, the burden
Of each twilight spent

Staring at the cupboard's contents,
All those tiny jars, so different.

(Hers is a love
Explosive, every moment

In her gaze
A long night and a short day.)

But now she has arrived:
She stands behind the table,

The supper laid
Like a Bingo card,

And gestures with an open palm
At all the offerings.

She smiles, never speaks, poses
Like a sculpture—a god in the finest

Old tradition—and then she leaves
In a cloud of suspicion and temptation:

A string of black pearls,
Inscrutable and good.

No Fool, the God of Salt

No fool, the God of Salt, beloved by all,
Has learned the difference between

Passing on and *passing through*.
She's been reading Einstein, once again,

To Solovine: "An infinite world is possible . . .,"
Stoking herself on caffeine and Turkish Delight,

Feet in square heels on a piano stool
In that little café off the Avenue.

You know the one? The Weimar?
Where once that tiny Lebanese chanteuse

Burst into flame? The God of Salt
Was there, as always, everywhere it seems,

But never much help,
Her minions stoic in their prisons,

Her skirt hiked up,
So many promises to break.

And the lovely singer caught, then sizzled,
Smoked, then raged, consumed.

The God of Salt? She looked up
From her book—as ever, Einstein,

"One should expect a chaotic world which cannot
Be grasped by the mind in any way . . ." —

And she licked her lips.
(Those lips, O, those lips.)

And she used the very pointed tip of her tongue.
(That tongue, O, that tongue.)

Two Poems

Daniel Halpern

Dusk

She never happens upon a garden at dusk
   doesn't wander into such magical light
   filtering through trees

the sun at so radical an angle
   its rays bent harshly across the vegetation
   carry dust from her steps as she enters

carry the million bodies of hovering sunset insects
   Her sky gray and the mist holds only
   infinite particles of water

The colors of the city chronicle black
   and white the surface of everything
   damp metal painted with drained pigment

She's not interested in relinquishing city landscape
   won't leave behind the chrome and cheerless
   The garden just beyond formalities of the city

darkens so quickly the abandoned sun remains as
   portrait in the high glass windows of the city
   a brilliant light held against the darkening below

Resurrection

Remember the sage and wild thyme nagging their sandals,
the stones and sand underfoot the carriers
who held your body vertically and placed it
under rock to hold back the natural world.

Remember those who held you and hold you still,
walk with you in their hearts. Piero
brings you back triumphant, stick in hand
above the sleeping soldiers who guard you

if only in dream. The Artist imparts
hues of the good earth, earth of the Renaissance
to locate the moment of your reappearance.
The Poet takes you off the rock and down

into the valley with the heat of primary color,
raiment of wildflowers. And the valley
bears wildflowers that no longer
draw blood from your ankles. The poet

Machado wrote of your second journey,
There is no road walker, you make the road
by walking. By walking you make the road,
and when you look backward you see the path

that you never will step on again.
And when you've crossed the fields fired
with wildflowers, you do not look back
but come to an eddy and there find,

held over the swirling water, a temple
where your first woman of this flesh
lights candles in her window at sundown.
Does she await your arrival? The cliffs

so steep here, the wind so like her
fierce breathing, so close to your own
breathing. Now you stand above the shore
on these green mountains, the way back overgrown.

The Nest

Tom Wayman

"*Y la sombra es el nido cerrado . . .*"
                    —*Miguel Hernandez*

Now shadow is
the closed nest
—tangled shadow: fibres
of a coarse mound
or effervescent tendrils

The nest
may be clenched
or darkly willing
—ready to open, trembling
because of events
thousands of kilometres
distant
or near to hand,
cajoled, teased, impressed,
so many kisses,
breathed on, spoken to
in tongues, answering
in the glossolalia
that remains an authentic
language of the nest

And now the nest is
dim water
—mysterious moisture
on the canyon floor,
rivulet or pond
constrained by shale banks,
then a creek
dodging past bullrushes,
coarse grass,
widening toward
swamp maple, flowering broom,

an odor of birdsong
that flickers amid the reeds,
river-bottom of clear sand,
sharp calls of robin,
wren, nuthatch,
attar of wild rose,
the slow lift of heron,
hulking pelt of bear
disappearing between
cottonwoods

But when light
becomes the nest,
a beam of fire,
a glowing orb,
conjoin,
flash
like molten metal
sparkling, or a fire
that has caught on fire,
where flame breaks out
atop other flames

in whose radiance
the faces, bodies
of grandparents,
grandchildren
swirl, ablaze
in a nimbus, glory

Cities, too,
cabinetry manuals, scythes,
jet engines
nestle in that scorching cup

nest of ancestors
nest of world

Figures on a Human Scale

Timothy Liu

So it was a disaster: butterfly nets
in the hands of children racing
through a landscape sown with buried
mines. Did someone say their bodies
looked like "flowers opening"?—
cries and shouts from a common crowd
gone mute. Regard the fallen form:
Manet's *Dead Toreador* cut out
from a larger scene. Yet would we
mar eternity with the oil from
our fingertips?—a portrait by Vermeer
shoved into a waiting van, our faces
still held captive by what remains
unsolved. All that we could not save.

Two Poems

Wisława Szymborska

Hatred

*Translated from the Polish by Joanna Trzeciak
and Marek Lugowski*

Look, how spry she still is,
how well she holds up:
hatred, in our century.
How lithely she takes high hurdles.
How easy for her to pounce, to seize.

She is not like the other feelings.
At once older and younger than they.
She alone gives birth to causes
which rouse her to life.
If she sleeps, it's never for eternity.
Insomnia doesn't take away but gives her strength.

Religion or no religion
—as long as she kneels at the start
Motherland or no-man's land
—as long as she's in the race.
Even justice suffices at first.
After that she speeds off on her own
Hatred. Hatred.
The grimace of love's ecstasy
twists her face.

Oh, those other feelings,
so sickly and sluggish.
Since when could brotherhood
count on milling crowds?
Was compassion ever first across the finish line?
How many followers does doubt command?
Only hatred commands, for hatred knows her stuff.

Smart, able, hardworking.
Need we say how many songs she has written?

How many human carpets she has unrolled
over how many plazas and stadiums?

Let's be honest:
Hatred can create beauty.
Marvelous are her fire-glows, in deep night.
Clouds of smoke most beautiful, in rosy dawn.
It's hard to deny ruins their pathos
and not to see bawdy humor
in the stout column lording it over them.

She is a master of contrast
between clatter and silence,
red blood and white snow.
Above all the image of a clean-shaven torturer
standing over his defiled victim
never bores her.

She is always ready for new tasks.
If she has to wait, she waits.
They say hatred is blind. Blind?
With eyes sharp as a sniper's,
she looks bravely into the future
—she alone.

The Turn of the Century

Translated by Joanna Trzeciak

It was supposed to be better than the others, our 20th century,
But it won't have time to prove it.
Its years are numbered,
its step unsteady,
its breath short.

Already too much has happened
that was not supposed to happen.
What was to come about
has not.

Spring was to be on its way,
and happiness, among other things.

Fear was to leave the mountains and valleys.
The truth was supposed to finish before the lie.

Certain misfortunes
were never to happen again
such as war and hunger and so forth.

These were to be respected:
the defenselessness of the defenseless,
trust and the like.

Whoever wanted to enjoy the world
faces an impossible task.

Stupidity is not funny. Wisdom isn't jolly.

Hope
Is no longer the same young girl
et cetera. Alas.

God was at last to believe in man:
good and strong,
but good and strong
are still two different people.

How to live—someone asked me this in a letter,
someone I had wanted
to ask that very thing.

Again and as always,
and as seen above
there are no questions more urgent than
the naive ones.

Children of the Holocaust

Gabriel Motola

Claude Lanzmann's *Shoah* opens with a Polish survivor singing a few lines that he first sang as a thirteen-year-old prisoner on the streets of the village of Chelmno. Lanzmann brought Simon Srebnik, forty-seven years old when he appears in the film, from Israel to that Polish village where the Nazis first began to exterminate Jews in gas vans before burning the dead bodies in newly-constructed ovens. Of the hundreds of thousands of men, women, and children who perished there, he was one of only two who survived. Midway through the nine-and-a-half hour film, after having given additional accounts of what he endured and witnessed, Srebnik explains that the work details of which he was a part had to clear the vans of the bodies immediately after each tightly packed "shipment" of eighty people were gassed and put the corpses into the ovens. He recounts a particularly harrowing incident. After a mechanical breakdown, still living but not fully conscious victims tumbled out of the van and, slowly coming to, began writhing on the ground. Despite being alive, however, they were thrown by the work details into the fiery ovens:

> When I saw all that, it didn't affect me. . . . I was only thirteen, and all I'd ever seen until then were dead bodies. Maybe I didn't understand. Maybe if I'd been older, I'd have understood, but the fact is, I didn't. I'd never seen anything else. In the ghetto in Lodz I saw that as soon anyone took a step, he fell dead. I thought that's the way things had to be, that it was normal. I'd walk the streets of Lodz, maybe one hundred yards, and there'd be two hundred bodies.[1]

Memory, Nietzsche asserts in *Beyond Good and Evil*, yields to pride when the two are in conflict.[2] Because pride is inflexible and memory indefinite, the self, if in danger, does what it must to protect itself, including the conscious or unconscious distortion of truth. Shame, on the other hand, is both the antithesis and nemesis of pride, because truth, unable to resist, recoils before it. Although at opposite ends of the emotional pole, both pride and shame are nevertheless interconnected by the moral imperative with which—through what it calls conscience—society governs. Throughout his work, Primo Levi has alluded to or specified the effects shame had on himself as well as on his fellow sufferers. In fact, in his most detailed analysis of the emotion, he writes in the chapter of *The Drowned and the Saved* entitled "Shame" that while few survivors feel guilty about having deliberately harmed or stolen from a companion "almost everybody feels guilty of having omitted to offer help."[3] While Levi applies the term "almost everybody" for the shame felt, he is apparently specifying men—since he does not speak of women while he was in Auschwitz. Women, in fact, seemed not to be similarly affected by their incarceration. Indeed, the difference in gender often accounts for the difference between the way men and women endured and consequently remembered their ordeal.

Basically, women because more nurturing were better able than men to endure their degradation despite suffering the same, or even worse, deprivation than did the men. This is especially apparent in the texts of female survivors of the Holocaust. From them, we see that women tended to look after each other, to share their food more liberally, to listen and provide comfort to each other. Men on the other hand generally hoarded their meager supplies for themselves and, worse perhaps, endured their emotional grief in silence, refusing to communicate their fears and despair and discouraging their fellow sufferers from doing so. This is not to say that shame causes men and women to remember the factual horror of the event differently. If anything women were probably aware that they suffered greater physical burdens than did the men, who were relatively better fed and housed because of their more valuable potential as workers.[4] But the felt memory is more profoundly compounded in those who had to endure humiliation, the moral and emotional degradation of self, than in those, who despite undergoing the same physical and emotional pain, could at least look back without shame at what they endured. Clearly the manner in which the individual bore his or her moral responsibility during captivity was a primary factor in the way he or she coped with the memory of the ordeal long after it was over. Children, too, depending on how young they were and, therefore, on their moral development when swept into the concentrationary universe, recalled an existence through a morally-charged memory different from that of either their mothers or their fathers.

In the chapter entitled "The Gray Zone" of *The Drowned and the Saved*, Levi describes the moral and ethical ambiguity grasped by the prisoners almost immediately upon their entry to the concentration camp. Because the clearly demarcated world of good and evil they had inhabited no longer existed in the concentrationary universe, the victims had to accommodate themselves to a new moral condition. In fact, Levi asserts, most survivors had to collaborate to one degree or another in order to get the extra nourishment essential to their survival.[5] What is crucial in terms of affixing blame is the phrase "to one degree or another." Those who performed certain tasks and thus given extra rations but who did not participate in the brutality or killing of their fellow prisoners were not to be judged harshly. Kapos, on the other hand, who often identified with their oppressors and thus became as brutal as they were, are to be so judged and condemned for their actions. Thus, though the moral universe shifted, it did not altogether disintegrate for those who had inhabited such a sphere before being thrust into a world in which such words as decency, morality, and justice were rarely if ever uttered. There were instances, however, of a moral conscience being so strong that it refused to yield even when life itself was at stake. Levi tells of 400 Greek Jews from Corfu who were ordered to work in what Levi calls the "Special Squad" (the same, apparently, as what Srebnik calls the "work details"). Instead of participating in the gassing and burning of fellow human beings, these Greek Jews without exception refused and were immediately gassed to death.[6]

Should a thirteen-year-old, taking part in actions that 400 men considered so reprehensible that they chose death rather than perform, be condemned for his participation? Should any prisoner, regardless of his age, associated with work details or special squads be condemned when his only alternative was death? Levi urges suspension of moral judgment of those who did choose life. But what he cannot suspend is the guilt, including his own, that most survivors felt after they were freed. That guilt, he asserts, is one of the main reasons survivors committed suicide— sometimes immediately, sometimes long after liberation.[7] Levi refers to the "civilian" moral code,[8] the sense of right and wrong that had been suspended in the camps, but which resurfaced after liberation, as that which caused the shame felt by survivors after, but which remained inoperative during the war because then all one focussed on was surviving. But what if what was "normal" before the camps was also normal during the time of the camps—as was the case for Srebnik? As a result, perhaps, of not being burdened by a civilian moral code significantly different from that which was his during his imprisonment, he seems equally unburdened by the sense of guilt most other survivors endured. Srebnik's assertion to Lanzmann upon recalling the sight of living people being thrust into the flaming ovens— "it didn't affect me"—is consonant with that of children who, having experienced a lack of empathy, as Daniel Goleman puts it, are incapable of a moral posture that society values.[9] When people are subjected to violence that they cannot combat or escape, over which they have no control, they relive the memory of such violence, no matter how much time has passed, as if it had just occurred. In fact, according to Goleman, the brain itself undergoes a biological change when traumatic stress strikes the individual. Although most research on this malady is being done on adults at the National Center for Post-Traumatic Stress Disorder, which culls its information from a network of Veterans' Administration hospitals, in which many patients still suffer from the trauma of their combat experiences, "these insights apply as well to children who have suffered severe emotional trauma."[10]

In At the Mind's Limits, which first appeared in 1966, Jean Améry, the philosopher and survivor of Auschwitz, anticipated the findings of institutional research on trauma by describing his own mental state years after being tortured: "Whoever was tortured, stays tortured. Torture is ineradicably burned into him, even when no clinically objective traces can be detected. . . . Twenty-two years later I am still dangling over the ground by dislocated arms, panting, and accusing myself."[11] And like the laboratory findings of the National Center for Post-Traumatic Stress Disorder, Améry's assertion that trust in the world will not be regained for those who have been tortured certainly applies to children who suffered the emotional trauma engendered by the Holocaust.

The texts of children of the Holocaust—at least those among its most effective and powerful chroniclers: Anne Frank, Danilo Kis, Norman Manea, and, most recently, Binjamin Wilkomirski—reveal a depraved universe whose brutality and despotism finally result in an apocalyptic landscape littered with the bodies of the dead and dying. Anne Frank, spared for a while but ultimately part of that doomed landscape, started keeping a diary when, on the verge of adolescence, she was forced into hiding with her family.[12] At thirteen years of age, Srebnik to the contrary, most individuals are already fully morally formed; that is, even if not yet legally responsible for their actions they know the difference between what their society deems right and wrong, good and evil. In fact, what makes the diary entries so powerful is Anne's acute sensibility that is nourished by an equally astute moral dignity. Nevertheless, nearly two years later, at not quite fifteen years of age, she remains an innocent, grasping at what she feels is the world's potential goodness despite what she sees and hears all around her: "And in the evening, when I lie in bed and end my prayers with the words, '*Ich danke dir für all das Gute und Liebe und Schöne,*' I am filled with joy, then I think about '*das Gute*' of going into hiding, my health, and with my whole being of '*das Liebe*' that will come sometime, love, the future, happiness and of '*das Schöne,*' which the world means. The world, nature, and outstanding beauty of everything, everything that is exquisite and fine"[13]

Her prayer of thanks to God for providing the Good, the Love, and the Beauty that now are or will be hers is directly related to the traditional morality she has willingly accepted as her own. And through the apprehension of the Good, the Love, and the Beauty, the essentials that both comprise and bestow morality, one is filled with Joy—a sentiment rarely if ever mentioned in the writings of survivors.

Aware of the intricacies of a moral life before as well as after she and her family went into hiding, Anne Frank, having broken no laws, was nevertheless classified a criminal solely because she was Jewish. Recognizing that the new world order instituted by the conquering Nazis was corrupt and malevolent, she nevertheless continued to abide by the traditional moral values she had gotten from her parents. Norman Manea's morality, on the other hand, was still in the process of being formed when at five years of age he was sent with his parents from their native Romania to the Ukrainian internment camp of Transnistria.

In *October, Eight O'Clock*, his remarkable collection of interrelated stories, many of which are clearly autobiographical, Manea traces the protagonist's evolution from a five-year-old survivor of the concentration camp through adolescence and adulthood, after returning to his native country. While in the camp, the boy becomes aware, as does his mother, of his father's love affair with a young cousin whom the boy himself had a crush on and had hoped would increase the family to four instead of being the cause of its figurative dissolution. But despite the obvious pain the love affair causes them, neither the boy nor his mother passes judgment on the father's behavior. It is as if the lawless conditions of the camp, having excised the civil rights they enjoyed before their enslavement, caused the captives to relinquish the constraints that constituted their moral precepts before the war. In "Proust's Tea," which takes place after their liberation, the victims congregate in a waiting room of a train

station where they are attended to by nurses who serve them tea and biscuits. The biscuits, which should have been representative of care given,
call up instead, in ironic tribute to Proust's madeleine, the horrible experience of the past: "The biscuits tasted like soap, mud, rust, burnt skin,
snow, leaves, rain, bones, sand, mold, wet wool sponges, mice, rotting
wood, fish, the unique flavor of hunger."[14] Having grasped such basic
human characteristics and emotions as language, love, and loyalty during
his five years in the camp—where language is harsh and restricted, where
love and loyalty have become twisted—the boy comes to learn their
value, paradoxically, through having borne witness to their perversion.
After his release, when asked what he most feared in the camp, the boy
replies: "Beautiful evenings . . . Crows . . . Silence."[15]

While it is understandable that crows, and even silence, may instill fear
in a boy, it is difficult to understand how beautiful evenings can do the
same. His response is in sharp contrast to what Frank continues to value
most highly while still in hiding: "The world, nature, and outstanding
beauty of everything, everything that is exquisite and fine." Shielded from
the reality of the horror by being closeted in the attic with her family,
Frank continues to believe in the permanence of the world that was and
longs for the dreaded aberration to pass so the world can resume its past.
But for Manea at five years of age who only knows the world as dangerous
and impermanent, where children die and families lose their love for each
other, beautiful evenings, like silence, may presage their opposite.

When he is given a book of fairy tales as a reward for being a good stu-
dent after returning to his native land, the boy's life is changed. The
book's lesson is that anything could become anything, including a little
pig who became the emperor's son at night: "It scared him; everything
could change in one night, a night five years long—the emperor's son
could become what he had just been, with no one to recognize or save
him. The fairy tales were real, and each one held a threat. . . .The fear
had come back."[16] Thus the book of fairy tales has recorded the transmo-
grifications in such a way as to fascinate and enthrall the young boy. But
having been witness during a night that lasted five years, the boy, like
Kafka, aware of the potential horror of such metamorphoses, is once
again beset by the fear that was his in the camp. The boy, recognized
throughout the work as bright and perceptive, has oratorical skills which
he uses to describe his years in the camp. He is thus made a welcome
guest in family celebrations and official functions, recognized by the
authorities as having the potential to be of value to their political cause.

In "The Instructor," the longest and most complex story of the collection, nearly four years have passed since his release from the concentration camp. The boy is being tutored for his bar mitzvah, a ritual he is reluctant to participate in. His instructor is a complex and bitter man, who as a lawyer defended a Communist Party official, when the Party was still outlawed, and was disbarred in the process, but who then publicly insulted the man when the Party came to power and is thus reduced to poverty and humiliation. In addition to teaching the boy his Torah portion which he must recite in Hebrew on the day of his bar mitzvah, the instructor explains to him how he must put on his tefillin, the two black cubes containing scripture. "'These are placed, one on the left arm, the other on the forehead. . . . The arm is bound first. Preference is given to the deed, to action. When we made the covenant, we promised that we would carry out the commandments, and only later would we try to understand them.'"[17] But the boy, intelligent and visionary, ready to repudiate his religious heritage and embrace the Communist credo that promises equality and justice, conceives in his head a film that pits a couple of prominent rabbis against God. A rabbi from Berdichev demands that God "'be judged by all who suffer and die to sanctify Your name, Your laws, and Your contracts!'" Another rabbi roars: "'I require that justice be carried out! That the Supreme Legislator subject himself to his own laws!'"[18]

If reluctant to participate in the ritual of confirming himself as a Jew in the synagogue, the boy is adamant in refusing to adorn himself with phylacteries which, for the initiated Jew, constitute a public and visible reminder of his covenant with God outside the synagogue. A Pioneer at an international Communist Party camp he was chosen to attend, he discovers the phylacteries that his mother had secretly put in the suitcase she packed for him. But concealing them throughout his stay at the camp, he ultimately throws them away. Recognized both for his oratory at describing life in the concentration camp as well as for heralding the new political state, picked to star in a film being made about the Communist camp while continuing to create in his own head the film of his life, the boy is taken under wing by a camp official who now becomes "the instructor." Thus, as he first discovered in the concentration camp and then in the book of fairy tales where anything can become anything, the religious instructor has been converted to the political instructor. Among the duties with which the boy must assist his instructor is the reading and censoring of the mail of his fellow campers, a task which rankles the boy's conscience. While the religious instructor had merely insisted that the boy perpetuate a ritual that no longer had any meaning, the political instructor induced him to spy on his fellow campers. The boy, though recognizing such spying to be immoral, knows too that doing so constitutes power.

The boy at the conclusion of "The Instructor" is now referred to as the "young man."[19] In one of the last reveries that fill the screen of his mind, merging the political and religious instructors into one "Comrade Berdichev," the boy insists on being heard: "'Didn't you teach me that judgment must remain above influence, unswayed? It must . . . Yes, you are right, I tasted power. Yes, I swallowed the poison, my instructors hoped that I deserved this honor, this horror. . . .'"[20] Confused and alone, on the verge of manhood, the boy is buffeted by all facets of an engaged life: politics and religion, loyalty and honor, family and state, cowardice and courage, reality and art, time and its passing, the documentary of the camp with the film of life—all colliding and merging as he realizes he is made to be a traitor to the religion of his parents, an exile in his home-land. Recognizing his having been morally tainted by the power bestowed upon him by the state, he also recognizes, oddly enough, that his extraordinary odyssey "demands an inkwell." This insistence on the metonymic "inkwell" is his assertion that he will be a writer, that the film in his head must be transcribed to paper, the recognition of which makes him think of himself as a "conceited little prig."[21] Thus, because of the awareness of his own corruptibility of which pride may be the single most powerful component, the boy paradoxically maintains a moral posture precisely through his acknowledgment of having lost it. This moral ambivalence is rooted in his memory of anything capable of becoming anything else which he first observed in the camp and which was rein-forced for him through the language of the book of fairy tales given to him when he emerged from the camp. His initiation—his bar mitzvah, if you will—into the world of the religion that caused such torment for him and his family and into the world of politics that immediately revealed its own corruption also awakens in him the world of art, into becoming the creator who must transmute the materials of life into the language of literature so as to determine meaning in a world that otherwise has none.

Norman Manea and Danilo Kis, both child victims of the Holocaust, are among the most profound and challenging writers of our time.[22] Both of them have written extensively, in fiction and nonfiction, on subjects that go well beyond their earliest childhood experiences. But both have also written the most eloquent and provocative, the most challenging and complex literary accounts composed by children of the Holocaust.

While Manea was sent with his parents to a concentration camp where their degradation became his own, Kis remained at home, witnessing the humiliation and beating of his Jewish father before he was deported to his death. Just as Simon Srebnik of Lanzmann's *Shoah* viewed being surrounded by dead and dying bodies as normal and hence had no moral compunction in witnessing the burning of living beings, Manea and Kis as boys must have viewed as normal what was done to their parents, since all Jews were suffering a similar fate. Unlike Srebnik, however, both Manea and Kis, still under the moral guidance of their parents, were therefore aware that what was being done to them was evil. Other children of the Holocaust, including Elie Wiesel, Janos Nyiri, Louis Begley, and Magda Denes—have written accounts of how they too coped with the pervasive evil—some by fighting it, others by identifying with it, all apparently having their moral compass distorted by it. Aharon Appelfeld, whose fictionalized accounts of the Holocaust experience have received international acclaim, is peculiarly silent in terms of his own experience as a child of the Holocaust. After escaping from the Romanian concentration camp in Transnitria in 1943 at the age of eight, he survived the remaining war years hiding in Ukrainian forests which were under Nazi control. An orphaned adolescent among displaced Jewish survivors after the war, he lived on the Italian coast before migrating to Israel in 1947. Unlike almost all the other major writers who, having suffered the concentrationary universe, needed to expose the agony of their existence to the world, Appelfeld writes not about his existence in the camps or in the forests. He writes instead of the time immediately before or immediately after the Second World War, almost invariably depicting the Jew as oblivious to the ominous signs surrounding him, as disdaining the painful memories etched deep within him, as presuming that the problem with the world was created by the Jew's own failure to become an invisible part of it. *Tzili* is the only one of his novels that deals with a child caught in the Holocaust. But here too, he writes less of what the Nazis are responsible for, focussing instead on the heroine who is abused by her own people, forced into prostitution before falling in love with another Jew who dies and is then, like Appelfeld himself, put on a ship at war's end and sets sail for Palestine.

Not quite twelve years old when the war started, Wiesel was almost fifteen when he and his family were deported. In *Night*, first published in France in 1960, he writes that after he and his father along with the other Jews had suffered constant abuse and humiliation he "accused" God of all that had befallen His people, thus causing Wiesel on the eve of Rosh Hashanah in Auschwitz to stand alone, apart from the praying congregation, a stranger in his own midst. Later, his ailing father having become an overwhelming burden, he admits that if he had allowed himself to explore "the recesses of my weakened conscience," he would have found himself relieved by his own father's death. Having no tears left to weep for his dead father, he could find only the words "free at last!"[23] Thus, shorn of his belief in God's virtue, Wiesel also finds himself denying the moral imperative to honor thy father.

Unlike Manea and Wiesel who survived the camps and who wrote of their experiences there as young men, Nyiri, Begley, and Denes, having survived either by hiding from or staying one step ahead of the Nazis, waited four or five decades to publish their stories. While Nyiri and Denes narrate their actual experiences through fiction or memoir, Begley apparently conceives of experiences that will forever change the moral being of the protagonist, whom Begley identifies himself with. In the very first paragraph of the introductory section to *Wartime Lies*, Begley writes of an older man who like himself—"fifty or more winters on his back, living a moderately pleasant life in a tranquil country" —thinks of the story of the boy who became just such a man.[24] And the man, Begley writes, calls the boy, Maciek, the protagonist of the novel. The man whom Begley clearly models after himself "has become a voyeur of evil, sometimes uncertain which role he plays in the vile pictures that pass before his eyes. Is that the inevitable evolution of the child he once was, the price to be paid for his sort of survival?"[25] The assumption the reader is therefore encouraged to make is that the first-person narrator, though called Maciek, is related to Begley who, having been himself a child in hiding in Poland, is profoundly concerned about what happens to the child's moral center, after being forced to witness and engage in lies and deception in order to survive. Maciek, the Polish-Jewish boy, reveals throughout the work the lies and deceptions his aunt engages in in order to save him and herself. But those "wartime lies" that save him from death are also responsible for causing him to become in effect as corrupt as the enemy he ultimately identifies with. And thus, though he has physically survived, the child he once was has died: "He became an embarrassment and slowly died. A man who bears one of the names Maciek used has replaced him. Is there much of Maciek in that man? No: Maciek was a child, and our man has no childhood that he can bear to remember."[26] While Begley imagines the man who grew from Maciek as being not only "a voyeur of evil" but also a participant in that evil as a result of his childhood experiences, thus causing the "death" of the boy, Nyiri and Denes write of their actual experiences and how those childhood experiences, like those of the man of Begley's narrative, formed the basis of their later lives. Unlike Begley's protagonist who is forever changed by the wartime lies he had to endure, the childhood selves of Nyiri and Denes, having been fortified by those experiences, are able as adults to join the world on their own moral and psychological terms.

Born in Budapest in 1932, but now living in London where he works in the theater both as playwright and director, Nyiri fled Hungary after the 1956 uprising against the Russians, which he describes in his first novel, *Streets*. In his next novel, *Battlefields and Playgrounds*,[27] a fictionalized account of actual events in Hungary during the Holocaust, Nyiri describes the survival of a family modeled on his own. The narrator and protagonist, Jozsef Sondor, eight years old when the novel opens, is already a religious skeptic. And his skepticism is matched by his incorrigible, mean-spirited, and churlish behavior—brought on in large part, no doubt, as a result of a profligate father separated from a now destitute mother. Trying to keep a step ahead of the invading Nazis and their collaborators, the Hungarian Arrow Cross, the family is forced to move constantly.

When Jozsef and his mother and brother are taken in by Hungarians who think they are dislocated Gentiles, Jozsef, after having condemned it throughout the work, proclaims his Jewishness.[28] He does so as much out of his usual perversity as he does out of his insistence on honesty. Immediately realizing the danger he has placed his family in, however, Jozsef is uncharacteristically remorseful. Fortunately, the Hungarians who have taken them in are opposed to the wanton brutality and assure them that not all Christians—in fact, no true Christian, they say—behave as do the Nazi and the Arrow Cross tormentors. Having been exposed to selfish and cruel individuals as well as to ethical and humane ones, both Jewish and Gentile, Jozsef is thus able to conceive for himself a code of conduct proper to all areas of life, including playgrounds and battlefields.

After the defeat of the Nazis, Jozsef, his mother, and brother are among the very few Jews to return "home," to his grandfather's village. Forced to grapple with the concurrent disintegration of his family, his people, and his country, Jozsef hears the taunts of the villagers, who complain that "Ten went away, and twenty came back."[29] Walking to the synagogue which lay in ruins, Jozsef wonders whether, because his life was spared, he is now supposed to believe in God. Given his honesty and integrity, he would immediately refuse such a deal. But through the cracks of the walls of the destroyed synagogue, he hears the incantations of the dead:

> *Let my right hand forget her cunning,*
> *Let my tongue be stilled for ever*
> *If I forget thee, O Jerusalem.*[30]

Jozsef Sondor thus chooses to remember and thus acknowledge the tradition of his people. Having helped lead them out of the wilderness, that legacy sustained and fortified them throughout the millennia as they created a civilization based on the moral wisdom of the law. Despite witnessing the ravaging of his community whose only crime was to honor its heritage, despite personally enduring the insults, the privations, the brutality because he was born a member of that community, Jozsef, as he approaches manhood at age 13, having just affirmed his compact with the members of the religion he was born into, now appears ready to honor and to embrace just such a heritage, appears ready, that is, to be a moral if not a religious Jew.

Remarkably similar to Nyiri, Denes reveals in *Castles Burning* how her father left her and her brother and mother in very dire circumstances in Budapest.[31] Taking all their money, selling all their possessions for the cash he claimed he needed to go the United States (with a stopover in Paris that he didn't want to miss), forcing the mother and two children to move in with her parents in a squalid apartment, the father abandoned his family knowing the Germans would occupy Hungary and that Jews especially would be in extreme danger. And, like Nyiri and his mother and brother, Denes, her mother, and brother are forced into hiding to escape the Nazis and their collaborators, the Arrow Cross. Furthermore, both the fictionalized Jozsef Sondor and the actual Magda Denes share similar characteristics: both affect superior airs; both are antagonistic and petulant; both are too clever for their own good. Unlike Nyiri's fictionalized account, however, *Castles Burning* is straight memoir, told from the perspective of the child Magda, from when she was five in 1939 until just after the war when she was twelve, but as remembered by the adult, Dr. Magda Denes, a practicing psychoanalyst in New York, who unfortunately died of a heart attack just after the book was published.

Denes seems to have had an extraordinary memory. She remembers, for instance, complex conversations that took place between adults using their sophisticated language, names of numerous people met in passing, and specific details of places and scenes all of which occurred more than fifty years ago. She records a conversation she remembers having with the only person she looks up to, her beloved brother, when she was four;[32] when she was ten, she remembers him saying: "In name only. I am a firm believer in capitalism. Better yet, in a meritocracy based on intelligence,"[33] and so on throughout the book. She also remembers knowing at age ten that "I was impossibly sarcastic, bigmouthed, insolent, and far too smart for my own good. I had been told that. Often. Be it resolved then, I thought, henceforth for all time, I will be nothing but shell-shocked, imbecilic, ignorant, and stupid, stupid."[34] She does not, of course, keep her resolve, continuing to be sarcastic, bigmouthed, and insolent—and to make intelligent decisions that even her mother, aunt, and grandparents abide by.

What makes for such an incredible memory? Such contributory factors as a superior intelligence, early verbal mastery, and the ongoing trauma occasioned by the Nazi invasion and brutality are obviously exceedingly important. But the infallible memory, as opposed to the uncertain memory that, for instance, Ida Fink evokes through the remarkable richness of ambiguity in her Holocaust-based novel, *The Journey*, is determined in *Castles Burning* by the moral certainty that Denes displays. "What if," the eleven-year-old Magda asks, "truth was just the power of one person over another, or of many over one? What if what I knew was nothing without a witness? All my witnesses were dead. How is truth preserved? . . . Where do you hide truth to make it safe? And when does it spread its everlasting golden wings for all to see?"[35]   The answer to her questions is that the truth of the child remains safely hidden in her memory until the adult publishes the book that allows the truth to spread its golden wings for all to see. But how is that hidden truth determined? Through the moral imperative, it seems clear, that she refines for herself from the code of conduct that the community has formulated. At the conclusion of *Castles Burning*, as the twelve-year-old Denes comes to terms with her brother's death at the hands of the Nazis, she writes: "The Bible has to have it wrong . . . It says, 'The race is not to the swift, nor the battle to the strong.' Not always, but often it is. To the very swift, and to the very strong. That is what I must become. An arrow and an anchor."[36] Surer of herself than of the Bible, sure of her rectitude, of her truth, of the moral certainties that have determined and will continue to determine both the direction and station of her life, she must become what in effect she has always been.

Her sense of her own moral integrity is so strong from the very beginning of her memoir, from the very beginning of her memory in fact, that whatever she says or does, believes or conjectures, is in fact historical as well as emotional truth. And who can doubt her truth? Whatever else memory is, particularly that memory which is comprehensive and incontrovertible as is Magda Denes's, it is the truth by which she records and defines herself. The moral force of memory may well determine, in fact, what *is* to be remembered.

Men and women as well as almost all adolescents were formed morally and socially by the time they either entered the camps or went into hiding. Hence they had had an established ethical code of conduct by which they lived and from which they could gauge their descent into the moral maelstrom. Children in the concentrationary universe, however, had no way to independently measure or maintain a morally social structure since, by and large, such a structure had ceased to exist before they were able to be integrated into it. But because most children who survived were kept with their parents or older siblings in the camps or in hiding, they were able to reckon from their elders an approximation of what was once and what was still morally appropriate—albeit a difficult determination since the adults, suffering immediate humiliation and privation, were almost all made to abandon their moral and social principles and thus turn topsy-turvy the world from which they had been ruthlessly banished. The children, therefore, those most vulnerable socially and morally, not to mention physically, were exposed to and had embedded in their memories a world inconceivable in even their worst nightmare. And those memories were recalled with varying degrees of emotional force by the adults who suffered the horror as children. Which is to say that social memory, dependent in large part on the moral content which informs it, determines in equally large part the existential "truth" of the experience. As Frank and Manea, Wiesel and Denes, among so many others have shown—however much they questioned and found wanting their received morality, however blurred and distorted it had become—the moral contract still provided these children to a greater or lesser degree the social structure of their communal existence. And the force of the moral contract, whether disdained or upheld by the recipient, deeply touched his or her felt memory of the lived experience, providing it with a texture and a heft not associated with rote or mechanical memory. In a class all alone, however, Binjamin Wilkomirski found himself in the concentration camp at the age of three or so without mother or father, without older siblings, and without, consequently, a moral guidon to follow.

Having witnessed the murder of the man he believed to be his father; having stood at the deathbed of an emaciated woman whom he believed must have been his mother, because she gives him her last morsel of dried bread; having been separated from four or five older brothers—he's not sure how many—who have all presumably died, Wilkomirski, from the point of view of his three-year-old self, tells the disjointed story of his survival and of what he witnessed in *Fragments: Memories of a Wartime Childhood*.[37] Having grown up with his secrets partly because he was ashamed of what he considered to be his unique experience, partly because society either refused to listen or was incapable of listening, he remained silent for decades. But because his memory could not be erased, because he wanted his own voice and certainty returned to him, he started writing. He explains how, in contradistinction, say, to Denes who remembers everything from her earliest childhood, he spent years doing research, traveling back to those places where he remembers things happened, having numerous discussions with specialists and historians, all of which helped clarify for him and to make a more or less chronological sequence of his bewildering shreds of memory. Most significantly, he concludes: "I wrote these fragments of memory to explore both myself and my earliest childhood; it may also have been an attempt to set myself free."[38]

At the beginning of his memoir, Wilkomirski acknowledges that he had to write his fragments in a foreign tongue, asserting that his own language had its roots in the Yiddish of his elder brother, Mordechai, overlaid with what he calls the "Babel-babble of an assortment of children's barracks in the Nazis' death camps in Poland."[39] He lets us know he is in Switzerland telling in fragment form what befell him. He had been taken to an orphanage there after the war ended for him by one Frau Grosz who, with her husband, subsequently adopted him. Almost immediately in the Swiss orphanage, after having been given amounts and kinds of food he had never before had, after having been given his own bed with clean linens, after—in a word—having been treated like an ordinary child in a comfortable home, he dreamt of escaping so he could return to the camp where the deaths of children from mass executions, from arbitrary torture and privation, from despair and terror, from starvation and disease, were commonplace. Even at so early an age, he felt compelled to preserve his memories of the camp because, unlike the orphanage in Switzerland with its strange ways, he understood the rules of survival in that loathsome place.

Although he does not elaborate on what those rules were, it is clear that they constituted the normal code of conduct, moral and physical, of the camp, that the inmates immediately had to learn upon their arrival if they hoped to survive the first days of their internment. He knows the "gray uniforms," which is what he calls the guards, male and female, can be relied upon to kill, beat, and torture the children. But those he could trust, including the woman he believes to be his birth mother, who gave him her last piece of bread before dying, and an older boy of twelve or so named Jankl who shared with him his stolen pieces of rotting food, help establish in him a primitive sense of morality and ethical behavior, so that the sharing of food and vital information is valued as a good while betraying a comrade is considered an evil. What the "gray uniforms" do, however, killing children or sending them on the transports for the smallest transgression is not necessarily an evil, but the expected norm.

One of the most harrowing incidents the three-year-old witnesses is the sight of rats coming out of a mound of dead women's bodies. Simultaneously puzzled and sickened, he thinks that once women give birth to rats they die. And so he wonders:

> Am I a rat or a human? I'm a child—but am I a human child or a rat child, or can you be both at once? . . .
>
> Nothing connects to anything else anymore. Nothing is in its right place. Nothing has any value . . .
>
> There are no feelings left. I can't feel if I'm breathing. I can't feel my ever-present hunger or thirst.
>
> I'm just an eye, taking in what it sees, giving nothing back. But I'm cold.[40]

Reminiscent of Levi, whose scientific training influenced his precise, objective prose style, Wilkomirski describes his experiences as if his whole being is a cold eye, "taking in what it sees, giving nothing back." In fact, his prose style throughout the book is that of "just an eye" which is what makes it so powerful. Cold emotionally as well as physically, he sees and feels dispassionately for the most part, thus engendering in the reader the exact emotional antithesis because the adult reader, unlike the child victim, has a moral center which assesses and assigns blame, which demands justice as it laments its absence, which recoils from the unspeakable horror that the boy views as normal.

In a particularly moving passage, Wilkomirski describes his reaction and that of his older mentor, Jankl, when two bundles were thrown into his barracks. The bundles turned out to be newborn babies wrapped in rags who, having literally starved to death, chewed the flesh off their fingers during the night so that in the morning all that was left on their tiny hands were bones. When Binjamin asks Jankl what had happened, if the babies were sick, Jankl replies that, yes, the babies had a sickness called hunger, that their frozen fingers no longer hurt so that during the night, they chewed their fingers to the bone before they died. Wilkomirski writes, "Jankl had spoken in a quiet, soft voice, but for the first time since we'd been together. I heard something sad and bitter in his voice, and as I looked at him in surprise, I saw that he was crying."[41]

He is less moved by the image of the dead babies, by their having eaten the flesh off their own fingers, than he is at the reaction such a sight caused the desolate Jankl. Wilkomirski is surprised by such sadness since he presumes, even at such a young age, that all children are eventually killed or die of sickness and starvation. Even when Jankl on whom he was most dependent, who shared with him food he had stolen, who taught him how to tie his shoes, who instilled in him a sense of right and wrong, however elementary, was publicly executed because he was caught stealing food, the three-year-old showed no emotion, thinking only that now he was alone.[42] But his awareness of his own lack of emotion, of his being just an eye, of "giving nothing back," as a child victim continues to plague him as an adult. In a later chapter, hidden by women laundry workers under piles of clothing, he hears boots thumping through the place accompanied by shrieks and screams of the women. He is able to see two bundles being taken out, but does not know what is in them. Later he discovers that inside the bundles were, "babies on their backs, arms and legs outspread, stomachs all swollen and blue. And where once their little faces must have been, a red mess mixed with snow and mud."[43] Sick, almost paralyzed, at the sight, he nevertheless manages to run to safety. Despite the passage of years, unable to rid himself of this image, he continues to reproach himself for not having felt anything for the babies, wondering if he had become so brutalized that there were no feelings left, neither sympathy, nor pity, nor even anger: "Because I felt nothing then, nothing but disgust and my own icy terror."[44]

What he does feel as a boy, but only after he was out of the camps, is shame. When Frau Grosz insists that he call her "mother," he does so reluctantly. Aware that the woman who gave him her last morsel of bread must have been his birth mother, he now "felt more ashamed than I had ever felt in my life. I felt as if I'd become a criminal, my mother's betrayer. I felt filthy and wretched, and my skin began to crawl and itch again."[45] But his feeling of being a criminal has less to do with betraying the memory of the woman he never knew than it does with being rejected by the boys he'd left behind in the camp. He's afraid, in fact, of their taking revenge on him for becoming a traitor because he'd be unable to cover up so terrible an act as calling Frau Grosz "mother."[46] The first time the notion of "shame" is alluded to in the book, in fact, is not in connection to an awareness of his contravening an established moral order, but to his being discovered as a "traitor" by the other boys he'd been in camp with—to whom he still longs to return, despite the intolerable conditions. And the main reason he longs to return is that he knows what is expected of him in the camp unlike the confusion and abuse he suffers in the Swiss school where his adoptive parents had placed him.

One day, the teacher of his class was holding up a picture of William Tell who was aiming his bow and arrow at a little boy with an apple atop his head. As the teacher and the other students in the class speak fondly of their national hero, Binjamin, who knows that "heroes" in the German Reich have no qualms about killing anyone, including children, thinks William Tell is aiming the arrow at the boy. The teacher calls on Binjamin to explain the picture, to describe what he sees. When he says the hero is shooting children, the other students in the class begin to snicker at and mock him. The teacher, becoming angrier and angrier, insists he continue. Now nervous, trying not to cry, Binjamin says it is "not normal."[47] For the moment the reader is relieved, thinking that Binjamin believes shooting children is not normal. But as you read on you discover that what he considers not normal is the wasting of precious ammunition on children. When the teacher demands to know why it is not normal, Binjamin responds: "'Because our block warden said, "Bullets are too good for children," and bec-bec-because only grownups get shot. . . or they go into the gas. The children get thrown into the fire, or killed by hand—mostly, that is.'" Outraged, the teacher tells him to sit down and stop talking "drivel."[48]

Still haunted by his betrayal of his birth mother by calling the woman who adopted him mother, he is also tormented by the memory of a boy's death he feels responsible for. While in the camp a new boy was placed at night in an upper bunk opposite him. Having no knowledge of the workings of the camp and in desperate need to urinate, the frightened boy screamed in the dark asking what he should do since the bucket used had already been filled up and taken away. No one answered him. He pleaded for help, for someone to tell him what to do. The young Wilkomirski, shocked at hearing his own voice in the darkness tell the boy to urinate in the straw, realized he had said aloud what he believed he was only thinking. The next day the new boy, who had heeded

Wilkomirski, was identified and taken away, the sound of his crunching bones heard by everyone. He was never seen again. Wilkomirski knew he was responsible for the new boy's dereliction, but he said nothing that might have saved him because he was terrified at what the other boys would do to him. Long after his release from the camps, as a senior in high school in Switzerland, his guilt over the boy's death and of what he considers his betrayal to his birth mother continues to plague him:

> I had handed over the new boy; I was inextricably caught up in the fact of his death. It was only because I was a coward that they killed the new boy. I might perhaps have been able to save him, and I didn't do anything.
> I had betrayed my mother and now called a stranger "mother."[49]

This stranger whom he calls mother is responsible, he says, for insisting that he never speak of the camps so that he was forced to harbor an existence which was made to be shameful but one he did not experience as such. As a result of having to hide so terrible a truth especially from those who considered themselves his parents, he was undoubtedly made to feel that he was forever locked in a dark but excruciating secret—the secret of the camps themselves—from which there could be no escape. In fact, he laments the fact that nobody had ever said to him that, yes, the camp really did exist but you are safe now—"There *is* another world now, and you're allowed to live in it."[50] Never having been allowed to publicly acknowledge his existence in the harrowing world of his youth, he was forced to continue inhabiting it alone.

But because his memory could not be erased, because he wanted his own identity restored and his own voice asserted, because he wanted ultimately to free himself, he began to write. And in releasing his memory, in making what was hazy and uncertain, explicit and focussed, in proclaiming the reality of the past, the writing apparently helped ease the torment that the guilt-inducing secrets of his early existence had instilled in him. But if the writing of this extraordinarily important and moving work helped strengthen his memory and thus ease the guilt, the work itself also reveals that because he still feels no shame, he is still "a cold eye," feeling guilty that he is, paradoxically, without feeling. Having lacked the received morality that informed the lives of those other children, Wilkomirski consequently lacked the attendant shame in the world he inhabited as a child. Thus while his memory itself is without feeling, his knowledge of bearing such a dispassionate memory of so vile a time paradoxically now evokes the emotions that should then have been his. It is as if he is intensely and passionately watching a documentary film of his own childhood which shows him as little more than a cold eye indifferently enduring and witnessing the most brutal and repulsive acts. But now in the darkened theater of his soul the painful emotions—the anger and frustration, the despair and the shame—are inwardly directed for not having the very same emotions then. For Wilkomirski, as for Srebnik, part of the normal human condition meant the killing of Jews. And for him, as for Srebnik, the moral condition of children who knew no other morality, there is no shame or despair associated with killing or disposing or viewing of emaciated and disfigured bodies—only disgust and fear.

Similar to a prisoner in jail having adopted a code of behavior he abides by while acceding to the greater societal authority that put him in prison in the first place, the innocent Wilkomirski has had created in him an emotional state that is paradoxically guilt-ridden but shame free. Unlike most prisoners who have been incarcerated because they are guilty of a crime, those in the concentrationary universe were innocent of any crime other than that of being born Jewish. As such the overwhelming majority of imprisoned or hidden Jews knew they were innocent according to the established morality that they had followed and continued to abide by. The very same morality, incidentally, their assailants were supposed to be ruled by. But having been thrust into the infernal world before he had learned the established principles of decency that guided his parents and older siblings, Wilkomirski expected the brutal and harsh treatment he received because all those around him suffered the same fate. But the others knew they were suffering though innocent of a crime and were thus both guilt-free and filled with shame, the young Wilkomirski felt guilt only when he betrayed the tenets of his fellow inmates but felt no shame at all while in the camp because, like Srebnik, what he experienced was normal.

Having been robbed of his name, deprived of his language, banished from his native land, having seen his father killed, his mother on her deathbed, his brothers disappear, the orphaned and rootless Wilkomirski, representing the fate of European Jewry itself, is the epitomic symbol as well as the literal embodiment of the Nazi goal. But having restored what he thinks is his birth name, in searching his own past in order to recover the memory, however painful, in refusing to be sucked into the black hole of his existence, Wilkomirski readies himself to rejoin the community, however shattered it now is, he was born into. In addition to writing these fragments to recover the memories that would help set him free, he published them in the hope that those who suffered a similar past would discover they are not alone—"would find the necessary support and strength to cry out their own traumatic childhood memories, so that they too could learn that there really are people today who will take them seriously, and who want to listen and to understand."[51] Finding solidarity in each other's shared anguish, proclaiming their mutual care and concern, these fellow survivors would be able to publicly disinter their buried past and thus possess more unfettered lives in the present.

But no matter how laudable his intentions are his conclusion should in no way be taken as a kind of spiritual triumph either for Wilkomirski in particular or for survivors in general; the loss is irreplaceable; the harm irreparable. From such evil good cannot come. The Nazis not only extirpated the thousand-year-old communal presence of Jews from all over Europe but also sanctioned their goal to collaborators and sympathizers who participated in the devastation. If many of those who took part in the offense today feel remorse for what they did or failed to do, there are still many men and women as well as some governments that, denying they were part of such an unholy alliance, have issued no proclamation condemning or apologizing for their past affiliation with the Germans. For them, the perpetrators and bystanders who embraced the goals of the Nazi philosophy and abided by its legal code, the very ones whose concept of normalcy children like Wilkomirski and Srebnik ironically accepted as their own, there is no need to apologize because where there is no guilt there is no shame.

Shame, though often a concomitant of guilt, is just as often independent of it and may indeed be brought on though no law, spiritual or civil, is broken. Levi points out in *The Reawakening*, for instance, that the Russians who liberated Auschwitz felt profound shame for what they saw had been done to fellow human beings. The hubris-filled Germans and their henchmen, on the other hand, who were responsible for the obscenity not only did not feel shame, but, in carrying out *their* law, apparently felt morally justified hence inspired because they believed they were ridding the land of a blight that had defiled it. So the guilt-free Russians felt shame while the Germans, eventually judged guilty of having violated the basic laws of humanity, felt none at all.

For Wilkomirski, as for Srebnik, part of the normal human condition meant the massacre of Jews. And for him, as for Srebnik, the moral condition of children who knew no other morality, there is no shame or despair associated with killing or disposing or viewing of emaciated and disfigured bodies—only disgust and fear. Unless and until Wilkomirski realizes he cannot feel shame for what he experienced as normal, he may well continue to be haunted for life. If not all the children of the Holocaust feel the absence of shame as a wrenching hole in their moral existence it is because they had had instilled in them, before the catastrophe befell them, the moral tradition that had been passed on from one generation to another for thousands of years. But the absence of shame that characterizes the young Wilkomirski's moral state was also clearly absent in the perpetrators responsible for the devastation. Unlike Wilkomirski who continues to be deeply affected by such a lack of feeling in his early moral being, many perpetrators—individuals and governments alike—feel no sense of shame for what they did because they continue to deny responsibility for their behavior or, worse, believe that such behavior because not illegal then absolves them from guilt. Unless and until they acknowledge their complicity, their silence will condone similar carnage now taking place in various countries throughout the world. And such silence will continue to be recorded in the annals of world history with profound shame.

Notes

1. Claude Lanzmann, *Shoah* (New York: Da Capo Press, 1995), 91-92. This version contains the complete text of the film. It was revised and extensively corrected by Claude Lanzmann for Da Capo Press. The original published version appeared in France in 1985.

2. Fredrich Nietsche, *Beyond Good and Evil*, in *Basic Writings of Nietzsche*, trans. and ed. Walter Kaufmann, (New York, 1968), 270.

3. Primo Levi, *The Drowned and the Saved*, trans. Raymond Rosenthal, (New York, 1986), 78.

4. See, for example, Liana Millu, *Smoke over Birkenau*, trans. Lynne Schwartz, (Philadelphia: Jewish Publication Society, 1991), 165.

5. Primo Levi, *The Drowned and the Saved*, 50.

6. Ibid., 58.

7. Ibid., 76.

8. Ibid., 81.

9. Daniel Goleman, *Emotional Intelligence (New York, 1995)*, 104-106.

10. Ibid., 203.

11. Jean Améry, *At the Mind's Limits*, trans. Sidney and Stella P. Rosenfeld, (New York, 1986) 34, 36.

12. Shortly after the War, her father, Otto Frank, the only one to survive of

those hiding in the attic, published a version of her diary which he himself edited. By the early 1950s, the still expurgated *Diary* had been translated into several European languages. In 1986, with financial support of the Dutch government to determine the authenticity of the work, the *Critical Edition*, of her Diary was published. See *The Diary of Anne Frank: The Critical Edition* ed. David Barnouw and Gerrold Van Der Stroom (trans. Arnold J. Pomerans and B.M. Mooyaart-Doubleday), New York, 1989. More recently, the "definitive edition" of the *Diary* was issued by the Anne Frank Foundation in Basel, Switzerland: Anne Frank, *The Diary of a Young Girl: The Definitive Edition* ed. Otto H. Frank and Mirjam Pressler (trans. Susan Massotty), New York, 1995.

13. *The Diary of Anne Frank: The Critical Edition*, 519.

14. Norman Manea, *October, Eight O'Clock*, trans. by Cornelia Golna, Anselm Hollo, Mara Soceanu Vamos, Max Bleyleben, and Marguerite Dorian and Elliot B. Urdang, (New York, 1992), 40.

15. Ibid., 45.

16. Ibid., 79.

17. Ibid., 85.

18. Ibid., 95.

19. Ibid., 116.

20. Ibid., 116.

21. Ibid., 116.

22. For a discussion of Kis use of the son to chronicle with luminous complexity the physical destruction of the father by the forces of evil paralleled by the ultimate spiritual victory of the father over those same forces during the Holocaust, see my "Danilo Kis: Death and the Mirror," *The Antioch Review*, Fall, 1993.

23. Elie Wiesel, *The Night Trilogy* (New York, 1988) *Night* Foreword by François Mauriac, Translated from the French by Stella Rodway, pp. 75, 116.

24. Louis Begley, *Wartime Lies* (New York, 1991), 3.

25. Ibid., 5.

26. Ibid., 198.

27. Janos Nyiri, *Battlefields and Playgrounds*, trans. by William Brandon and the author, (New York, 1995). First published in London in 1989.

28. Ibid., 447.

29. Ibid., 531.

30. Ibid., 532.

31. Magda Denes, *Castles Burning* (New York, 1997).

32. Ibid., 121.

33. Ibid., 148.

34. Ibid., 93.

35. Ibid., 227.

36. Ibid., 384.

37. Binjamin Wilkomirski, *Fragments: Memories of a Wartime Childhood*, translated by Carol Brown Janeway, (New York, 1996). First published in Germany in 1995.

38. Ibid., 155.

39. Ibid., 3.

40. Ibid., 87.

41. Ibid., 71.

42. Ibid., 76.

43. Ipid., 104.

44. Ibid., 105.

45. Ibid., 123.

46. Ibid., 123.

47. Ibid., 129.

48. Ibid., 130.

49. Ibid., 147.

50. Ibid., 150.

51. Ibid., 155.

Shubshi-meshre-Shakkan

—Babylonian

Adapted-Rendered by David Ferry

Hymn

I sing this hymn in praise of him who is
The wisest of all, raging in darkness, or,
In the bright morning, calm, the wisest of all.

The storm of his anger it is that lays the land low;
His breath in the quiet morning stirs but a leaf;
The flood of his anger cannot be withstood.

He is the lord who pities and forgives.
The sky will buckle under the weight of his hands;
He holds the sick man gently in his hands.

The thorns of his whip cut into the flesh and it bleeds;
His poultice cools and eases the body's pain;
It eases the pain and the wounded body heals.

He has but to frown and the strength departs from a man;
The strength departs from a man and the man is weak.
The Lady Fortune departs, seeking out others.

He smiles and the personal god comes back to the man,
His strength comes back to the man and re-enters his body.
The Lady Fortune returns from where she had gone to.

Narrative

I

Everywhere around me there is confusion.
Enlil and the other gods have given me up.

The personal god has gone away from my house.
The Lady Fortune has gone to somebody else.

I see the omens everywhere I look.
The king, the sun that shines on his happy people,

The king is angry and he will not hear me.
When I go to the palace now, they look at me.

One person blinks and another looks away.
What are these omens? How is it I should read them?

When I lie down to dream I have nightmares.
In the street I see the others looking at me.

I see how people point their fingers at me.
I hear them talking about me in the street.

One says: "I made him want to end his life,"
One says: "I will take over his position,

I'll be the one who goes and lives in his house . . ."
Six or seven talking in the street,

Six or seven gathered in the street,
Storm demons raging against me in the street.

*

The year has turned and everywhere I see
Wherever I look the signs of my bad luck.

I cannot find out anywhere what is right.
I pray to my personal god and he doesn't answer.

I pray to the Lady Fortune, she will not listen.
I went to the dream interpreter, he poured

Libations to the gods but they said nothing.
The zaqiqu spirit said nothing; nothing was what

Could be done by the one whose charms can charm away
The evil spirits. Everywhere around me

There is confusion. Everything is strange.

*

It is as if I did not pray to the gods.
It is as if I did not properly say

The name of the goddess before I eat my meal.
It is as if I did not teach my household

How to honor the gods. It is as if
I taught my household people how to neglect

The holy days and festivals of the year.
I kept the rules; to worship was my joy;

The music of the procession delighted me;
Before I ate I spoke the name of my god;

I taught my people how to honor the gods,
And to honor the king as if he were a god.

I taught my people how to respect the palace.
I wish I knew these things would please the gods.

I wish I knew the meaning of these things.
Who knows the will of the gods in heaven? Who knows?

Maybe the gods despise what men think right.
Maybe what men think wrong delights the gods.

Who knows the ways of the gods of the Underworld?
What man has ever learned the ways of the gods?

Today he is dead who was living yesterday;
From gladness to sorrow is but the blink of an eye;

He sings in joy this moment who wails the next.

II

Around me everywhere there is confusion.
Everything is strange. A storm wind drives me along.

Sickness has come upon me. An evil wind
Has blown in from the horizon. As new little plants

Come up through the ground in spring when their time has come,
The Weakness comes up through the ground. The Coughing comes up,

It comes up horribly laughing out of the abyss.
The Headache comes up out of the Underworld.

The Bone-Ache comes from the surface of the waters.
The Lamashtu-demon comes down from the mountain.

All of the demons gather themselves upon me.
The phlegm fills up my throat and my throat chokes.

Whatever I eat is vile. Beer, solace of men,
Is vile in my mouth. Grain is vile in my mouth.

All night the demons torment me, What are they saying?
I cannot hear what it is that they are saying.

Where has my dignity gone, and my good looks?
The exorcist has nothing to say. The diviner

Has nothing to say. My personal god has not
Come to my rescue. The Lady Fortune has not.

My chest was broad, my arms were strong, and now
A boy could easily wrestle me to the ground.

My looks are strange. The flesh is loose on my bones.
I try to walk. My feet have forgotten how.

My knees are fettered and bound like the busu-bird's.
At night I lie in my shit like an ox or a sheep.

My grave is open already and waiting. Already
All the funeral things have been prepared.

He who gloats gloats when he hears about it.
She who gloats gloats when she hears about it.

The day is dark for all my family.
For all my friends lamenting the day is dark.

III

His hand was heavy upon me, I could not bear
The weight of his hand, I could not bear the fear

Of the storm wind screaming against me and blowing against me.
I lay awake or else I was asleep.

There was a young man, beautiful, wearing new garments.
I dreamed a priest was holding in his hand

A bough of tamarisk that purifies.
There was a young woman came to me in my dream.

Beautiful, wearing new garments. She spoke to me:
"Here is deliverance from your wretchedness."

There was a young man came to me in my dream,
Bearded, wearing a headdress. He carried a tablet

And on the tablet written was a message:
"Marduk has sent me. I come to bring you luck.

To Shubshi-meshre-Shakkan I bring good luck."
The storm of Marduk's anger was quieted down.

A lion was eating me. Marduk muzzled the lion.
Marduk took my hand and raised me up.

He who had thrown me down he raised me up.
My knees, which were fettered and bound like the busu-bird's,

My knees were freed from their bonds and I could walk.

My throat, which was closed, was opened, and I sang.

Hymn

The Babylonians saw what Marduk had done
And everything they said proclaimed his greatness,
The storm of his anger it is that lays the land low;

His breath in the quiet morning stirs but a leaf;
The flood of his anger cannot be withstood.
He is the lord who pities and forgives.

Who would have thought this man would see the sun?
Who would have thought this man would walk again?
Who would have thought we would see him on the street?

What god but Marduk could bring back the dying?
Who would have thought this man would see the sun?
Who would have thought we would see him on the street?

As far as the land extends and the sky above it,
Wherever the sun god shines and the fire burns,
Wherever the waters are and where the winds blow,

Wherever the creatures are whom the goddess Aruru
Fashioned of clay, endowed with breath and life,
The black-headed creatures, men, who walk the earth,

Let there be praise for Marduk for what he has done.

Contributors

A native of Cardiff, Wales, **Dannie Abse** published his first book in 1948. Since then, he has published nine more volumes of poetry in the United Kingdom, as well as his *Selected Poems* (U.K. Penguin, 1994). His books available in the U.S. include a book of poems, *White Coal, Purple Coat* (Persea Books, 1989) and a collection of prose, *Intermittent Journals* (Dufour Editions, 1995). He recently edited *Twentieth Century Anglo-Welsh Poetry* (1998). ★★★ **Paul Breslin**'s poems have appeared in *Agni*, *American Poetry Review*, *Poetry*, and *TriQuarterly*. ★★★ **Ami Sands Brodoff** is the author of the novels, *Can You See Me?* and *Love Out of Bounds*, and a volume of stories, *Bloodknots*. She was awarded a River City Fellowship in Fiction (winner, 1997 awards) and a Yaddo fellowship. She teaches writing to formerly incarcerated women at Bates House near her home in Princeton, New Jersey. ★★★ **Marcus Cafagña**'s first book, *The Broken World*, was a National Poetry Series selection. He has new poems in *Field* and *Xconnect* and forthcoming in *Quarterly West* and *Cherry Orchard Review*. He teaches creative writing at Southwest Missouri State University. ★★★ **Peter Cooley** has published six books of poetry, including *The Van Gogh Notebook* and *The Astonished Hours*. His most recent book is *Sacred Conversations* (Carnegie Mellon University Press, 1998). His poems have appeared recently in *The Kenyon Review* and *Sewanee Review*. He teaches creative writing at Tulane University. ★★★ **Robert Cording** has published three books of poetry, *Life-List* (Ohio State University Press, 1987), *What Binds Us to This World* (Copper Beech Press, 1991), and *Heavy Grace* (Alice James Books, 1996). He has poems appearing or forthcoming in *DoubleTake*, *Poetry*, and *Gettysburg Review*. He teaches at Holy Cross College in Worcester, Massachusetts. ★★★ **Fred Dings** has written two books of poetry, *Eulogy for a Private Man* (forthcoming from TriQuarterly Books, fall 1999) and

After the Solstice (Orchises Press, 1993). His work has appeared in numerous periodicals, including the *New Yorker*, the *New Republic*, and *Poetry*. ★★★ **Stephen Dixon**'s latest books are the story collection, *Sleep* (Coffeehouse Press, 1999), and the novel, *30* (Henry Holt, 1999). ★★★ **Edward Falco**'s short story collection, *Acid* (Notre Dame, 1996) won the Richard Sullivan Prize and was a finalist for the Patterson Prize. His stories have appeared widely in journals, including the *Atlantic*, *Playboy*, and *Ploughshares*. ★★★ **Beth Ann Fennelly** received her B.A. from the University of Notre Dame and her M.F.A. from the University of Arkansas. She is currently the Dianne Middlebrook Fellow at the University of Wisconsin. She has published poems in *Shenandoah*, *Michigan Quarterly Review*, *Poetry Ireland Review*, and the *Best American Poetry 1996*. ★★★ **David Ferry**'s most recent books are *Dwelling Places: Poems and Translations* (University of Chicago Press, 1993), *The Odes of Horace: A Translation* (Farrar, Strauss and Giroux, 1997) and his translation of *The Eclogues of Virgil* (Fall 1998). ★★★ **Laurence Goldstein** is the author most recently of a book of poems, *Cold Reading* (Copper Beech Press, 1995), and a book of literary criticism, *The American Poet at the Movies: A Critical History* (University of Michigan Press, 1994). He is Professor of English at the University of Michigan, where he edits *Michigan Quarterly Review*. ★★★ **Marilyn Hacker** is the author of eight books of poetry, including *Winter Numbers* (W.W. Norton, 1994), which won the Lenore Marshall Prize from the Academy of American Poets; and *Selected Poems 1965-1990* (1994), which won the 1995 Poets' Prize. ★★★ **Daniel Halpern** is the author of eight collections of poetry, most recently *Selected Poems* (Knopf, 1994), *Foreign Neon* (1991), and *Tango* (Viking Penguin, 1987). Knopf will publish a new collection of his poems, *Something Shining*, in the fall of 1999. He has received fellowships from the Guggenheim Foundation and the National Endowment for the Arts, as well as the 1993 Pen Publisher Citation. ★★★ **Bob Hicok**'s most recent book is *Plus Shipping* (BOA Editions, 1998). *The Legend of Light* won the Pollack Prize and was an ALA Booklist Notable Book of the Year. An NEA Fellow this year, he will have poems in *Best American Poetry, 1999*, and the Puchart Prize anthology. ★★★ Pulizer Prize winner **Yusef Komunyakaa**'s most recent book is *Thieves of Paradise* (Wesleyan University Press, 1998). His CD, *Love Notes from the Madhouse*, has been released by 8th Harmonic Breakdown. He teaches at Princeton University. ★★★ **Patricia Lear** is the author of *Stardust, 7-Eleven, Route 57, A&W, and So Forth* (Knopf, 1992). She had received an O. Henry Award, and her short story "After Memphis" was anthologized in *The Best of the Decade: New Stories from the South.* ★★★ **Rachel Levine** received her MFA in poetry from New York University. This is her second poem in *TriQuarterly.* ★★★ **Timothy Liu**'s books of poems are *Say Goodnight* (Copper Canyon Press, 1998), *Burnt Offerings* (Copper Canyon Press, 1995), and *Vox Angelica* (Alice James Books, 1992). He teaches at William Paterson University. ★★★ **Marek Lugowski** edits *A Small Garlic Press.* He co-edits *Agnieszka's Dowry* and is a contributing editor for *Cross Connect* at the University of Pennsylvania. ★★★ **William Lychack**'s fiction has appeared recently in *Best American Short Stories, Ploughshares, Quarterly West,* and *Witness.* He lives in New York City. ★★★ **Doug Macomber** has won numerous television journalism honors, including several Emmys. He is currently working with the poet Carl Phillips on a collaboration of photography and prose poetry. ★★★ **Jayanta Mahapatra** is the author of more than a dozen books of poetry, including *Shadow Space* (D.C. Books, 1997), *A Whiteness of Bone* (Penguin-Viking, 1992), and *Selected Poems* (Oxford University Press, 1987). His poetry was anthologized in the *Vintage Book of Contemporary World Poetry* (Random House, 1996). ★★★ **Gabriel Motola** has published essays, reviews, and interviews on writers of Holocaust literature in such journals as the *American Scholar, Paris Review, Sewanee Review, Antioch Review, Midstream, Southwest Review,* and the *Nation.* Two chapters of his novel, *Incisions,* appeared previously in *TriQuarterly.* He teaches at The New School in New York City. ★★★ **G.E. Murray**'s most recent books of poetry are *Oils of Evening: Journeys in the Art Trade* (Lake Shore Publishing, 1995) and *Walking the Blind Dog* (University of Illinois Press, 1992). He is co-editing an anthology of Illinois poetry in the twentieth century, to be published this year by the University of Illinois Press. ★★★ **Alan Michael Parker**'s first book of poems, *Days Like Prose* (Alef Books), was named a Notable Book of 1997 by the National Book Critics Circle. His second collection, *The Vandals,* was published in May by BOA Editions. Co-editor of the *Routledge Anthology of Cross-Gendered Verse* and editor for North America of *Who's Who in 20th Century World Poetry,* he teaches at Davidson College in North Carolina. ★★★ **Ricardo Pau-Llosa**'s third and fourth collections of poetry—*Cuba* (1993) and *Vereda Tropical* (1999)—were published by Carnegie Mellon University Press. His most recent book of art criticism is *Rafael Soriano and the Poetics of Light* (Miami: ed. Habana Vieja, 1998). ★★★ **Carl Phillips** is the author of three collections, most recently *From the Devotions* (Graywolf Press, 1998). He teaches English and African and

Afro-American Studies at Washington University in St. Louis. ★★★
Charles Rafferty's first book of poems was *The Man on the Tower*
(University of Arkansas Press, 1995). He has poems forthcoming in the
Dickinson Review, Greensboro Review, and *Poetry East* and is the book
review editor for *Hellas*. ★★★ **Mark Rudman**'s recent books include a
long poem, *Rider,* which received the National Book Critics Circle
Award in Poetry; *Realm of Unknowing: Meditations on Art, Suicide, and
Other Transformations* (1996); *The Millennium Hotel* (1996), chosen by
the VLS as one of the 25 best books of the year; and the final volume of
the trilogy, *Provoked in Venice* (1999), all from Wesleyan. His translation,
with Katharine Washburn, of Euripides' *Daughters of Troy* appeared in the
University of Pennsylvania Series. He teaches at NYU. ★★★ **Ira
Sadoff**'s most recent book of poems is *Grazing* (University of Illinois
Press, 1998). The *Ira Sadoff Reader* was published in 1992, as part of
UPNE's Breadloaf series. His recent stories have appeared in *New
England Review* and *Ploughshares*. ★★★ **Peter Dale Scott**'s poem "Second
Retreat" is from *Minding the Darkness,* the unpublished third volume of a
trilogy that includes *Coming to Jakarta* (New Directions, 1989) and
Listening to the Candle (New Directions, 1992). He has also published
Crossing Borders (1994), and translations. ★★★ **A.A. Srinivasan** is cur-
rently at work on a novel. "Tusk" is her first published story. She lives in
Los Angeles. ★★★ **Wisława Szymborska**, winner of the Nobel Prize for
Literature in 1996 and the Goethe Award in 1991, was born in 1923 in
Kornik, Poland. She has written nine volumes of poetry, including, most
recently *Koniec I Poczatek* [*The End and the Beginning*]. ★★★ **Ann
Townsend**'s first collection of poems, *Dimestore Erotics* (Silverfish
Review Press, 1998), won the 1997 Gerald Cable Prize. Her fiction,
poetry, and essays have appeared in such places as the *Kentucky Review,*
the *Nation,* and the *Southern Review*. She teaches at Denison University.
★★★ **Joanna Trzeciak**'s latest book is a translation of Tomek Tryzna's
Panna Nikt [*Miss Nobody*] (Doubleday, 1998). She has been an authorized
translator of Wislawa Szymborska since 1989. Her translations have
appeared in the *New Yorker, Harper's,* the *Times Literary Supplement,* and
the *Atlantic Monthly*. ★★★ **Mary Yukari Waters**' fiction has appeared in
Glimmer Train and Shenandoah and was recently awarded a Pushcart
Prize. She lives in Los Angeles. ★★★ **Tom Wayman**'s most recent collection of poetry in the U.S. is *I'll Be Right Back: New and Selected Poems
1980-1997* (Ontario Review Press, 1997). He teaches at Kwantien
University College in a suburb of Vancouver.

the Green Hills
LITERARY LANTERN

Featuring

Dennis Saleh
Sofia M. Starnes
B. Z. Niditch
Simon Perchik
Donald Levering
Gayle Elen Harvey

Ted D. Barber
Dika Lam
Seteney Shami
Scott Jones
James Longstaff
Bruce Tallerman

Recent Contributors

Jim Thomas
Mary Winters
Chris Dungey
R. Nikolas Macioci
Nancy Cherry
David Wright

Walter Cummins
Doug Rennie
Geoffrey Clark
Ian MacMillan
Leslie Pietrzyk
Robert C. S. Downs

Current Issue
Available Now, Price $7.00

Send Orders to:
the Green Hills
Literary Lantern
P.O. Box 375
Trenton, MO 64683

Or Order by e-mail:
jksmith@netins.net

Published at:
North Central Missouri College

Financial assistance for this project has been provided by the Missouri Arts Council, a state agency.

ekeppel

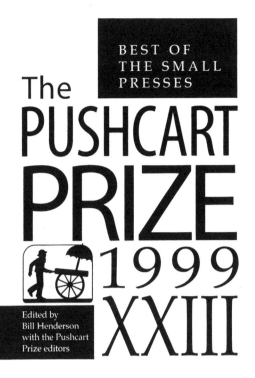

The

BEST OF
THE SMALL
PRESSES

PUSHCART
PRIZE
1999
XXIII

Edited by
Bill Henderson
with the Pushcart
Prize editors

"A distinguished annual
literary event."

ANNE TYLER
NEW YORK TIMES BOOK REVIEW

"The cream of the small
press crop."

WASHINGTON POST

THE PUSHCART PRIZE has
been selected many times as
a notable book of the year
by The New York Times Book
Review, and has been
chosen for several Book of
the Month Club QPB
selections. Pushcart Press
and its Prize were named
among the "most influential
in the development of the
American book business
over the past century and a
quarter."

PUBLISHERS WEEKLY

"THE BEST READ ANNUAL THAT IS PUBLISHED –
READ AND NOT MERELY SOLD AND COLLECTED
ON A SHELF."   Russell Banks

THE 1999 PUSHCART PRIZE is one of the largest in
the history of the series—over 600 pages of
stories, essays and poems as selected from
hundreds of presses with the help of over 200
distinguished Contributing Editors.

HARDBOUND $29.50
PAPERBACK $15.00

PUSHCART PRESS
P.O. Box 380
Wainscott, N.Y. 11975

TriQuarterly thanks the following past donors and life subscribers: